# THE PAGE

## The Year Of The Dragons

By James Warren McAllister

# THE PAGE

## The Year Of The Dragons

Cover design, artwork, and photograph
By
James W. McAllister

Title Lettering
By
Robyn Dickson

To Dad, for all those times you sang "Puff, The Magic Dragon" to me.

I've finally figured out what "ceiling wax" is.

# CONTENTS

# The Good King

The light mist collected in drops on his torn and bloody armor as the exhausted King Gingalain rode slowly through what remained of the battle-scarred village. The dismal day's grey sky was further darkened by the smoke and soot from the smoldering shops and homes he rode past. A dog cried off to his left, as the foul stench of some burning fuel other than roof thatch and timber assaulted the royal nose.

Gingalain had first come into this place after the Great King's death. He was looking for a quiet country home to spend his life in, having tired of the war, politics, and petty dramas that so frustrated him as the youngest Knight at the Great King's Table. The kindness of the people here, and the beauty of the rolling countryside had warmed his heart.

He first rode into this village still clad in the azure and gold of the Great King. He had stayed for a time, aiding the evacuation of Camlann, as best he could. But his father had already departed, the heartbreak of the task driving him away. Gingalain stayed for a few days after that, but with Gawain, his father gone, the castle in ruins, and the Great King dead, there was naught to tie him to the place.

That day so long ago, Gingalain had ridden into the village and stopped at the inn for a meal. While there he sought to acquire suitable land to retire upon. As he entered the inn, the great commotion of politics assailed his senses. It seems that with the Great Kingdom fractured by the war, a score of local nobles had gathered to determine their best course. Gingalain's keen ears picked up the gist of the arguments, finding them so unlike the self-serving rhetoric he had heard over the past few years, that he stepped closer. For these men acted as the Great King had taught, in the best interests of their people. This was the final string that would bind him here for the rest of his days, though he did not know that for some time.

Suddenly, the room snapped into silence as all eyes beheld the tall knight, most with suspicion. But on one face a grin of recognition bloomed into a smile, then bright eyes burst into a hearty yell; "Sir Gingalain! By God man! Come and sit! Enjoy our hospitality, as we hope it may purchase a bit of your wisdom!"

Gingalain squinted in the lantern light, for if he believed his eyes as to the man standing, it had to be... "Sir Aglovale? By the heavens, mine eyes are gladdened at the sight of you!" Gingalain strode powerfully into the room as Aglovale moved to meet him. The two men embraced as only those who had fought death side by side would.

"Come, my friend. We have need of you greatly now."

"Aglovale, my years of service may have been spent already. No longer does a young heart, full of lust for adventure and glory, beat in my chest. These days I seek a homestead to live upon, and perhaps, God be willing, to raise a family."

"Gingalain, I came here upon a similar quest just under a year ago. I've been tasked to protect, eh, something for a short time, perhaps for the rest of my life. This is the place, blessed with good land that is tended by good people. Stay with us, that your wisdom may guide us onto a better path."

"I never could stand against your silver tongue." Gingalain scowled at his old friend, "I remember that lame horse you sold me..."

"Now, now, that horse sired many fine steeds from which you profited quite handsomely, as I recall!"

"Ha-hah, so he did, my friend. Now, what has your good people here so anxious?"

King Gingalain recalled that night, and the actions he had recommended. He remembered the battle he said he would not fight in, for he had tired of war, yet there he was, shouting commands and swinging his long broadsword as the reaper at the harvest. Something about these people, and something about the pretty maid who served his dinner and his mead with an enticing blush, had bade him to stay, to become involved. How things had changed from his plan.

For after he helped defend the land from the North Sea invaders, he did become involved. He had purchased an old keep upon a gentle hill. He commissioned to have a modern home, comfortable yet secure, built from it. He spent many an hour advising on standards for the region, rules the nobles must live by before they could expect the populace to abide by them.

Time and again the most difficult disputes found their way before him. His advice was always given with the remembrance of the Great King's teachings. The people must have liked it, for soon he was arguing with the nobles why he should not be made their king.

Gingalain recalled how he was nearly ready to pack up and move, but his friend, Aglovale, came to see him.

"You canna go, Gingalain."

"I will not be enslaved by politics again, my friend. That is reason enough to go, in absence of a reason to stay."

"I have it."

"You have wha…" Gingalain stooped, openmouthed, and stood. It could not be that!

"My brother brought it to me. Percival told me the Great King's last instructions; I was to hold it until the Chosen One came to me. He told me you would send a young man to me."

"I… Aglovale, I…" Speechless, Gingalain sat back down, staring blankly at a spot on the table.

"My friend, I too was tired, worn out. Sometimes things place us where we need to be, where we are supposed to be, where we must be. Tell me, have you ever been happier then the times you've had here?"

"No, my friend." He let out a large sigh as he sat back. "This land is as comfortable as my mother's breast. The people here, they've made me one of their own."

"I know one who wishes you would make her your own. Why haven't you?"

"My friend, the thought of asking her frightens me!"

"Ha-hah-hah! The Brave Gingalain, honest to a fault! I've fought next to you against entire armies, and never has even a single hair on thy head known a drop of fear! Yet a simple maiden blushes and smiles, and such a quivering mess you've become!"

"A true friend would comfort and advise in one's time of trouble!" Gingalain scowled.

"And should I stop poking at you, you would assume I no

longer cherished your friendship. As would I, should you become 'polite' in that regard!" Aglovale stepped closer, his voice becoming lower and kinder as he advised his friend. "Ask her, Gingalain. Stop torturing yourself. You deserve this little happiness, my friend. Things are coming..."

The king remembered the ceremony in the small chapel he had built within his castle. His battle-grimed face had to smile at the beauty of her that day, and the wonder of her that night.

Gingalain recalled the next ceremony in that chapel, how his friend had touched his head and each shoulder with THAT sword. He couldn't help but glimpse the blue-silver steel blade with platinum Damascus waves, simple hammered-iron cross guard and gold pommel with its azure jewel, and night-black leather grip. As the blade touched him, he cast his eyes down. The pale blue glow had to have come from the sword as it touched him; with each touch of that blade, a tingle, not free from pain, ran straight through to burst within his soul.

Now he was here again, riding through the evidence of his royal failure as king. He was too late, too slow to bring the army. Those animals from the North Sea had attacked this village. Gingalain arrived in time to kill them all, but not to spare the village from suffering at their hands. That thought weighed very heavily upon the man the people here called The Good King.

Aglovale rode up beside him, his helmet off, and his armor rent and torn from a northerner's powerful blows. He took a measure of the burden his friend carried.

"Remember, there is another purpose for you, My Good King."

"Aglovale, sometimes that purpose seems ready to crush me."

"A friend of ours once told me, 'Think only of the urgency, of the importance, and the nobility of your task, and you shall gather an ample strength to accomplish it!' You would do well to take to heart the Great King's words!"

"Surely The Liard Himself has placed you as the walking staff for my soul, my old friend!"

"Did you hear that? I think...it comes from the house of Ualas! Come, Gingalain!"

The two men dismounted their panting steeds and carefully entered the stone building, the remnants of its thatched roof still

4

smoldering. The bodies of a raider and the home's master lay just inside the portal.

The noise was obvious now, a young one was sobbing quietly. Moving to the back of the house, Gingalain saw him first; a very young boy, perhaps two or three years old, standing over the body of one of the raiders. A knife was buried to the hilt in the back of the savage's neck.

"Mommy!" the sobbing boy pointed to the dead man.

Aglovale rolled him over, and the two knights gasped at the woman, bloody cloths ripped off of her, an ugly wound on her head where her attacker had struck the fatal blow.

The two knights stood in silence for a moment, hoping the scene before them would transform. Aglovale felt his friend's blood begin to boil.

"What is this lad's name?" Gingalain quietly asked Aglovale.

"Padraig Ualas, Sire. His father was a good friend. His mother a kind woman."

"Aglovale, bring the Ualas boy to my wife. We shall raise him as our own. Our lack of offspring is not due to a lack of passion; perhaps there is a greater reason for that and this abomination around us. I have some urgent business across the North Sea. We shall not be raided again, or I shall not return. By God, Kintyre shall be free of this!" Gingalain turned and strode out of the room.

Aglovale had seen him like this before, many years ago. He was very glad he did not live where these raiders came from.

# The Young Boy

"May we eat, *now*, your Majesty?" The king detected just a trace of whining in the voice of the young page as they trudged through the waist deep snow. The page had not asked this question for a whole day, by his own count; surely it was time now! The boy's face was red with the cold, winter night, his eyebrows caked with frost combed from the stinging wind.

"Soon enough, my little one", answered the king, his words steaming through his smile in the cold of the winter night.

The king had raised the page since he was two years old, artfully deflecting all who inquired about the origins of the child. As he grew, young Padraig had taken the duties of the Good King's page, and in time people had come to call him by that title as if it were his name.

Each mid winter the king had trekked out through the snow, bundled with supplies for the entire season. Where or why he set out each year, the Page did not know; each time he had asked, the king had only replied, "everything in it's own good time!" Last year, the page had timidly asked the king if he could go with him, a request that had been swiftly denied on the assertion that the page was not strong enough for the task. All year had the boy prepared himself to rebut that charge, and this year had nearly demanded of his Mentor the permission to accompany him.

The king treated his ten-year-old charge as a son. Although he was not his son, he was never spoiled or positioned above others, as a prince would be. Unless, of course, he had truly earned that elevation. "Now, hurry, my boy! Hurry!" The king's exclamation, the excitement in his voice added to the boy's energies as his pride in the boy's determination added warmth to his own smile.

King Gingalain was a large man, and a strong one, in many ways. He was known as the Good King not by any decree, for if he were to choose, it would be 'the reluctant king' that would fit him best. Still, all who knew of him called him the Good King, for it was what his subjects knew him to be. The Good King assured that Kintyre was kept free from the northern raiders, and

Gingalain never tolerated cruelty of any kind. The people of Kintyre were taxed little for their security, and each according his prosperity so that all contributed, but none were burdened.

He carried a large load of firewood in his strong arms and a bundle of furs upon his broad back as he trudged tirelessly through the blowing snows. The young page struggled to keep up with his much lighter load of smoked meats and cheeses, trudging along in his master's footsteps. The boy did love looking at the broadsword that swung from the king's belt, protection against the bears, tigers, and wolves about these parts. On through the deep, crisp snow they went. To where, for what end, the young page knew not. He only knew that he could not feel his feet, and that his face was frozen from the blowing snow and biting cold.

"Never mind the hardships of this trek my boy! Think only of the urgency, of the importance, and the nobility of our task, and you shall gather an ample warmth from it," the Good King advised his charge. "After all, it is not so far that we travel."

If I knew *what* our task was, that would help, thought the boy. "For seven days and seven nights, it is not so far, you say!" the Page muttered under his breath. The good King smiled at his Page's struggles, but he knew that a much higher level of humanity would one day be required of this boy.

"Think not of your body's hardships; focus on your soul's purpose, Page. Remember, each of us is placed where we need to be, so we may help those we know can lest help themselves. It is our duty, assigned from above! Take heart, and know *this* is your reason for being born so smart, so brave, and so strong," the king offered to his page. His heart ached to reach down and place the young lad upon his back, but there was a lesson here. The boy would be a better man for having learned it now.

"I will, my Sire. I tire, but I still try!" Youthful pride had driven the page on, until this expression of pride in him by his king rekindled his soul. This approval from his king would keep the page focused and determined, until that time, years to come, when the Light of Truth would illuminate his true purpose for him.

After a time, and a most difficult passage, the pair came upon a small, ill-repaired cottage with a large cross, painted in azure and gold, upon its simple door. "Here, my boy. This is our destination!" The king exclaimed as he knocked thrice upon the door.

As the small door opened, the page was astonished to see an old woman, nigh twice the age of the king. Her shining hair of lustrous silver was streaked here and there with a few bright copper strands. She wore a clean yet discordant azure and white frock. "Who calls here?" she asked.

"Your humble servant and his page, M'Lady." The king replied softly.

"Come on in, and warm thee by my fire, for it is all I have to offer thee." The woman offered.

"Come, Padraig, warm yourself, quickly, lest all of our host's heat be lost to the night!" the king ushered his page into the small home.

"Sir Le Bel Inconnu, speak kindly to the young one, for he must be one you treasure to bring him so far in this weather just to see me!" the widow instructed.

"Aye, M'Lady. He is an important lad, but he does not yet know it."

The page's eyebrows rose at this exchange. But his attention moved quickly, as it will with all boys his age. He gazed about the small room, noting the sparse furnishings and lack of adornments. He was a bright and observant boy, accustomed to living in the household of a modest king. He did notice the king's apparent comfort with the plainness of the clean, single room dwelling. Being an observant boy, he also noticed a glow in the room above that which the fire should have produced, yet he could spy no source for it. The single adornment Padraig could spot was a wondrously glowing silver cross, inlaid with azure stone, placed upon the wall over the fire.

The boy's eyes widened as the king then knelt before the woman, and bowed his head as he spoke, "Here, M'Lady, allow me the pleasure of this small appreciation of thy hospitality." The page quickly knelt and bowed his head after his king's lead, for he was a smart boy, and he sensed it was the proper thing to do, even if he did not understand why. The Good King offered his burdens to the woman, and placed his bundle of fuel where it would be handy near her fire. Turning to his page, the king nodded once. Page carefully placed his bundles in the most appropriate spot he could find, for he sensed his guardian wished him to act with care and thought. The Good King smiled his reward.

"Thank you, my knight." the woman answered with a grace in her voice that surprised the page. "May I offer ye some sustenance, meager as it may be?"

"We would be honored to partake, M'Lady!" The Good King replied. As the old lady began preparing the meal, Gingalain turned to instruct Padraig, "Notice, my page, that the cold which you feared would overcome you, has fled before M'Lady's kindness?" The boy looked at the fire, and then looked at the wood the Good King had set near it. It now seemed twenty times the bundle of wood the king had carried; yet only one log had Padraig seen before the royal burden was laid there.

"Aye, Sire." was all the young page could meekly say. Yet he did notice warmth that seemed to spread directly from this Lady to his heart, into his arms, his legs, and with it came a renewed vigor and strength. This warmth was fueled just as much by the understanding that the king made this journey on a cold night at The Feast of Stephen each winter.

"My Lady, please be kind enough to accept these tokens of my servitude. This fuel. These furs. And these foods are for thee, from your people, through me, your humble servant." the kneeling king beseeched the woman.

Page noted that the furs were the same ones the king would buy each spring from traders, for 'emergencies' he would claim.

"Good King, thy generosity and kindness grow each year. Rise and accept this token of my loyalty to thee. Eat, with thine page, the humble offerings of this poor widow."

So the three sat at the simple table. The widow served the victuals to her guests, then herself. She then bowed her head and clasped her hands and said, "And He took the bread, gave thanks, and brake it, and gave unto them, saying, 'This is my body which is given for you: this do in remembrance of me'. Likewise also the cup after supper, saying, 'This cup is the new testament in my blood, which is shed for you.' Let us now eat!"

And so the Widow, the Good King and Page ate a simple fare of bread and soup, in a simple room, of a simple cottage, in a simple woods. As he was eating, eyes on the Good King, as always, Page noticed the food tasted richer than anything he had ever eaten in the king's banquet hall. It was better than anything he had ever eaten anywhere. He also noted that while the Good King had several helpings of soup and bread, as did Page, the loaf never shrank, and the soup pot never emptied. A smart boy was the page, for he did not ask for explanations of these miracles. That knowledge would come to him, but not for many years.

After supper and some simple conversation, the Good King and his page bid farewell to the widow and began their trek home. After a time, the page spoke to his king, in running, rapid-fire thoughts as the young his age so often do, "Sire, how is it that the same cold wind which bit so sharply at me on our journey out, now is but a trifle? How is it that a simple meal of soup and bread satisfied so much more than any feast in your banquet hall? Is it that we are not burdened by the loads we had carried on our trek out? And, Sire, why do you carry such a load out so far; surely you could have your servants perform such a menial task?"

At each question the Good King merely smiled in response, but at the last query Gingalain stopped in his tracks. He turned and looked down upon the boy for some time before answering. "My page, you learn fast and well. You see the truths that wise men miss. Tonight, you see, but have not understood completely yet. You have this to learn; our task tonight was not menial in any way." The Good King smiled as he continued, "Yes, my boy, you are learning lessons unspoken." King Gingalain knelt in front of his page to place his royal face at the level of his chosen pupil. He placed his hands upon the lad's shoulders, looking him squarely in the eyes.

"Certain acts, by unburdening the loads of others, will in kind serve to unburden *our* loads, while they also strengthen our souls. Remember that which Friar Colum Cille has taught. Search your heart, for therein The Laird God has set the answers ye seek, but hav'na asked. They lay there as much as in any of my words. Now, promise me this; that whate'er you shall undertake, where'er you shall travel, whate'er fortunes you shall acquire, you will ne'er forget this night, the meaning of The Feast of Stephen, or the satisfaction and sustenance from the simple meal eaten this night."

Not quite understanding, and a little awed by his guardian's intense attention, the page replied, "My king, I promise thee, I shall never forget this night."

This promise, as with all he made thereafter, the page kept for his entire life.

Once, some five years after their first winter trek, King Gingalain lay ill with a fever, and could not consider a trip in the snow. His loyal page, now a strapping young man, took it upon himself to run the affairs of Gingalain during this time. And a fine job of it he did; none would question his authority to do so, for all who had dealings with the king knew of his pupil. And Page did it not to glorify himself or raise his station. Rather, he did what he simply thought needed to be done, no more, no less.

When the day came at hand for the annual trek, Page undertook it alone, with double the burden. Yet the weight he felt was not that of the furs, fuels, and foodstuffs he carried, but of his king's health, and the old women's well being.

Upon delivering his parcels, the woman greeted Page and inquired as to the Gingalain's whereabouts. Padraig was truthful; the widow placed an old hand on each side of his face, drew it down, and kissed his forehead.

The two sat for the usual supper, and again the widow bowed her head for the Grace; but instead of speaking the Word, she simply requested, "Dear Padraig, would ye be so kind as to say the Grace this night?"

Padraig nervously began, hoping he could remember all the words, "And He took the bread, gave thanks, and brake it, and gave unto them, saying, 'This is my body which is given for you: this do in remembrance of me'. Likewise also the cup after supper, saying, 'This cup is the new testament in my blood, which is shed for you.'"

"Amen" the widow said softly. "Well said, Sir Padraig. Ye have remembered the words; does ye understand the meaning they carry?"

Padraig's eyes opened wide at her utterance of that accolade, reserved for a status higher than he had aspired to since his youthful dreaming. Yet he only answered the question of the widow, rather than task her with his own queries. His answer brought a smile to the face of the old woman. "I was taught by Friar Colum Cille that The Savior spoke these words at His Last Supper, M'Lady. He suffered for us, for our sins, so that we may know everlasting life in Him."

"I see Gingalain has spared no effort in thine education, Sir Padraig."

"I believe that to be true, M'Lady." Padraig added to himself, "But, as I am not his son, I know not why he would do so."

After the supper of bread and soup, as he prepared to take his leave of her, Page knelt before the widow, for it always seemed the right posture to take with her, and asked, "These five years have I come with the Good King to visit you, and I do not know your name. What may I call you, M'Lady?"

"Call me Gwenever, young knight. Now, I must repay thine chivalry and compassion towards an old widow. Here, this has been set-aside for thee, for quite some time, from mine own house at Camlann. The time is right for thee to take charge of it." She handed him a flat, oval bundle of bright but worn azure and gold cloth. Page was amazed as he took it from her single hand, for the weight was such that he could barely avoid dropping it until his second hand steadied the weight. He slung it where it seemed to belong, across his left shoulder, and kissed the old widow's forehead.

She then bade him to make haste in returning to watch over the king. When Padraig arrived back at the castle, he first checked on his mentor, for there his greatest concerns resided, and told him of the visit with the widow. When he related to the Good King that the widow had asked him to say The Grace, Gingalain's face beamed brightly while his eyes filled with tears. "She gave you the bundle, then, Sir Page?"

"Sire, the kind widow did that, and she also called me 'Sir Padraig', and 'Sir Knight'. I am not a knight, Sire!"

"Knighthood is only *recognized* by the king's sword, my good lad; it is *earned* well before that ceremony. I will formalize that status with the Rights next Wednesday. If The Great Queen has stated it, so it shall be done!" The king smiled. "Now, Sir Knight, go, and examine that which the Great King's widow has bestowed upon you! Oh, but such a contented rest I will have now!" The Good King beamed as Padraig had seldom seen.

Page returned in trembling confusion to his rooms. Surely I am not worthy of this, he thought. What did the Good King say, the widow was, could it be? Artair's Gwenhwyfar? Yet, The Great King's widow was said to have died long ago, and Sir Gawain and all his sons, as well. Yet the widow had bestowed the bundle upon him, and had knighted him in word if not in deed! The king has raised him as his own son, so he cannot be dead! The Good King, Sir Gingalain, still lives, and would perform that deed this week, after he had explained to his Page the lies that were spread about the fall of Camlann. But Padraig still wondered, what is the bundle?

With hundreds of thoughts running in his head, Padraig laid the thing on his bed, and bent over it to unwrap the fine Roman cloth from the heavy bundle. When this was done, he stood in awe; before him was a large shield, bearing the marks of many a battle, yet looking new and fresh, a brightly shining silver thing with a great cross quartering it; in the upper left quarter, a lion, the upper right, an eagle, the lower left, a galley, and in the lower right a fish, all rendered in azure blue and gold upon the silver background. Near the leather armband and handhold he found a dark copper stain; could this be the blood of the Great King, Artair? Legend spoke of such a shield, but such was the humility of Page that he believed this just a simple gift, no more; he shut such thoughts of grandeur from his mind.

It was the last winter the old widow would see from this earth. It was also the winter when Page learned that life was not about seeing exotic locations, or having fun, or adventure, or excitement, but perhaps that life was about your duty to the people you traveled life's path with.

# The Inn

Padraig Ualas rode Gilda into the small town. He sat un-armored atop his red roan mare this early spring morning, save for the azure blue and silver shield hung behind his left shoulder. His only weapons were the dirk hung at his left waist and the light mace swinging off the right of his saddle. So early in the morn was it that none were about to take notice of him. This was as he had planned it, avoiding the attention an armored knight would command upon entering these towns. The townsfolk's lives were hard enough without having to pay homage to him; it took more from them than it would ever give to him. After all, he was here to help them. He was not here to collect their admiration.

Page had been through this town with the king Gingalain twelve years ago, during this very season. The village had been full of life and vitality then. He remembered the king had bid him to stay at the inn while he attended to business "not suitable for young pages." He remembered two things of that bright time; he had spent a hard three days working with the smithy as he forged a new sword for the king, (the very same sword that he had shattered but two morns ago), and that this had been the only time the king had removed him from inclusion in his business since he had met the widow Gwenever. The king returned with a slash across his right arm and numerous bruises. Padraig later learned that Gingalain had been at war. Now it seemed as if the damp, grey skies echoed the waning life of this place.

His eyes moved quickly around the village. These were humble homes, some mere piles of stone with turf roofs, and some showing signs of recent fire. The streets, some cobblestone paved, most not. A Roman-built stonewall protectively encircled them all, yet the jumbled heaps of stone which had once been homes bore witness to the inadequacies of it. Page spied three toed footprints throughout the unpaved streets. His hand moved to his mace and gripped it tightly, knuckles blanching as he scanned the skies.

Dragons!

He had been taught about those vile banshees, though he had ne'er seen one. His training fueled his anger at their presence here, as well as his apprehension over that fact. Was he fit enough to handle them? His tutors, from Master Zin to Friar Colum Cille to Sir Bohrs, the old Master at Arms, had told him he was, but still...

He rode up to a small building with signage proclaiming "The Good King's Common Inn," searching through the mist fogging the village as well as the skies above with eyes and ears. Page noticed a tall boy tending to horses behind the Inn, and a girl with a basket emerging from the chicken coop. Not having been observed so far, Padraig dismounted and walked confidently to the inn's door.

He knocked thrice, as was his custom, and patiently waited.

Presently the door opened to reveal a white bearded man of moderate build and confident bearing. "Yes?" the innkeeper peered at Padraig, studying every inch as his gaze traveled up and down the very tall, stout young man before him. "How may I serve thee, Sir Knight?"

"I will require a room for the night, meals for the day, and boarding for my horse, good man. Pray that there is such available for thy humble servant?"

"Your speech is of the house of the Gingalain, Sire. My hearth and home is yours, as it would be his, for as long you require."

"Humble am I to accept your hospitality, good sir. Please accept this purse as a down payment on my account." Padraig offered a leather pouch, heavy with coin, but not overly so, to the man.

"You are too kind, Sir Knight." The innkeeper said as he accepted the purse. "How may I address thee?"

"Most call me Page, innkeeper" Padraig replied, out of respect for his mentor, as only the Gingalain and the widow Gwenever had ever called him by his given name. "Now, please, tell me of the dragon sign I see throughout this good village."

"Please, Sir Page, speaking of such things is forbidden by the sheriff," The old innkeeper's frown colored the nervous whisper.

As he ushered Page quickly inside the vestibule, his bright and alert eyes searched for any eavesdroppers nearby.

"Then speak of it not, and allow me entrance into thy inn, that I may rest there and break my fast."

"Please, good Knight, come in–this way to break your fast." The innkeeper called to his stable boy, "Edan! Son, take the good knight's mount to the stable and see that she is cared for properly!"

As the bored-looking teen took the reins of the knight's steed, Page rubbed his blonde head and placed a coin in the lad's pocket, missing the brief frown cast across Edan's face. Before entering the Inn, he turned his back to the Innkeeper briefly. The old man glanced at Page's shield slung across his broad back, and as the azure blue color and triple crowns registered, his eyes widened.

The public room of the inn showed modest furnishings befitting the small village in which it resided. Page was shown to a seat in the public room for his refreshment, and soon the morning's fare was placed before him. A shy young girl, the same he had spied leaving the chicken coop earlier, gave him service of the meal. She was wearing a simple garb suitable for a modest lass. Her long, golden hair, her bright eyes, and her upturned nose captivated Page. He made sure to thank her each time she came to serve him. But try as he might, the only response to his attempts at conversation was a blushing smile as she turned away.

When the innkeeper returned to assure the knight's satisfaction, Page asked of him, "Innkeeper, the kind lass serving me, would she be thy daughter?"

"Yes, kind Knight. She is my flower, my life. Her mother passed at her brother's birth, and now these two alone command my soul. Pray thee to be an honorable man?"

"Fear not, kind sir. I have no vice nor malice in heart nor mind for you or yours. Please, may we speak of the signs I have noted throughout this village? Is there a winged plague which troubles this humble place?"

Nervously the innkeeper looked about, and in hushed tones replied, "Dragons be here, Sir Page! Three of them, and they do the bidding of the sheriff, Rascur. Half of this village and the surrounding farms have fed them, all at the pleasure of the sheriff. I would speak not, but my Flower has he cast his eyes upon, and I fear so for her! So young! Please, Sir Knight, help this old father to protect his Flower, for her brother Edan is too young, and I am too old to stand against Rascur!"

"Fear not, good father. As long as I draw breath, no father shall know that fear for his offspring. This I pledge by the name of Gingalain, the Good King, who raised me as his own."

"It *is* you! Heavens be praised!" The innkeeper fell to his knees, and through his tears exclaimed, "You 'ave come home as promised, and we will be saved!"

# The Sword

"What is this you speak, good father? Who has promised what to you?"

"Gingalain was here when Gwen was but a babe. He told me that some day, when all seems to be forever dark, the Chosen One would bring the Light and lead us along the Way to Salvation. Could he be speaking of any but you, Sir Page?"

"You cob some very large boots for me, Innkeeper. Help you I will, but Salvation? The Laird God administers that divine Grace, not this mortal Page. Tell me, good man, what of the dragons? What of the dread you hold around your flower?"

"Her name is Gwen, Sir Page, my Gwenellen. The Sheriff, Rascur, has decreed that every maiden of age shall be sacrificed to the dragons. We think he keeps them in his dungeon for himself. God only knows how he has control of the dragons, but all who oppose Rascur they rip apart. My Gwen is of age, and the bastard Rascur has cast his eye her way. He's told me to send her to him, to spare her the dragon's fire. I fear I've almost done that many times this year!" the innkeeper sobbed.

"Not much older than her am I, yet you place all your faith in me, good father?"

"My faith is in God and Christ, good Knight. Yet, I know you are sent for our relief. Gingalain brought you home those dozen years ago. Wise he was in choosing you. I feel it."

"Is there a blacksmith nearby? I was besieged by meirleachas, and my sword was shattered on those robbers' heads. I shall require a sound blade of more weight than my dirk and mace to defend the honor of one so fair as your lovely Gwenellen."

"The smithy was killed by the dragons nearly as they arrived. He was alive as they opened him up and ate his liver in the village square. But, I may have what you need." The innkeeper looked around quickly. "Come." And he went through the kitchen door with Page close behind. Down into the root cellar, behind the ale and wine casks, there stooped the innkeeper holding his candle.

"Down here, Sir Ualas."

A hidden door! Down again, into the damp, dark hole painted by the flickers of the candle. Then, behind a crate of turnips, the innkeeper brushed the dirt off of a package.

"My brother brought me this long ago. Of the Table, was he. The last to see the Great King alive, and this he brought to me, to keep here. Afraid, was I, ever to e'en gaze upon this legend again. He wrapped it and placed it here, my brother did. He stayed and guarded it, until he slept, never to awaken. That was the day my Edan was born and his mother was taken. To the Good King I told this tale. For you he told me. This is for you!" The old man trembled as he lifted a cloth-wrapped parcel in his shaking hands. As long as Page was tall, and Page was a tall man, this parcel was. Page watched the old man lift it with one hand, and offered it to a puzzled Page.

Amazed that an old innkeeper could handle a package of that weight with one hand, Page nearly dropped the parcel in surprise at its heft. Setting it down across his lap, carefully, as if he was unwrapping The Savior in the manger, Page stripped the cloths from the package. A glint of metal, and the dark cellar became awash with a brilliant, pale blue light. The warmth of it returned thoughts of the Widow's cottage to Padraig's mind.

"Could it be? My Laird! It can not be, but it could only be!"

"Yes, Sir Knight, it is!"

"Excalibur?" Page whispered in awe.

"Aye!"

Wide-eyed, Page held the legendary sword aloft in one hand as he stared at its beauty. If e'er a metal object could awe a true Christian, Excalibur would have been that object. The blade was bright bluish-silver steel with platinum Damascus waves, the cross guard simple hammered-iron, the grip wrapped in night-black leather, and the gold pommel held an azure jewel. The blade was so sharp it seemed to cut the light somehow. And the balance! This blade was made for him, and him alone! He felt it. Could the Great King have been his size, his exact size? Or did the Sword, that mystical thread back into Celtic lore and legend, somehow adapt to his size, strength, and style?

"Picked you, Sir Page. Selected you, the Sword has." The innkeeper quietly declared. "My brother could barely hold it, and half a head taller than you was he. Never balanced in his hand, not meant for him, he said. Scarcely able to lift its dead weight was I, 'til you were here. In your hand, Sir Knight, 'tis alive again. In the Great King's hand I 'ave seen it, glowing as now. Measures you heart it does, good Knight."

"You knew Artair? How so? You're not old enough!"

"A young lad was I. Fetching his armor was my task. The iron cross-guard, he said, made from the very Roman nails used on the Savior. I saw him wield it in battle but once; such a terror, that sight! Singing, it was, and a brilliant light all about it, like an Angel's sword! When it struck, it moved too fast for the eyes to see," the innkeeper tapped his temple, "and these were eyes of a young man then." Trembling, the innkeeper went on; "My brother, much older, served at the Table of the Great King. Later, I did also. As did King Gingalain, though he is younger by far than I. That Good King is a cousin of the Great King, and came to rule Kintyre after the Great King's passing.

"A full score of love God gave me with my wife, Grace. Then he gave me Gwen and Edan, and took Grace from me. So I could care for my two without distraction, I would say. Sixty-eight years have I lived. Time's a-comin' for another to care for my flowers." The innkeeper's eyes suddenly became bigger as he stared at the glowing sword.

"My good Knight, the Sword, it be singing."

And it was. As Page held it, the shining masterpiece issued forth a quiet chorus, as Angels would sound, just below the level of hearing. The singing was there, but as if from far away. Page felt a slight vibration in the hand holding the Sword; rather than distracting, it increased his comfort and made The Sword feel weightless.

The innkeeper took all this under his gaze, and stepped slightly back behind the knight. The shield he gazed upon also glowed with a cool, pale blue flame, and the old man could see the three golden crowns aglow on the azure field. It was! It was the Great King's Azure Shield!

Page was awed, excited, yet he felt calm, a peace he had not felt since king Gingalain had last been with him. How he missed his old mentor. Why had he just ridden off that day over a year ago? To where had he gone?

"Dear sir, what is your name?"

"You would know my name as Aglovale, Sir Padraig," whispered the innkeeper.

"Sir Aglovale! Your brother was…"

"Percival"

"Sir Percival!"

# The Sheriff

"Tell me, what of dragons, Sir Aglovale?"

"Please, good Knight, dunna use my former title! The sheriff would burn me if he knew! The village folk know me as Vale."

"As you wish, Vale. Tell me of the dragons?"

"There are three of them. All do as the sheriff bids. Ugly, cruel incarnations they be. Tall as a horse, are they, yet with wings, and talons as an eagle, and heads as snakes. Fearsome and cruel."

"Where did they come from?"

"No one knows for certain. They came with the sheriff. Perhaps he brought them with him from Caledonia. He came with little, and then the dragons came and he prospered. Now he's rich, while we all suffer the loss of our daughters. Without our daughters, there can be no new families. Without new families, there will be no future for this village, for this county."

"Perhaps tomorrow would be a good time to meet this sheriff."

"Care you must take in that, Sir Knight. He would seek you out as soon as he knew you were here. Going to him would be advisable, but you must be careful."

"Vale, I am always careful." smiled Page. "Now, where may I find this, sheriff?"

"Rascur rules from the hill north of the village. He taxes as a king; but no king is he!" The rancor dripped off the old knight's words as they passed his lips.

"There is more to being a true king than amassing taxes and dispensing suffering. The Good King taught me that in many ways."

"Aye, and the Great King Artair lived by that Way as well. No dragon from the Heavens nor from Hell could stand before him, let alone a mere man."

So the two men shared their understanding of the Way things were; that Kings and Heroes dwelt on a level apart from that occupied by mortal men. But not only in their powers and deeds; for kings such as Artair could often elevate mere mortal men far

22

above their own dimension. A true king, through the Grace of God, empowered those loyal to God and Country in ways inconceivable by mere mortals.

And so Page sheathed the legendary sword; his scabbard seemingly made for this blade alone. He bade Vale well and left the good man to tend his inn, mounted Gilda and rode for the hill to the north of the quiet village. As he gave one short glance back, he thought he spied, just for a heartbeat, the form of a young maiden peering out of the second story window. Real or imagined, Page decided, the thought lifted his spirits to a smile. "Remember", he recited to himself the lesson the Good King had taught him so well, "Strive not for your own glee. Strive but to serve others, and your own happiness will be thus assured."

On he rode through the surprisingly quiet village. He recalled being here once before, many years ago, with the Good King; he recalled a busy, vibrant, alive community, full of laughter and commerce. Now, he could nearly smell the damp gloom that had moved into this place.

"Easy, Gilda, easy, girl! Calm your fears. Remember that He is with us, as always." Page soothed his nervous mount. The young filly was strong, very quick, with good wind, and fiercely protected her rider. When Page had tried to tame a large stallion last spring, that horse had thrown him and seemed certain to trample him until Gilda jumped three fences to land squarely between the fire-hearted stallion and Page. For several long moments did the larger stallion stand and stare at this young filly, just half his size; then he bowed his head and backed away slowly, as if commanded by a higher master. Gilda had remained near Page most of his living hours ever since.

"I wish you could tell me, Gilda, what has you so en garde? Be it dragons? I doubt a warren of the beasts could give you pause, now could they?" Page soothed himself with his words as much as his mount.

Up the hill to the gate amid stonewalls fit for the residence of a king, rather than a king's servant, rode Page. Four armored men gave presence at the gate, and challenged him, as his approach became known.

"Hrmpf! Halt! What business 'ave ya 'ere?" the largest snarled to Page.

"Good captain, I have come to see your sheriff Rascur, at the behest of our king!"

"Hrmpf! King! Hrmpf! None 'ave we 'eard from that old one fer two moons! Hrmpf! Be gone, the sheriff needna be troubled with the likes of ya!" the captain of the guards squinted at Page.

"Good captain, I come as the king's representative to hear of this village. Here, sir, please inspect his seal. And know that I shall have audience with your sheriff." Page's powerful bass voice lowered to nearly a whisper, "and, should your neck beg to sharpen my blade beforehand, I willna protest that much." The captain thought he saw the young man flinch, then felt the warm trickle below his left ear. The young man reached down and wiped some red stain onto the captain's cloak from his dirk. The captain's hand shot up and he felt the small slice begin to sting along the left side of his neck. "Your cloak looks adequate to remove your blood from my edge." Padraig's words seemed to be squeezed out by his narrowing eyes.

Noting the seal of the king, and bleeding from the stranger moving faster than he could see, the captain caught the golden glint from the formidable main blade at the side of this tall stranger. He bade one of his soldiers to go find the sheriff.

"Tell His Excellence an agent of Gingalain is 'ere for him."

"Thank you, kind captain!" Page offered with a flourish. He felt his mount quivering, as if readying for a charge at the man.

"Hrmpf!" was the captain's reply. Page couldn't help but think that this man seemed to grunt that way quite much too often.

Soon, but not soon enough for the captain, whose nerves frayed more with each second he spent under Gilda's glare, the soldier returned and gave word to him. After several more "Hrmpfs!" the captain led Page to the house.

The disgruntled guard led Page through two more gates and an imposing portal with heavy wooden doors. Page found himself waiting in an ornately, yet darkly decorated gallery. To pass the time he studied the lugubrious portraits adorning the dank hall.

"How may an 'umble sheriff be of service to an agent of the king?" a gravelly voice broke the long wait.

Page turned slowly and measured the owner of that voice. Short, middle aged and fat, this was no active man, but a slovenly usurper of the labors undertaken by others, Page thought.

"Greetings, sheriff. I come seeking word of our king! I understand he passed this way not too long ago?"

"Of the king, I've no news to share with ya. Many a time have I sent word, seeking a visit from the king, yet ne'er has he 'onored me with his presence. What business with the Good King brings ya to my little protectorate?"

"As long as I have cause to be here, perhaps an accounting of the king's taxes and tributes would be in order." Padraig felt the damp, dark chill of a dishonest man spreading from this sheriff.

"Maybe, young man" muttered the sheriff darkly. "But first, let me prepare a room for ya to refresh in, afore we dine, yeah?"

"Most gracious, but I will keep residence in the village until my business is complete." Lest I become separated from my head as I sleep, Padraig thought.

"Oh, but ya must stay 'ere! I insist! Besides, it may not be safe in the village, e'en for a gentleman such as yerself." The sheriff squinted at the large sword scabbard hanging from Page's waist, with a leather cover protecting the pommel from prying eyes. "Or, should I say, Sir Knight?" The sheriff cast a suspicious eye to Page's face.

"My other business is not of your concern, so long as the accounting of the king's taxes is acceptable. Neither is my name nor my title, other than that you know I am the king Gingalain's agent." Such was the firmness and authority of Page's words and the manner of their delivery that the sheriff felt forced to step back twice.

"So be it, Sir Knight." Rascur turned and stormed out of the room.

As soon as he was out of sight, Page heard the faint rumbles of far off shouting, along with another wailing sound he could not quite place, except that it chilled him to his very soul.

Presently, the captain of the guard returned, explaining that the sheriff had appointments all night but would be happy to host him early in the following morn, just after sunrise. The captain then ushered Page out of the house and pointed Page to the road that led off the grounds.

Page mounted Gilda, who seemed both relieved for his return and nervous about something. As they passed the first turn in the road they were met with such a shriek that Page feared his ears would burn off! A shadow spread over them in the twilight, a shadow of a thick yet snake-like body carrying leathery scalloped wings before a forked tail.

Dragon!

# The Dragons

So well had Page trained, so diligently had he studied and practiced, yet it was almost all for naught. He hesitated. Only for a brief instant. But with dragons, hesitation most often meant death.

It was Gilda that saved him.

The faithful young mare saw the dragon's shadow and reacted as if she were winged Pegasus; she leapt so high the shocked dragon froze in mid strike. Instead of dealing a deathblow, he came under the fury of four sharp, instinctive hooves lashing with unbearable force. Gilda's forelegs caught only the wings, but completely shredded those leathery appendages. Her powerful hind legs came up next as she spun when her forelegs grounded, and these caught the beast full in its unholy chest, crushing the bones inside and silencing the beast's ghastly shriek of surprise by crushing the air from him.

Page had been thrown from Gilda as she struck at the beast, but time seemed to slow for him now as Master Zin's training quickly took hold, and good training it had been. Page hit the ground on his feet even as he reached for Excalibur; how his mystic weapons surprised him as Excalibur was in his right hand before that hand had reached the scabbard, and the Azure Shield on his left arm even as he thought of it! Without hesitation Page swung the shield up high, followed by the singing blade, up and to his left, as he turned his hips to bring all his power into his swing. Page felt a terrific impact hit the shield, using the force of the blow to add momentum to the glowing blade. Excalibur flashed in movement faster than any mortal arm could swing or any mortal eye could follow, parting the crimson skin, the sword seemingly guiding his strike in an arc that ended with the fabled blade back in his scabbard, his shield slung across his back! Page panted breathlessly as he watched the two pieces that had but a second before been one rather large dragon hit the ground, parted in two from its left shoulder to its right knee. Its wings shredded, what most would call the breast of the crimson beast looked as though a score of maces had used it for a target. Sharp, six-inch long talons on the large hands and feet, with slimy, yellow-green fangs grinned at the front of the snake-like, protruding mouth. All of it now bathed in the foul, putrid stench of coal black dragon blood. And the eyes, set on each side of a narrowed head, so as to give vision forward over the long snout. Dead. Black. Cold. Bottomless. Unearthly, evil eyes.

The entire encounter had taken but three seconds. Page felt rather than saw the shadow come up behind him. The familiar wet nose gave him a tap on his shoulder, Gilda's way of telling him it was time to go. "Good idea, girl. Are you alright?" For, as he had felt his trusted mount draw near, he also now sensed a dark, terrible danger among the grey clouds ahead over the town.

A frisky head shake and snort gave him his answer, and though two talons had cut her flank, her wounds were not deep. Page mounted her and let her choose the speed back to the inn. She went at a defiant trot; head high, daring another attack even as she and Page kept a more watchful eye about for just that occurrence.

Padraig knew there were two more dragons. That is where his sense of dread was centered. Not for Gilda or himself, but for the villagers. They would be two very angry dragons.

Just as his apprehension peeked a bone-chilling screech filled the air, with a second added before the first had finished.

"Gilda, faster, girl-GO!" Page urged, flashes of the innkeeper and the face of his daughter passing before his mind's eye. But the young mare already had hit her full speed at the sound of devilish screeches harmonizing over the village ahead.

The two dragons!

As they neared the wall, the two beast's horrid cries were joined by the terrified screams of villagers, those he was charged to protect. Even faster Gilda galloped, her earlier nervousness banished as her muscles were fed by her master's anger.

Page's blood boiled as he imagined what was happening to his charges. The inn! He had to get to the inn! The girl, the old knight, and the stable boy were the only souls he had seen outside of the sheriff's palace since he arrived. He knew he had to save them, there was a *reason* they had been placed before him! He just *knew* it!

Through the gate, and he saw them. One, twice the size of the beast he and Gilda had killed, and a second, even larger yet. Low they flew over the thatched roofs, and where they passed, the roofs burned.

Screaming villagers ran from the burning homes, some afire themselves. Into the streets they fled, right into the slashing talons of the dragons. Page watched horrified as a woman with smock aflame ran into the street. Page anguished as she was slashed from behind by one dragon, then from the front by the second. Yet too far away to save her, Page saw the beasts playing with the screaming woman, their talons picking and cutting her flesh at will as they hit her between them, from one to the other and back. How long it took to close the short distance, Page thought, as every slash of the woman's skin he felt as a dagger thrust straight through his own soul.

Padraig watched in horror as the larger dragon looked straight at him, grinning even as Gilda nearly flew to close the distance between them. Excalibur was in his hand, no matter he had not yet reached for it. The Azure Shield was upon his arm, though he never pulled it from his back. Up Excalibur went to smite the grinning beast. But, fast as Gilda was, and as quickly as Padraig moved in battle, they were not fast enough.

"NO!" Page roared as the grinning dragon opened his pointed snout wide, and then turned and snapped it closed about the woman's neck, removing her head just before Page was in range! Up the dragon jumped, wings unfurling, flapping, that blood chilling screech being echoed from behind him...

The second dragon hit Page from behind as he was distracted by the first. The blow was of such force it threw Page off his mount, and pushed Gilda to the earth as well. Both knight and horse were stunned, Page unmoving as Gilda scrambled to her feet. Without any speed the horse looked an easy target, but she would not leave her master. As one dragon dove on the brave animal, the other would try to dive on the fallen knight. Dragons this size were powerful beasts, but possessed nothing close to the power of an average horse. And Gilda was far superior to any normal steed. Even with Gilda's power and quickness, she could not stop every attack on the knight, but those talons that did strike at Padraig found only the incredibly hard metal of the Azure Shield. When dragon flesh hit the three crowned shield, the dragon flesh burned.

Page moved up to his knees quickly, twisting in a blur of motion, and then stood again with Excalibur in his hand. The wondrous singing from the sword drowned the screeching of the dragons from his ears; the pale blue light from it shone all around the knight, growing stronger and stronger as Padraig regained his wits.

The dragons changed their plan and attacked Gilda now. This was no easy challenge for dragons even this large, for one strong, well-placed kick from the aroused equine could prove fatal for a dragon. But the two coordinated their dives, and did manage to move her away from Padraig enough to slash her deeply twice.

A third attack was coming from front and rear when the larger dragon was hit by a spinning blur, the Azure Shield. Sir Bohr had made Padraig practice this so many times that he didn't have to think, the spinning shield unerringly hitting the dragon edge-on square in his chest. The living metal burned through the dragon where it stuck, nearly halving him. Where the Azure Shield's three crowns touched the beast, the dragon burst into a bright, pale blue fire that quickly engulfed him, spreading out from the wounds to completely consume the unnatural abomination.

Page raced to where the dragon would fall, wanting to prolong the fatally injured beast's pain as much as he could. The face of that tortured woman, eyes pleading, was etched on his vision; Padraig's rage ensured that this beast would get as she had given.

Pulling his shield from the dying beast, Page looked for the last red-scaled monster. He caught a streak of red diving to his left, near the inn.

Page ran as fast as he could, moving faster than even Gilda could run. It was not far, but to Padraig it seemed a world away. He could see the smoke. As he turned the corner before the inn, his heart burst; the inn was aflame. There, with an old sword still clutched in his powerful grip, the blade dripping black dragon blood, lay the innkeeper, the old knight Aglovale. Breath still was in him, but not much.

"Sir Aglovale!" sobbed Page, "you killed it? The last dragon?"

"No, my son. Only a slash along her cheek." The old knight cried, his laments escaping as whispers from his crushed chest. "She has wounded me mortally in return!" And the old man coughed blood onto the ground. After a moment, he continued, quietly, "My Flower, my Gwen! Gone, taken by that beast!" The old knight's tears poured out faster than his blood.

"Fear not, good Knight, I will find her and deliver her back to you!" Page struggled to give the man a reason to cling to life. The effort was valiant, but the injuries too severe in body and spirit.

"Save her, Sir Page. For I will ne'er look upon her again."

"The armorer for King Artair! You are called!" Padraig meant to command sternly, attempting to rally the knight with his call to duty, but his words only trembled through his tears.

"No, Sir Padraig Ualas. My calling was complete when Excalibur found you, for that is what Merlin tasked me. Use the tools you have been given, and save my two flowers!"

And after he said those words, Sir Aglovale looked into Page's eyes, and then he breathed no more.

Page began to sob, for the old knight, the woman, the other villagers, and for Gwenellen. A great sadness crept into his soul, but for a brief moment, forgetting that he had never told Sir Aglovale his true name. His despair submerged him in his own failures; he was too slow, too clumsy, too inexperienced to save these good people.

Just as that bottomless pit began to open beneath him, his shoulder was pushed from behind. And pushed again. The third push woke him to reality, as he turned to see Gilda staring straight into his eyes. The young mare cocked her head to the side slightly, and snorted. Padraig was sure that he heard the widow Gwenever's elegant voice saying, "Well, Sir Padraig, what are ye waiting for?"

# The Quest

"To the sheriff we go, then. How are you, girl? Feel up to it?" Page reached up and gently stroked the red roan's cheek. Looking into Gilda's eyes, the young knight saw no fear, no pain, but only a steadfast determination that quickly fueled his own.

Brushing down her sides, Page was thankful the wounds seemed shallow. But he had missed one long, deep gash near the saddle. Clumsily he moved to fix the Azure Shield to his mount's saddle, and spotted the gash just as the blue metal touched the wound. Page gasped as the wound closed at the shield's touch! Gently, yet with great urgency, he applied the relic's healing wherever Gilda showed injury. Soon, she was as if ne'er a talon had touched her.

Back along those same roads to the sheriff's house Gilda carried Page at a determined pace. Both the horse and rider's eyes vigilantly scanning the dark grey clouds for any sign of the red beast. The growing darkness gave witness to the setting sun as they came upon that now familiar gate.

Padraig could determine no sign of the guards they had passed just a short time ago. The ev'ning mists reflected the gloom Page felt as Gilda quickened her pace to the house. Rounding the bend where he had met the first dragon, Page saw that the body was not there, although the creature's blood still glistened under the rising moon. Slowing now, Gilda gave an alert as she sniffed the air; Page also picked up the acrid scent of fire!

Coming up to the house, a gruesome sight met the intrepid knight and his mount. The sheriff's guard, dozens of men, brutally slaughtered and dismembered, lay strewn about the grounds. Page worried for Gilda as he dismounted her, but was reassured, as she snorted, standing tall and defiant before him. Into the house ran Padraig, noting that the scent of smoke from numerous small fires did nothing to mask the coppery odor of fresh blood. The hall was as if painted in red, so numerous were those grisly streaks and splatters. Padraig stepped over parts of more guards, arms, legs, heads; it was all Page could do to keep down the bile this scene bade him to wretch.

There! The stairway! Up the stairs Page flew, his purpose submerging his nausea as he took a pair of steps in each great stride. More carnage; what had this weasel of a man, this "sheriff", wrought? More fires in the sleeping chambers gave Page pause; after all he had seen here, would there be anything still living in this gruesome reflection of Hell? Padraig stopped, turning back in preparation of descending the stairway.

"Help!"

Did he hear that? So faint, could it have been the girl? Page turned as his deep voice boomed, "Where! Where are you?"

"Here," came the faint reply, "the last room!" Down the hall rushed the driven knight, fearful of finding the girl only as she succumbed to death's embrace.

"Help" again came the forlorn plea. Page now knew this was not his damsel by the gravely voice even as he entered the once grand chamber. If the hallway had been the display of an Evil butcher's wares, this bedchamber was that butcher's slaughterhouse. Gore hung from silken drapes, pieces, chunks of flesh were strewn about as if feed for the hens. "Here. Help me. Please!" the fading voice pleaded from the floor. Page entered the room and was drawn to a scurrying and low, dark movement; the rats fled at the knight's approach to reveal the sheriff, or what remained of the mousey little man. Lying in his own blood; armless, legless, with each stump and most of his torso burned over by the dragon's breath, and then gnawed away by the vermin of his own house, from which he was powerless to defend or escape. The man's wounds had been inflicted to give a slow, painful death. "It hurts so! Please, sir knight, end my pain!" gasped Rascur.

"Where did the beast go? Where did she take the girl? Answer, and I shall end your pain."

"She took the girl with her. Look to the north, well past Oban to the Isle of Skye. There would she have gone, for that is from whence she came!"

Sir Page left the house of death to the fires, but after he had kept his promise to release the sheriff's suffering.

Mounting Gilda, he started up the path to the main road, the knight suddenly felt drained by both the days' events and the task laid before him. Skye was many days from here, and he knew not how much of that great isle he needed to search. To reach the Isle of Skye, he would need a boat. How far ahead was the beast? How far could it fly carrying the girl? These questions weighed upon Page's strength as he pondered them; their burden aided the fatigue from the days' battles in pulling him down.

He fought to remember Gingalain's teachings as he rode on recalling the words out loud; "Remember, each of us is placed where we need to be, so we may help those we know can least help themselves. It is our duty, assigned from above! Take heart, and know *this* is your reason for being born so smart, so brave, and so strong!"

Gilda jumped as they approached the gatehouse near the road, lifting the young knight out of his gloomy slog. The loyal mare whinnied softly and pointed, as smart horses are known to, with her nose at the road just past the gatehouse. There stood a large, pure white stallion, a knight's saddle of pure black leather done in the old style easily carried upon his broad back, reins tied to the gatehouse post. At the feet of the fine young horse sat a figure, cloaked in a well-worn, dark blue cape. Page noted the end of a pure black leather and oak scabbard past the sliver hem of the cape.

"Good eve'n to you, Sir..." Page's greeting was cut short as the figure in the cape stood and turned, gazing at him with a steadfast determination from bright brown eyes under a tussle of dirty blonde hair. The inn's stable boy!

"Good Sir Knight, I beseech you to accompany me on my quest."

"Son, a task of mine own occupies me now. I have not the time for the indulgences of adolescent adventurousness." Page replied firmly, yet with a gentle tone. The boy had lost his master to the beast today. "By what means have you outfitted yourself, boy?"

"These are my rightful possessions, formerly my... father's" the young one choked somewhat on the last two words, but quickly regained steadiness. "I am the offspring of Sir Aglovale. These are now my things. I am tasked with the return of my sister, Gwenellen, whom the dragoness has carried off. My cause is just and true, Sir Knight; I ask that you join me in my pursuit."

"Dragons are not for little boys to play with!" Page shot out, and immediately wished he had not.

"I am not a little boy!" the small figure declared in a steady, stern and quiet voice as he reached beneath the cape and capably withdrew an adult sized sword.

"Courage and control you have beyond your years, lad! Hear that I share your quest already. You may accompany me on this journey, as your services may prove useful to me." Padraig realized that the defeat, weariness, and gloom that had been crushing him had vanished. Curious, he thought. "Come, we can make some good distance this night before we must camp. What is your name, brave little one?"

"Call me Edan, Sir Knight."

"Well, Edan, whose name means warrior! Is this your horse? He is quite a large steed for one your size. Will you be able to handle that powerful young mount? Are you even able to climb up on him?"

"I have ridden Greg since he was large enough to carry me. He knows what I want as I think it. We will be fine!" And with that, the small figure turned to the pure white horse, which knelt before his master without word or gesture, and the former stable boy easily mounted the young stallion.

All this time, Greg and Gilda had been locked in an expressionless stare. Page noted that the two mounts gave a quick nod in unison as Greg rose up to his full height. While a young stallion, Greg was already larger than most adult steeds, and half again the size of Gilda. He waited patiently, as a gentleman does, and then assumed a place slightly behind and on Gilda's left side as the two proceeded ahead into the night. Greg was taller than Gilda to the extent that the stable boy's head was even with Page's own.

When, after a few hours, the moon hid behind thick clouds, Page decided they should make camp for the night as they came upon a convenient stream. After unburdening the mounts, the horses drank their fill, then grazed alternately on the spring grasses; one keeping watch as the other ate. Padraig marveled at the sight of this teamwork; never had he seen horses work together this way. As Edan had the foresight to pack bread and cheese, and Page had only a wrapped, smoked haggis and some dried venison; the two made to eat the bread and cheese, as these would spoil sooner.

With the food laid on a cloth before them, Padraig began, "Thank Thee, Father, for that you have placed before us. The Laird is my Sheppard; I shall not want. He maketh me to lie down in green pastures: He leadeth me beside still waters. He restoreth my soul: He leadeth me in the paths of righteousness for His name's sake. Yeah, though I walk through the valley of the shadow of death, I fear no evil: for Thy rod and Thy staff, they comfort me. Thou preparest a table before me in the presence of mine enemies: Thou anointest my head with oil; my cup runneth over. Surely goodness and mercy shall follow ma all the days of my life: and I will dwell in the House of The Laird forever. Let us eat!"

Edan stared at Page for a moment, and then said, "Wait, Sir Knight. One moment." The young one rose and went into the bundles yet again, returning with a leather flask. "Sir Knight, this wine has been consecrated by the Bishop just last New Moon. If you would please, Sir Knight!"

Page gently took the wine from the youngster, and poured into the cup that was with the flask, and began solemnly; "And He took the bread, gave thanks, and brake it, and gave unto them, saying, 'This is my body which is given for you: this do in remembrance of me'. Like wise also the cup after supper, saying, 'This cup is the new testament in my blood, which is shed for you.'"

The two bowed heads as they gave thanks. They did not notice their mounts had paused in their grazing, and stood facing the two as they too were in prayer, heads down as well.

The two Christians then ate.

"Sir Page, how can we e'er hope to overtake the beast that flies?"

"I seem to remember that dragons can only fly a short distance. With the added burden of Gwenellen she can fly each day less than a day's ride for us, from what I can recall. The beast must stop to hunt quite often, so your sister will likely be bound. We will know we are on the track by the leavings of its meals." Page looked up at the adolescent boy, judging his age to be twelve or thirteen. An idea formed in Padraig's mind.

"Edan, tell me, have you had training with your arms?" Page asked the stable boy dressed in a knight's cape.

"My father taught all his children how to defend the weak from aggression. I can use these tools to good effect; but do not assume these are his arms, for my father was wise, and made each of his offspring learn to use the appropriate tools of defense. Our father taught us that we are ne'er unarmed, and my sister will be unafraid to strike when it is prudent to do so," the boy stated, as if explaining how his mother cooked lamb.

"Your father was a wise and good man. The broadsword you have, it is a design I have never seen. What of it?"

"Much as your blessed sword, but lighter, yet longer and more powerful than a Roman or Saxon blade. Father named it for the local smithy; Claymore was his name."

"Had I not this exquisite blade, I would offer you a handsome sum of gold for that!"

"The blade you have, Sir Ualas, can not be defeated while in your hand. My blade has no such assurance, yet sell it could I never. This means much too me Sir! Do not ask such a thing!"

"A compliment to your father and the smithy was all I intended, young one. How did you know my name?"

"My father told me all, Sir Padraig."

"Tell me, have you been trained as a page or a squire?"

"I understand the duties of a squire, Sir Knight." Edan said quietly, head canted to the right as wide eyes considered Page. "What is your intent in asking?"

"Will you squire for me, Mister Edan?"

"I am honored to do so, M'Laird!" came the whispered reply.

"Good! Now, it is time for sleep. Gilda will watch over us as she can, and my thought is, by observation, that Greg will take up while Gilda in turn sleeps. Sleep well, Edan, for the morrow will bring us, besides the beginning of your training, many other challenges, I fear!"

"Good night, good Knight!" a smiling Edan giggled, with a

voice seemingly younger now, Page thought.

Page slept well; for now that he had some one to pass his training onto, the self-doubts flying around in his mind had been banished by the planning of his lessons.

Morning found Page awakened by a firm nudge from Gilda, and greeted by the smells of a roasting rabbit as well as the warmth of the rising sun.

"I see you have been active this morn, Edan!"

"We need a good meal to start our journey, Master."

"Your father has gifted you with a well rounded education. After we eat, bring your dirk and we will see how well you have learned your father's training."

"Yes, Master," grinned Edan.

Their meal passing quickly, knight and squire faced each other over an open spot near the camp. Edan standing ready with his dirk drawn, and Padraig with his still in its scabbard.

Without a word, Page drew his dirk and as he turned, swinging it in an arc aimed to land at the base of Edan's nose. Page moved quickly, more quickly than any other knight could have, but not at his full speed. A smile came to his face as the young Squire's dirk met his, deflecting the blow down and to the side; Edan's dirk continued in its motion quickly up and around to stab the shoulder of the attacker while his dirk arm was down. Except neither the shoulder nor the knight was there! Instead, Page's dirk now lay across Edan's throat, and the knight's other arm pinned the Squire's dirk arm to his side from behind.

"Your reactions are very good, Edan. Now, as we ride," Page said as he released the Squire and stowed his dirk, "you must think of how to do what I just did. But, first, it is time to bathe in the stream!"

And with that, Page stripped his clothes and ran into the water. Edan just stared, wide eyed, looking most terrified at the prospect.

"I-I bathed w-while you slept, Master. I will prepare our mounts, as a-a squire should, while you splash about." With that, a red-faced Edan quickly turned and set about the declared tasks, pausing every now and then to steal an embarrassed glance at the naked knight.

Within a half hour the two were mounted, and moving down the road to Stonebridge Dunn.

Two more days did the knight and his squire travel northeast, past Loop, on up the peninsula of Kintyre. Each day at mid-morning, they would spy a glimpse of the dragon as she rose high above the land to be sure they followed. Neither commented on the bundle conspicuously carried by the beast.

Before them soon lay Stonebridge Dunn, and, as Page was beholden to pay his respects there, the pair rode up to the gates of the ancient citadel.

The seal of the Gingalain assured a welcome reception from the caretaker of the keep. Page knew him not, but had heard king Gingalain speak kindly of this huge man. This neighbor king had fought along side Gingalain when he had driven out the Raiders from the North, and had defended Dunadd after Artair's death, Aengus Mac Mor.

Aengus had welcomed them with the insistence that they partake of a fine meal. Led to seats in a large but modestly furnished hall, the knight and his squire bowed their heads while Aengus gave thanks.

"Thank ye, M' Laird, for these bounties o' this World that Ye have seen fit to place afore us. Amen!"

"Amen!" Edan and Page chorused.

"So, lad, what brings ye to ma 'umble Keep?" the boisterous host bellowed around a mouthful of mutton.

"In search of my King, Gingalain, at first. Now to rescue a fair damsel from a dragoness." Page stated plainly.

"DRAGONS!" Mac Mor exclaimed, rising from his seat. "Sir Page, there be more to yer tale! Out with it, boy!" the bright-eyed Great Celt thundered as he sat down again, raising his great quaich, and gulping a mouthful of mead from it.

"I had left home for Glenbarr and Torridale, searching for the Good King Gingalain. He had left on a short journey to those towns, he had told me. But a pair of new moons have passed since last we had word of him. My search for him brought me to a small village a few days travel from here. That is where I found the dragons."

"Aye, three ya'll always see, an young dame, a bull, an' a huge cow."

"And that was what we came upon. A self appointed 'sheriff', called Rascur, had some hold on them. He sent the bull after me, but my mount stunned him and I was able to halve the beast."

"Halved 'im! Ye dunna say!" Mac Mor squinted at the knight.

"Aye, kind host. The remaining pair took their revenge upon the village and the good people there" then Page's voice trailed to barely a whisper; "too slow, too hesitant, too inexperienced to save them was I."

"And cows jump over the moon as pigs fly past!" Edan's high-pitched voice exploded as the squire slammed both fists onto the table and stood tall. Padraig had not before heard the squire speak with such force. So shocked was the knight, that he could not speak. Edan's eyes burned while recounting the events of Sir Aglovale's death.

"The dragons descended upon the village with the twilight. First they burned every roof of every home. Then they attacked the good people trying to put out the fires. Torture, they wreaked upon us. I was occupied with the fires in the stables, for that was my duty, to free and save the horses there. A timber from the burning roof fell, pinning me to the earth. From there I had naught to accomplish but to view the..." Edan's voice, now breaking often, struggled watery eyes to finish the tale,"...the events as they unfolded. Mrs. Ashe, the baker's widow, was...the beasts played with her as a cat does with a mouse, then the dragon bit, she bit, she...bit...bit her head right........."

"Evil, an' vicious are these beasts. More Evil than a good man can e'er understand. Go on, lad. What then?" Mac Mor said, using a surprisingly quiet and soothing voice.

"Then Sir Page was upon them!" Edan exclaimed, the squire's voice bristling with excitement. "So fast, he was everywhere at once! He swung Excalibur, too fast for me to see the blade! Gilda, his mare, was on them as a lion is on the lamb, and then Padraig, he hurled his shield; it struck the dragon, parting her chest, and the dragoness burst aflame!"

Mac Mor gave Padraig a sideways glance, first to the young knight's face, then down to the hilt of his sword, barely visible to the Great Celt.

"Excalibur?" Mac Mor's awed whisper was barely audible. What should he make of this, he wondered? Is the squire a tale-spinner, the knight a sorcerer, or is there something else here? Deciding to wait for that answer, at least for now, Mac Mor turned back to the squire.

"Then what happened, brave boy?" Mac Mor urged.

"The dragoness attacked our inn. My father was there, his old sword taking its own toll from the dragon's flesh, for sure!" Edan's voice took on a somber tone as the squire continued. "Thrice he cut her, but age had drained his speed and strength. Padraig was running faster than a sparrow flies, but the beast had... dealt... Father..." again the squire valiantly fought back the tears, taking a deep breath to continue. "While father lay dying, the dragoness grabbed Gwenellen, my sister, and flew her off towards the House of Rascur. The flames had nearly reached me when Greg, my horse, pushed the burning beam off of me and pulled me free. Too late was I. But Sir Padraig, he saved the eight score that still live in our village, I doubt not! Those dragons were to shed the blood of every man, woman and child in the village that day. But he killed the large dame and drove the younger dame off.

"I saw to my fathers body. All my tears would not revive him. So, I made arrangements for the burial of Sir Aglovale," at this name, Aengus Mac Mor's eyes widened, he gave a loud gasp and clutched his chest as if Satan had reached for his soul, "and then I gathered my arms and headed after the dragon.

"I met Sir Page at the guardhouse outside Rescur's lands. He has been improving my skills with my arms since."

"An amazing tale, young squire" Mac Mor looked closely at the Squire; yes, this was Aglovale's issue, n'doubt; that fire behind the eyes told the tale. "Am I to understand that Sir Aglovale is yer father, and he breaths n'more?" he added softly.

"Yes, Laird O' The Isles, that is true."

Turning to the young Knight, Mac Mor asked through narrowed eyes, "Sir Padraig, how did ya acquire yer fine sword?"

"My father gave it to him, Laird O' The Isles" Edan blurted out.

"I asked the Knight, young squire! Answer 'imself, should he!" replied Mac Mor, eyes squinting at the young knight.

"It was the knight Sir Aglovale, my Laird, who presented me with Exca...this fine blade." Page responded.

"I KNEW it! That hilt, I 'ave seen before! The Great King himself wielded that powerful blade in me first battle! For it to be content with ye, well, I 'ave 'eard the stories, from me own father. He was the one Artair bade to fetch Percival, to take the sword to Aglovale. Whene'er any not appointed or chosen would to touch it, the man's 'and was burned through! Alive that blade is. And yer shield, Sir Padraig, it was the Great King's shield! Only that would halve a dragon! Chosen ye must be, good Knight. For what task, I know not. For Artair, I'm sure 'is task was to show us what good could be, what good men should do, and what can destroy that good. For you, I know not, but convinced I am still!" With that wide-eyed exclamation, the Great Celt lifted his quaich to his lips, took a great gulp of mead, set his quaich down, grinned at Padraig, then promptly fell forward and passed out cold on the table.

# The Hunter

The morning sun rose to find Page and Edan preparing for their departure. But first came young Edan's lesson, as Padraig would have naught of omitting it.

The two began by standing, facing each other. This morn, each held a sword in hand.

"Should you find an adversary before you as I am now, what is your approach?" Padraig asked the young squire.

"As my father taught me..." Edan moved quickly, slashing with the lighter claymore at Padraig's left side, "...take the initiative."

As Edan's blade flew down towards Padraig's hip, it met nothing but wind; Padraig was not there. Edan pulled the claymore up and to the left to block the expected downward slash of Padraig's blade. But this slash did not come. Instead, Edan found Padraig's blade fully across the squire's own exposed throat with Padraig standing on the right.

"You have another lesson to ponder this morning, my squire."

"It would seem so, Master!" Edan swallowed hard. How had Sir Padraig moved so fast?

The two quickly resumed the tasks of preparing for their quest. They soon had loaded up their mounts, as Mac Mor had left instructions during the night to give Page whatever provisions he required.

Half the day's ride out from Stonebridge they passed the village of Lochgilphead at the bay on Loch Gilp. Stopping only long enough to water their horses, they set out just past midday. Edan commented that they had not seen the dragon yet that morning.

Two hours down the road the knight and squire found themselves riding on increasingly agitated mounts. The two horses stopped dead as they rounded a bend just before a widening of the way. The afternoon sun, falling through the white ash trees, dappled the green grasses and spring blooms along the lane. But the travelers were blinded to that beauty by the horrific scene spread out before them. At the far corner of the bend a smoldering carriage lay upon its side, just off the edge of the road. The soot-smudged gild work was torn from the carriage. Six men, four of them uniformed, perhaps guards of some sort, two wearing more humble habiliments, lay dead nearby. Their bellies were splayed open, their livers gone. The sight served to remind Padraig of the carnage at the sheriff's house, such that he fought to keep his breakfast from achieving the violent escape it so strongly attempted. Three of the men were burned into faceless carrion, the smoke carrying a foul, repugnant odor to assault their senses. The previously springtime-sweetened air was here wrapped in the foul stench of burned flesh and the angry metallic breath of heavy bloodfall.

"The dragon has eaten here." Padraig whispered.

"Here, my Laird, was there a treasure taken from here? What use of treasure hath a dragoness?" Edan asked, lifting a small, opened strongbox from the carriage, revealing its vacancy by inverting it.

A dog's sharp yaps called them, breaking their fixation on the carriage.

"Sir Knight, here!" A young man's cultured voice cried out. "Please, Sir, this maiden." the voice sobbed.

Edan and Page's hearts stopped at the words. Off their mounts and on the run knight and squire flew to the voice.

"Oh, Laird, my, such a good, beautiful maid! 'Tis not right that this be done to her!"

Page and Edan stopped at the sight of a young man in simple green hunter's garb, longbow and quiver on his back, knelt weeping over a young maid with raven hair, a large hound whimpering as he fretted to and fro about them both. The beauty of her face was overcome by the gruesome wound where the dragon had nearly beheaded the beauty, hopefully before it had consumed her absent liver. The mournful stains of her life's blood eclipsed the fineness of her white, gold, and green frock. The knight and squire's relief that this was not the Gwenellen they sought lasted but a moment as their senses absorbed the abhorrent scene before them.

"Who was this Lady?" Padraig quietly inquired, gently placing a hand on the stranger's shoulder.

"She was Murron, the daughter of the Mayor of Cairnbaan. She was headed to Lochgilphead, to buy whisky and gowns for her upcoming wedding. We were...she....." The hunter took a deep breath before continuing through his tears, "we had played together as children, years ago."

"What is your name, young man?"

" I am...call me Rory, Sir Knight. Please, help me prepare her for burial. Her home is too far to carry her body splayed thusly, and I canna go to that town." Page looked at the open bag of money set between the maiden's feet and the carriage, then back to Rory.

It took the three of them the best part of two hours to perform proper burials of the maid and her guard. The hound kept his whimpering, yet followed the hunter at a trained distance, keeping his vigil as if always at the ready. While the men tended to the dead, the dog sat and watched. Soon Greg and Gilda moved up behind, heads lowered at the somberness shown by their masters. Other than the prayers spoken by Padraig over each grave, nothing was said until they had finished these mournful toils. As the last of the earth was placed upon the maiden's rest, the hound turned and looked up at the horses. The three then gave a slight nod in unison, as if at a signal.

"Rory, tell me what happened here." Padraig wiped his brow.

"I am not sure, Sir Knight, for I only arrived here the moment before you. I found the guards slain and the carriage aflame. I will hide naught from you this day; when I saw the carriage, I meant to make off with the gold." Rory indicated with disgust the bag and gold coins on the ground. "Then I saw..." the last word escaped his quivering lips only at a whisper, "...Murron."

Page noted that the gold Rory had mentioned was near the maiden's final position. This was not where it would have dropped had the hunter been carrying it when he spied the girl. While the young man was dressed simply, his garments were of high quality and his manners indicated a noble upbringing, as did the dress of the maiden along with the provisions and the number of guards present.

"The dragoness, did you see it?" Edan's concerned and compassioned voice whispered.

"No, but hear the rapine, I did, as my dog, Luag, had become excited. As I hastened my approach, the horses fled past me. Nearly trampled, I was. I spied the smoke, then the carriage, the guards, and the money. Then I saw… her…" his reverent tone trailing off to find whatever it was in the great distance along the road which claimed the focus of his gaze.

"Gather all the money. We will return it, all of it, to the Mayor; he has lost enough this day."

"Good Knight, may I ask, what brings you this way?"

"We follow the one that fed here. She took a maiden, the sister of my squire, so as to injure me for killing her two companions. Our quest is to rescue that maiden."

"Allow me to join you, Sir Knight. I beg you to accept me into your service. Give me the chance to avenge my betro…. this poor lady!" The tears were real, Padraig knew. This maid was more to him than a childhood playmate he planned to rob.

"I would accept, but you have no horse, and we need to keep a quick pace to overtake the demon."

"Sir Padraig, Greg is more than strong enough for both. Rory may ride with me until we reach Cairnbaan. We may procure a mount for him there."

"So we may, Edan. Rory, come along then! We go to see the Mayor of Cairnbaan."

Rory leap up onto the back of Greg behind Edan with surprising quickness. Page watched as Rory wrapped his arms around Edan, who turned, and with as stern a look as Page had e'er seen before, whispered with great intensity to the bowman.

"You will be well advised to keep you hands where they belong and your tongue silent on this matter."

Rory cocked his wide-eyed head to one side.

"You're a secret from the knight! How could this be?"

"He would not take me if he knew, and I need him to save my sister. A bargain I propose; you keep my secret, and I shall keep yours."

Padraig watched Rory released his grip on the squire, immediately nodding his ascension to whatever Edan had said. The conversation was too low for the knight to hear, but as long as his squire was content in the matter, Padraig would not intrude. The horses began their pace along the road, the hound trotting easily alongside Greg.

Only an hour's travel did the group make before the increasing clouds and the darkening night bade them to find a suitable cantonment. The three stopped to make camp where a clearing by the road touched a beaver pond. Rory proved a bigger help than Page had anticipated, nearly taking every chore from Edan until the latter stared in frustration at him.

Soon the evening fire was burning, with a rabbit for each now turning on the spit. The hound had flushed each hare into range of Rory's bow, and Edan had seasoned with fresh hathar leaves and blossoms, along with some salt from the Squire's well-planned provisions. The crackling fire and the roasting meat filled the camp with wonderful sensations of sound and smell. Edan again brought out the consecrated wine, over which Page recited the words again; "He took the bread, gave thanks, and brake it, and gave unto them, saying, 'This is my body which is given for you: this do in remembrance of me'. Like wise also the cup after supper, saying, 'This cup is the new testament in my blood, which is shed for you.'

"We thank Thee, Father, for that you have placed before us. The Laird is my Shepherd; I shall not want. He maketh me to lie down in green pastures: He leadeth me beside still waters. He restoreth my soul: He leadeth me in the paths of righteousness for His name's sake. Yeah, though I walk through the valley of the shadow of death, I fear no evil: for Thy rod and Thy staff, they comfort me. Thou preparest a table before me in the presence of mine enemies: Thou anointest my head with oil; my cup runneth over. Surely goodness and mercy shall follow me all the days of my life: and I will dwell in the House of The Laird forever. Amen."

Throughout the prayer Rory stayed on one knee, his head down, his hands clenched in submission as his eyes flashed quickly between the knight and the squire. His hound sat obediently behind him, adopting his master's stance as closely as a hound could.

"Now, let us eat!" announced Padraig.

At the end, the dinner passed with little conversation as the considerable effort the three had expended in the burial of the maid and her escort caused a more urgent use of their mouths. Rory shared his rabbit with the hound, whose name was revealed to be Luag, for he was quick to learn, and slow to lose.

As the last few morsels sped past their lips, Padraig offered comfort to their new companion; "Rory, Edan here has taken to washing the day's grit in the late evening, while my preference is to cleanse myself after my squire's lessons in the morn. You may join the one who fits your preference the better!"

Edan peered through widened eyes, first at Page, then at Rory for his response. The squire's face looked as if the dragoness herself had appeared when Rory said with a smile, "this eve'n, I believe I will bath in yon stream with your squire, Sir Knight!"

"Too exhausted, am I, to bathe this eve'n, Master! I'll turn in now, if you will." Edan spewed the words out quickly.

"As you wish, Edan. But the morning brings new lessons for you, remember!" Page replied.

"Good night, good Knight" Edan recited, as the squire had every evening since their common quest began. "Good night, *hunter*" the Squire said with a chill matching that of the deepening eventide.

"Good night, young squire. Sir Knight, tell me where you learned the words of prayer?"

"One of my teachers was Friar Colum Cille. He instructed me in the ways of the Church."

"Saint Columba! You seem to have had the best education, Sir Padraig! Who is your father then?"

"My parents died when I was very young. King Gingalain raised me as his own. And you, hunter? From where do you hail?"

"I was born near Dunadd, but I was raised on Éireann, near Ballynahatty. My father sent me to Lochgilphead to earn my fortune by my own hand."

"So, you've chosen to make your fortune as a meirleacha?"

"A thief in Lochgilphead lost his life in pursuit of my purse. That meirleacha was wed to the sheriff's daughter. Rather than face him, I left."

"That sheriff is a capable warrior I presume?"

"He is, but that is not why I left. There had been enough

bloodshed, and I wanted…" The hunter's gaze moved to a place far away. After a moment, he stifled a sob.

"Enough tonight then. Sleep well, Rory the hunter."

"Sleep well, my friend," Rory replied with a melancholy tone. Padraig noticed the briefest of simpers bloom on the young man's lips. A portend of an impish yet honorable nature, Padraig was sure.

Deep into the night, and deeper still into his dream of the widow Gwenever, Page woke suddenly at a splash from the not inconsequential pond. His training held well enough that he showed no movement; not even an eyelash quivered, but holding his breath controlled took even as much will as did keeping his pounding heart within his bosom. Slowly, imperceptibly Padraig rolled to the sound as if asleep, pulling his covers along. Through barely parted lashes his eyes scanned the natatorium for the agent of the disturbance, fighting an urge to glance to Rory's bed first. The water had given the signal, and the source would be there.

Over the water's moonlit patina Padraig sought out the source. There it was-a beaver? It seemed larger than a beaver should be, longer. The hound? No, for he was calmly lying at his master's feet, facing the pond without alarm. There! In the water, an arm? Not a beaver, but a man!

Now the knight cast an inconspicuous glance to Rory; finding the newcomer rolling his back to the pond, also pulling his coverlet with him against the cool dampness of the spring night. Then on to the next point of interest; Greg and Gilda. The roan mare was calmly surveying the surrounding area, while the young stallion was unconcernedly fast asleep.

The placidness of both the hound's and Gilda's manners relieved Padraig greatly. Just one more place left to check. As Edan's bedclothes seemed properly employed at maintaining the squire's warmth during the slumber beneath them, Page sat up and gazed fully at the pond. Finding the waters still and clear for longer than he could hold his breath, Padraig took a complete circumference of the camp, only to find Gilda staring at him as if his state of wakefulness was evidence of a total folly. Then Padraig felt Rory staring at him.

"Good instincts and training you have, Sir Knight. You heard the splash?" whispered the young man.

"I also spied a man raising his arm within the waters. Yet as I scanned the surroundings, no one rose out of the pond. Still, Gilda remains unconcerned, as does Luag, and Greg is sound asleep, so danger likely is not at hand" Padraig quietly replied.

"Your mounts are exceptional companions. I'll sleep better knowing they keep watch. Do they alternate, then, one at watch while the other sleeps?"

"Will you two let a soul sleep!" exclaimed Edan.

Page looked at his squire, tilting his head at the youngster.

"The splash was made by me. I could not sleep without my bath, and now that I've had it, I can't sleep with the din of you two chattering as love-struck crickets in the night!"

"Ha! Some one has learned their lessons well! Sleep well, then, my squire. And hunter, you as well."

"And a good sleep to you both" Rory grinned.

The rest of the night passing without notice, the three awoke as Luag nosed first his master, then Edan, and finally Padraig. Wakefulness reminded each of the aches of their bodies and their hearts brought by the day before.

Page noticed the horses at their station, soon joined by the hound. Edan broke the oatcakes for the morning meal for the three, and some dried venison for the hound. They ate after Page, as usual, said the Grace.

"Now, Rory, I will train my squire, not as well as my master trained me, but as best I can" Padraig announced.

The hunter squinted at the Knight, as though to read his intentions; for Rory has seen some who practice cruelty as training, and he could not allow that to happen here.

Presently the two drew their dirks and stood apart, two good strides between them. As with each day past, Padraig opened with a great slash that was as obvious as it was irresistibly fast. And as with each day past, Edan handily blocked and quickly countered the blow. Each day, Padraig moved from this engagement in a different way, as Edan changed the counterblow in a search for the solution. But Padraig moved with such speed, such precision, that he was always behind Edan before the squire's counterblow landed.

This day would be different, thought Edan, moving up the same counter that had failed at the first training. Just at the beginning of this counter, Edan suddenly dropped low and spun away from Padraig. The squire had thought to find the knight attacking from behind, but he was not there. Edan found the knight as Padraig sat on his squire, ending the scrimmage but not the training.

"Aargh! How can I beat you when you are nowhere!" Edan's high-pitched voice cried out from days of repressed frustration, fist slamming the ground.

"Ha-hah! May I, Sir Knight?" Asked the grinning Hunter.

"Please, Rory, I would be honored to hear your assessment."

"Edan," Rory began, "your focus is upon striking your opponent; perhaps that is not a good strategy against a superior foe. Remember, good squire, battles are more often lost than won."

At the end of those words, Greg gave a stomp and snort. Luag, enjoying himself greatly, lay with wagging tail observing it all.

Edan stared blankly at the hunter. "I have a knight setting on my back, and the hunter talks as if a riddle will lift him off!" Edan lay, chin in hand, waiting for the knight to grant his squire freedom.

"The hunter speaks wisely, Edan. Think on his words. Now, for me, a quick bathing and we shall be off!"

Presently Edan was busied with packing up their camp while the two older men bathed, the squire muttering all the while as Luag followed with great interest.

The three found themselves entering Cairnbaan at mid afternoon. Rory asked that they remain outside while he conveyed to the Mayor the news of the death of the girl. Padraig made no move to hand Rory the bag of gold, and the hunter did not mention it. While Rory had been almost cheerful company the entire day, a veil of dark solemnity and sadness covered his countenance as soon as the town came into view. Page thought he had seen the young man's body shudder, as from stifled sobs, but he sought to keep the hunter's dignity intact through kind discretion.

Some time had passed, and Padraig was readying to enter the house himself when the Mayor appeared at the door, beckoning the knight and squire to enter his abode. Padraig retrieved the gold from his saddle and handed it to Edan, advising his young squire.

"Be respectful when you return this to the Mayor," Padraig cautioned Edan. "It will remind him quite painfully of his loss."

With that, the three dragon hunters entered the Mayor's house.

# Meirleachas

The Mayor of Cairnbaan was a light haired, barrel-chested man, wearing the confident manner of one who was leaner some years ago, but now was comfortable and little stressed by his position. Padraig had noted the town was clean, and the folk he had seen about seemed happy and well off. He noted that the mayor's house was a modest one for a town the size of Cairnbaan.

"Sir Knight, it is an honor to meet you. I am Mayor Diarmad. The, eh, um, Rory, the hunter has informed me of your quest. I offer you my humble hospitality, but I understand and will take no offense that you wish no delay in your pursuit of the dragoness."

"Kind words from a grieving father, Mayor Diarmad. Our prayers be with you, and with her soul. Our need is only for a suitable mount for Rory, as we have welcomed his partnership into our quest." Padraig commented as the group moved outside.

"So he has told me. With his return of the dower, eh, our gold, a reward is in order. I have a young stallion being brought to the front of the house for him. He is the issue of my own faithful mare, and his name is Cailean. You will find him a useful companion, Rory," the mayor announced as his stable hands led a tall, coal black steed up to the hunter.

"Thank you, Mayor. Your kindness will be remembered." Rory stated simply, as he patted the horse's nose. The mayor bowed in reply.

"Mayor, I insist, in the name of the Good King, please accept this sum as payment for such a fine animal." Padraig pleaded, handing a small bag, adorned with the seal of King Gingalain, to Diarmad. The mayor, glancing at Rory long enough to note his subtle nod, thanked the knight as he accepted the payment.

The three made their good-byes, and rode off down the road to Dunadd, following their dragoness.

Soon the trio was nearly to Dunadd, making much better time now that the Hunter rode his own mount. Greg seemed to enjoy the lightened load as much as Rory enjoyed the newfound freedom.

Approaching the hill of Dunadd near dusk, Padraig spied the dragoness carrying her well bound parcel just above the next hill. Despite the previous days' difficulties, they had gained at least a little ground on the beast.

Page watched the horses as they stopped next to the River Add to make camp, the setting sun making but a shadow out of the ruins of Artair's once-shining keep. Greg and Gilda were watching Cailean as the three dragon hunters set camp. The new steed watched the two calmly, fully confident of himself, or so Padraig gathered. Best leave such matters for the horses to sort out among themselves.

After saying Grace over their modest meal, the squire, the hunter, and the knight settled into a discussion of the upcoming confrontation with the dame dragon.

"The she-beast will kill your maiden for sure if you press her too hard, good Knight," the hunter asserted.

"Sir Padraig is too fast for the dragon to do that! He would never let it happen!" Edan exclaimed.

"Edan, temper thy tongue. Our friend was giving his assessment and his advice, not assailing my skills. Sir Rory, what do you suggest?" Padraig snuck in the title to gauge the hunter's reaction to it.

But the hunter would not be distracted. His hand reached down and scratched Luag behind his ears as he explained, "I hold not the title of a knight, as you do, Sir Padraig. I do appreciate the respect you bestow upon me, but it is undeserved. As yet." The last two words added under Rory's breath, unheard by his companions. "We need to draw the beast into a confrontation. Distract it, with fresh game, perhaps with the possibility of revenge!"

"I will challenge the beast, alone. That it will take, for why else does she carry the maiden, Edan's sister, but to taunt me onwards?"

"You will kill it! It must know that, it's seen you kill the others!" Edan was too excited to contain the emotion swelling within; pride and fear mixed to color the squire's words.

Gilda and Greg each gave a snort.

"Shh! Quiet!" The Hunter admonished.

"I was not disrespect..." Edan's protest was cut short by Padraig's hand clamping the squire's mouth.

"Rory wasn't admonishing you, he was alerting us. Something is out there!" Padraig whispered, keeping his hand over Edan's mouth.

The squire's eyes grew wide as they scanned the dark woods around them. Rory motioned to the left, and Padraig nodded, releasing the squire. Padraig pointed to the right, and Edan crept slowly in that direction, only pausing to pick up the claymore.

Rory silently moved behind the uneasy horses, Page circling left, and Edan to the right. The three were nearly in position when the attack began.

Three robbers broke through the brush into the center of camp, the horses raising a terrific noise. Two more came in from the left, only to meet naught but the three meirleachas from the center. The five looked at each other, wondering where their prey had vanished to, when an arrow pierced the middle robber's throat.

Suddenly a brilliant blue flash startled the robbers, who turned to see the meirleacha on the left sliced in two by the light. The robbers fell to panic, backing into each other, glancing here and there into the darkness. Another arrow hit a robber as swords from Edan and Padraig sliced into the last two. After forty seconds, five robbers were dead. The two hiding in the brush ran away, Luag barking at their heels.

Padraig kept first watch as the others slept, until Edan relieved him three hours later. Two hours after that, Rory sat down next to the squire.

"You handled yourself very well there, for..."

"For what?"

"For a young squire, I was going to say. Your secret is safe with me, unless it endangers him." Rory nodded in the direction of Padraig.

"What care you of his fate?" Edan's suspicious tone challenged.

"Fear not, I do not love him as you do. I sense that he carries a special destiny, one that I am fated to defend."

"Then your secret is safe with me, as well, Aedan Mac Gabrain." Edan whispered into the hunter's ear, just before touching a feather of a kiss to his cheek.

"How did you know?"

"You and your father stayed at our inn four years past. Do you not remember?"

"Yes. I had forgotten that Sir Aglovale had retired to keep that inn. We were to meet Gingalain and Mac Mor that year, at Stonebridge Dunn."

"Your father is well?"

"He is dealing with matters a king should not be involved with. He has abdicated Dal Riata to my rule."

"Then why the deception?"

"There are agents about who would see me dead, the better to divide our nation into petty kingdoms. I met one in Lochgilphead. Best they know not where I am until I consolidate my rule. When I return to Éireann..."

"You can better secure the stability of our nation, Dal Riata."

"You are a sharp tack, aren't you! Sir Aglovale's blood runs strong in your veins, Edan. Proud would he be to see you now."

"Kind words, from a High King to a squire."

"When will you tell him your secret?"

"When my sister... when I can. Or, when I must. Or, perhaps ne'er."

"Edan, if you find the need for an ear, mine will judge you only as a friend."

Edan nodded, then rolled away with tearing eyes closed, begging sleep from beneath the bedding.

The next morning Padraig bade Rory to let the squire sleep while the two men packed the camp and readied the horses for the day's journey. Only when the breakfast was ready did they awaken the younger one.

The posture of Luag and the restless horses should have alerted the three, but the nets fell too quickly. Rory and Edan were caught without arms, but somehow Padraig had his sword out slicing the ropes. The twenty meirleachas had pounced by then, their mix of Roman and Pict arms poised to rain death down upon these three travelers who had dared to stand up to their kin.

The three horses were not of a mood to idly watch their master's slaughter. Gilda and Greg rose together to defend their masters. High into the air did their fore hooves raise, smashing again and again upon the would be murderers. First Greg was smashing aside a blow aimed for Gilda as she rose, then the roan mare protecting the huge stallion as he rose to the attack. Cailean had vanished into the woods, reappearing behind the meirleachas, striking several down while cutting off any escape.

The three horses began herding the remaining sixteen robbers away from the netted travelers, but with only limited success. The meirleachas began hacking at the brave steeds, Cailean taking several cuts from which much blood issued forth, yet he never slowed in his task.

"Enough wit' tha animals! Kill 'em, so then we'll finish our business wit' those in the net!" a large bearded meirleacha yelled, just as Luag leapt from the bushes and caught him by his throat. The robbers rallied, and set about their assigned task with great vigor.

But, they could not have known Excalibur was there. The light blue glow from the blade streaked among them, slicing their malevolent flesh as efficiently as a friar slices his bread. Padraig spun, swinging Excalibur as if it was a blade of grass instead of steel, slicing left, right, up, down. He was everywhere, slamming that sharp edge into them, slicing off limbs, hacking into ribs. Yet he was nowhere, nowhere the robbers' blades struck back, always gone before the meirleachas could harm him.

Three, four, five of the robbers went down, never again to rise. And then the Shield was on Padraig's arm, and he waded into the meirleachas, who, still corralled by the sharp hooves of the equine trio and harassed by the sharp fangs of the hound, began falling as the harvest before the reaper. So fast was he, only the fabled blade's blue glow gave the eye a clue as to his motions.

In short order it was done. The twenty would-be robbers lay in pieces around the camp, their blood staining the soil as well as Padraig's garb. The knight stood, tall and dominant in the center of the camp, panting as a lion after his kill. Luag walked up and lay at Padraig's feet, his hide slashed from several blows. He too panted open-mouthed, the robber's blood having stained his face. The three horses snorted from behind the knight, steaming cool spring morn.

Edan's awe filled whisper broke the silence; "See! See how fast he is! Ne'er has one been so fast and so true with a blade!" Adulation and pride, plus something more, colored the squire's soprano tones.

Rory stood silent. Too shocked to speak, the hunter tilted his head to one side while staring at the still glowing knight. Padraig, his wind recovered, rummaged through his supplies, and then walked about the campsite, dropping a single gold coin on each dead meirleacha.

"Why are you paying the dead, good Knight?" Edan asked.

"These men will have wives and children. They fed them through their evil deeds. I will not tolerate lawlessness, but I will not starve a widow or an orphan, either."

Slowly, the hunter moved nearer where the Padraig stood, and then bent down until one knee rested on the ground. Then the hunter bowed his head to the knight.

Padraig turned a surprised face to his new friend, stating, "Do not bow to me, hunter, for I am no royal!"

"I beg to differ, Good Knight! No mere knight has e'er God bid to move as you do! The world truly is yours to take, yet I know in my heart you would ne'er take it." Rory declared.

Edan had taken a knee beside the hunter. The squire looked up at Padraig with adoring eyes.

"Such a man is worthy of The Crown, if ever a man was." Rory added.

"I believe that the day shall come when I will pledge to you, Rory. Given the Good King's approval."

"The Good King would surely approve, Sir Page, since he is-"

"Aaaaaaaaaaarwk!" The scream from above cut Edan's revelation short as the dragoness flew low, carrying a bound and screaming Gwenellen. The beast swooped low enough for the three to see her worn and frightened face pleading for rescue. Then up, the beast climbed the air, away in the direction of Oban. Padraig quietly seethed as he saw the dragoness smile. The hunter could not remove the vision of the girl's face from his mind.

The three then turned back to their tasks. Once Cailean's wounds were attended to, the three mounted their steeds to resume their quest.

# The Sea Road

The hunter rode up alongside the squire to a position just behind Padraig. The road towards Oban was very rocky here, as it had never been close to Roman quality. Since the death of Artair, it was not traveled often and it was repaired even less; Rory looked at Edan, trusting Cailean to keep a steady foot.

"You will favor me by keeping our agreement, young one. Your youth has purchased your forgiveness this time; inexperience is a cloak you may only wear once." Rory said in a quiet yet terse voice.

The squire's eyes widened in alarm.

"I had thought it an appropriate time. Forgive me, but I see now that I was wrong to assume that decision for you!" Edan whispered the plea to the hunter.

"Your good will I can never doubt. Just see that your actions stay behind it, my friend." Rory rode Cailean up next to Padraig and Gilda.

"I beg your patience with my Squire, my friend. Remember your own youthful intoxication from that first battle well fought and won." Padraig greeted Rory as he rode up alongside him.

Rory gazed at Padraig for a long moment. Had he heard and understood? If so, what could he do about it?

"Often a young lad needs a father's touch to remind him of lessons learned, but set aside. It is a caring father that guides the lad along the proper path."

"Heh-ha! Your father, or your friar has taught you very well, for a life as a simple hunter!" Padraig grinned and gave Gilda a little kick, sending the roan bolting down the road full gallop.

"Oh-ho! Off we go then!" Rory slapped Cailean, the coal-black steed stretching his legs to catch Gilda, Luag off in hot pursuit. Bending low to lessen the wind, Rory felt rather than saw the huge white steed flash past him; Greg was the largest of the three steeds, and he carried the lightest load.

The three horses flew down the road at an astounding gallop, followed closely by the faithful hound; Luag's ears pinned back by his speed, his tongue flapping in the wind at the gleeful exertion. Greg was near Gilda's hip, Cailean now nearly even with Greg. The trio had been walking too much; they were born to run, and now running they were! They ran as three horses had never run before, as if flying with but a toe to touch ground on occasion. On they ran, and on, the three laughing riders now at the mercy of their mounts.

Several leagues passed before Padraig called "Enough!" As if by royal command, the three powerful animals slowed and stopped, in just the position they had run. Padraig looked at Greg and Cailean, unconvinced that chivalry had not kept the two stallions from overtaking his mare, even though he knew she had speed in reserve. As for Gilda, she bore the same regal expression as always, as if the lead position was hers by natural right. Just a moment behind trotted Luag, tongue hanging out of his panting mouth, with his tail wagging wildly as he joined the others.

"A good place to camp tonight; a slow stream to bathe the dust and blood from our backs." the hunter declared.

"Then camp it is! What fun, eh, my friends?" Padraig beamed.

Rory dismounted Cailean, and then gave a start when he looked at Edan.

"Good Knight, I believe those woods over yon should hold some deer. Would you hunt with me? I have an appetite for a bit more than rabbit or squirrel tonight!"

"Excellent idea! Edan, see to the camp! We shall be back with a feast for you soon!"

"At least an hour, to properly hunt and dress the kill, I think." Rory turned and winked at Edan.

"And I get to set up camp! I suppose you'll want me to butcher and cook the beast as well! So, good hunting then!" Edan smiled back at the two men as they faded into the woods. As soon as they were out of sight, Edan was out of the dusty, bloody clothes and into the stream, with Luag right behind.

Yet while Edan was unexposed to the eyes of Padraig and Rory, other eyes gazed upon the young squire. Leathery wings silently rode the evening air, searching for the day's nourishment in the world below. Those eyes spotted the bright young body in the stream. A plan of attack soon formed behind those dark eyes.

Edan bathed quickly, for there was much that needed to be done before the two returned. As the young squire rose out of the stream, Luag moved to the front of the squire with a low growl, Gilda moved up along one side, and Cailean onto the other. Startled, the squire looked all around for Greg and whatever had set the horses astir.

Greg stomped heavily around the others, head bobbing, up and down. Edan followed his friend's eyes, up, THERE!

"DRAGON!" Edan bellowed loudly and broke from between the horses. Into the pack, quickly, a shirt thrown over shoulders, unsheathe the sword, now turn, and swing up HARD...

The beast was close, but Greg would have none of it moving any closer to Edan. High in the air he jumped, placing himself between his master and the dragoness. He had no momentum to extend his leap, but his companions did. The roan mare rose high above Greg to land a fore hoof on the breast of the beast just as Cailean came up and hit the Dragon's hips with his sharp hoof.

The dragon gave a great cry, and flew off low over the woods. Edan watched as she approached the trees, and saw two arrows fly up and over the abhorrent thing. Missed!

Heart beating fast, Edan pulled fresh britches from the bundle and quickly donned them, while checking Gilda and Greg. Both horses had been unharmed. But Cailean's efforts had opened some of his old wounds, and Edan attended them, glancing often at the skies.

After tending Cailean, Edan picked up the claymore to sheath it, and gasped at the dark, foul smelling stain on the tip; dragon's blood! The young squire stood up just a bit taller.

The knight and the hunter were soon in camp with a good-sized deer. They had been nearly to the edge of the woods when they had heard Edan's shout. Rory had managed to loose two arrows at the beast, but it was too far for accurate shooting; the arrows missed, and the dragoness flew on.

While Padraig butchered the deer, Rory prepared the fire and Edan unpacked the cooking equipment. Padraig noticed that Rory again had taken on some of Edan's chores, but kept his tongue on the subject.

"Are you up to a new lesson this eve'n', good squire?" Padraig asked as the three sat about the fire, enjoying the smells of roasting venison.

"As you command, my knight!" the squire replied.

"Good! The lesson will be to always..."

"Keep your guard up, my Knight?" Edan finished the sentence from behind Page, his dirk flat across the Knight's upper chest, from shoulder to shoulder. Edan's cheek was next to Padraig's ear; a slight shudder passed through the squire at the nearness of the knight. "A short lesson indeed, Edan! Bravo!" Padraig beamed a huge smile. "You get first watch then, my squire!"

Mid morn the following day the road turned east. The three rode over a shallow rise to behold a sight that stopped them immediately.

There off to the right of the path, the midday sun shone brightly on the deep green waters of Loch Linnhe crashing onto the rocks below. The waves rolled in at a regular pace with the incoming tide. The emerald seas crashing into the rocky shore of Kerrera threw up a mist of diamonds that imprisoned the bright morning sun into a rainbow above the stony shore and jutting rocks. On that island, the peak of Carn Breugach rose directly before them, and the old, fallen stonework of an ancient keep called Gylen was barely discernable to the west through the mist cast up by the surf. Hundreds of puffins and guillemots flew about, causing Luag much excitement. The sea birds were suddenly very vocal at the hound's intrusion into their domain. The breeze off the loch brought the fresh smell of the sea up to the travelers.

"Thank the Laird for letting me see this view!" Padraig exclaimed quietly.

"Should we survive our quest, my friend, I will show you vistas as breathtaking by the score!" Rory promised, his voice tinted with his awe at the sight before them.

"It is grand, but shouldn't we get moving?" Edan broke the spell holding them there, and the three began moving slowly along the high, rocky trail.

A red flash caught Padraig's eye as he studied the rainbow below. He tried to focus on it, but it was gone. There! Again he saw it, better this time, compelling him to stop as Gilda bayed in alarm. The dragoness!

Far below their level, the dame dragon swooped in and around the disturbed guillemots, snatching a dozen of the fat ones for her meals.

"Almost graceful would you call it, if it wasn't such a horrid being!" Edan spat.

"Can we find where the Lady Aglovale is stashed, and end our quest today?" Rory queried.

"Where would you look?" Padraig replied. "We could but guess until she heads back, and then we would be too late to affect a rescue. Best we meet her at the end of her journey-it's on her terms, and though I dunna like that, it is our best option."

Padraig turned and faced his friends with the most earnest expression either had seen cross his handsome face.

"I have been thinking for some time about how best to attack that beast, and save Gwenellen. I now understand what we must do. I ask you now; does each of you pledge yourselves to follow me in this quest? To follow my directions without hesitation or question?"

"I do Sir Knight!" The squire chimed enthusiastically.

"I do, Sir Knight!" The hunter earnestly vowed.

"When we do engage with the beast, you will follow this plan; I will engage her while Edan frees Gwenellen. Rory will protect Edan and Gwenellen as they flee away. Greg is strong enough to carry the two. You will take her and ride fast and far, with ne'er a glance back. I will find you when all is done. You have pledged to me that you will do this without question and without delay."

The hunter and the squire stared at the knight with mouths agape. Before their objections could be made, Padraig had nudged Gilda into a trot down the road.

"I could ne'er leave him like that!" Edan sobbed quietly, fighting boldly to hold back the tears born of the thoughts of the outcome of the battle Sir Padraig had just laid out. "And I could ne'er leave Gwenellen! King Aedan, you must save my sister, for I can not, I will not leave that man!"

"I'm not sure I could leave such a man either, and I dunna love him as you do. When the time comes, we will all go down the same path to our destiny, together. I promise." With those determined words, the High King of Dal Riata urged Cailean after the knight. The squire, tears wiped from youthful cheeks, followed.

# Decision

Over a small rise the three warriors rode, and rounding a slight bend came upon the sight they had expected.

Oban!

The town sprawled out before them, yet their eyes were drawn to the massive keep, which rose high above the cliff side and extended straight down to the sea. Dark grey stones, wet from the sea spray, fit closely together to form the massive stronghold. Only a slim door allowed entrance to the safety within.

All around the great dunn sprawled the town of Oban. Smoke rose from the fishermen's homes, shops, shipwrights, blacksmythes and the like along the shores of the Sound of Kerrera. Along the roads and streets the three could spy no one out and about, despite the fine weather of the warm spring midday. The reason soon became apparent; the dragoness was circling about, setting aflame that which it could, ready to burn all that moved outside the Keep.

Padraig had seen this before, and drove Gilda to great speed down the path to the town. Never before had the she run so fast, for her blood boiled at the same vision her knight had seen.

Greg and Cailean lowered their heads and flew after the roan mare, black and white flashes urged by the resolute shouts and proddings of their riders, with Luag right behind. As falcons after a hare the three flew along the road, stallions after mare, but the dragoness had finished her mischief before they could reach the outskirts of Oban. Having plucked a good-sized lamb for her supper, the dragoness flew off low over the trees to the north of town.

The three riders eased their mounts to a walk, Edan and Rory taking a moment to catch and pull up alongside Padraig.

"The closer we get to that beast, Good Knight, the more my blood boils!" Rory panted.

"Which is why I must fight the dragoness alone." Padraig stopped Gilda, and turned to face his companions. He sensed that they were unhappy with his plans for fighting the dragoness.

"She has taken Edan's sister and killed the squire's father. She has killed your betrothed. Both of you have too much fire in your veins to battle her with your heads; you would rush in for vengeance, make mistakes, and the dragoness would feast upon your livers."

The hunter and the squire stared at the knight in silence for a time.

"You could tell, then." Rory said quietly, his wet eyes steady on Padraig.

"You are also more than a simple hunter, as evidenced by the dowry your betrothed carried. Your feelings for her were honorable if ill hidden; that is to be expected in such circumstances. Who you really are I dunna know. I leave your disclosure of that information to your own discretion. I have seen enough of you to know that you act honorably, and are bound by your words. That is enough for me to trust you, and to call you my friend."

"I am grateful for your patience, Good Knight. I have ne'er met a man with your insight and honor." Rory glanced quickly at Edan as he continued, "I ask you, though, is not the dragon's hostage the one who warms your heart? At the time of battle with the beast, willna your blood boil from the fire in your heart?"

"My friend, the girl is a damsel in distress, pretty and of good nature, and from a good line. Yet, I dunna know if she would warm to me, should my heart lead me that way. Too short was our time together for me to know the lass well enough."

"Still, Sir Padraig, we should discuss our strategy for that confrontation and look at other...options. How else will I learn?" Edan wore a poorly suppressed smile while sitting tall on Greg's back.

"Yes, well said, my squire. I see much of Sir Aglovale in you. No doubt you could sell spoiled wool to a shepherd the day before shearing, and at a premium price! Very well, we will discuss this as your lesson this eve'n." Padraig smiled as he spoke, then trotted off into town shaking his head slightly.

The three rode through the town together at a slow pace, and, finding no one about, moved to the Keep of Oban, along the north side of the town. There the three dismounted and left the horses to browse the grass, as Luag chased the mice they flushed. Padraig walked up to the narrow but stout looking portal, and banged three times upon it.

The iron cover over the viewing slit moved aside, and presently the narrow door opened.

"Hurry! Lest the dragon fall upon you!" The panicked voice urged from the darkness behind the door.

"Be calm, my friend. The beast has flown off with a lamb to dine upon. She will not return to bother your people this eve'n." Padraig reassured the voice's owner as he slid through the narrow portal, followed by Edan and Rory.

"Follow me, stranger." Was all the voice said as Padraig watched the boots climb the steep stairs.

Up the narrow passage the three went, climbing step after step in the darkness.

"Have we reached the moon yet?" Edan gasped.

"I think my squire has grown too fat from that deer!" Padraig chuckled.

"Perhaps your squire would benefit from a few days of running along with the hound." Rory offered.

"Funny. Ha-ha!" Edan croaked.

Suddenly a blinding light appeared just above Padraig. After climbing in near total darkness for so long, the three could only squint out a form passing through the brightness.

One by one they passed through the heavy oaken door at the top of the stairs, emerging into a great room brightened by several barred windows. Two dozen armed men ringed the hall, faces alert but with weapons sheathed. A large red haired man stepped forward, panning his eyes up and down the three strangers. His eyes abruptly stopped upon the patch of cloth Padraig wore over the hilt of Excalibur.

"The seal of the Good King, Gingalain! I am Magnus Dubhglas, Mayor of Oban. Who are you, Sir?"

"I am Padraig Ualas, Knight of Gingalain, and this is my companion, Rory the hunter, and my squire, Edan Aglovale."

"Sir Padraig, welcome." Magnus stepped forward, offering his hand to Padraig as he squinted a glance at Rory. "The Good King

Gingalain passed this way only fortnight before, and Laird Mor a few days ago, each at the head of a strong force. Come, let us celebrate the dragon's departure!"

The crowd gathered and greeted the travelers, soon joined by the rest of the men, women and children of the town. In good order, everyone moved down the narrow, dark stairs and into the streets. The crowds soon spread out, several men following the Mayor and the travelers along to the tavern.

The Tavern of Oban looked but a small local establishment from without. From within it, the great hall seemed thrice the size of the building that housed it. Soon the servers and cooks were at work, a fine young Bo Ghaidhealach was upon the fire. The aroma of the roasting beef filled the hall as the owner tended to his guests.

As the strong mead flowed the conversation became less formal and more to the point of recent matters.

"So, you are hunting the dragoness, hoping to free the girl. Why do you think, Sir Padraig, that the beast took the damsel?"

"To entice me to follow, I have no doubt. I slew her mate and her sister, and she wishes to cause me pain."

"Have you considered that she will kill the girl once you have pursued her enough? If she is tormenting you, my friend, then she is holding that disappointment as her triumph over you."

"I will not abandon the damsel, good Mayor. I canna do that."

"Nor should you, Sir. My point was only to be sure that you are aware of it. How may we assist your quest?"

"This good meal is more than we could rightly ask of your town, Magnus." Rory offered.

"Thank you, Sire...eh, Sir Hunter." The Mayor paused in a bow as he stumbled a bit over his words. Padraig showed no sign that he had caught the Mayor's gaff.

"Tell me please, Mayor Dubhglas, did King Gingalain tell you of his plans? And Laird Mor was with him?"

"Aye, that he did, Sir Knight. The Good King is off to Skye, to roust the lair of dragons there! Laird Mor was following in support, without the Good King's knowledge. Several of our young men joined Laird Mor on the quest. We have but the score of warriors left here, along with our fishermen and our sailors, to defend our town."

"Skye is where the dragon's sponsor said this beast was headed. What do you know of this dragon's lair?"

"Upon the part of Skye known as Rubha an Dùnain, they tell me, is a large compound of stone henges. They say that once, over a dozen grandfathers past, these henges were all across the land, from Hallsands to Durness. Nearby are three other henges. All are so ancient that none can remember the names of their builders." Magnus leaned forward and softened his voice, adding a certain fearful reverence as he continued. "When the weather is right, a summer's eve'n' with a bright moon and thunder in the clouds, the stones come alive; they glow with a red light, and the dragons fly out of a mist which gathers between them. Three at a time, a bull and his two dames come. Legend says that if you destroy the stone henges, the dragons canna come. It has been done before; those with selfish and evil intent rebuild the circles, and make pacts with the devil's creatures. Since the Good King drove the Northern Raiders from the Isle, no one has dwelt there. There has been none to assure that the stones were not restored."

"And Rascur had rebuilt them, and entered into a pact with these devils to satisfy his abhorrent desires. Dearly did he pay for his depravity."

"The Good King and the Laird are going the same place as the dragoness we hunt. Can we be sure that the dragoness is headed to the same place?" Edan spoke up.

"There is but one other place she would head to after losing her mate." The mayor turned his gaze upon the hunter before he continued. "Far west, across the sea to Éireann. There are two other henges there, near Portballintrae. The most ancient of all, I've been told. They are the only intact ones aside from those on Skye that I know of."

"The way is long yet to Skye. Would we be better off sailing there?" Padraig asked.

"Should we sail, and the beast heads west, we will surely lose the damsel. We should continue to follow the beast." Rory offered.

"The route of the beast is setting you up as well. Soon, it will cross Loch Linnhe, and you will be bound to trek around it." The mayor leaned forward to emphasize his point. "You will lose a week's time at least. And, consider this. If the dragoness finds a ruined lair on Skye, she is compelled to strike out for Portballintrae."

"Pardon this squire's ignorance, kind Mayor, but how does one destroy stone?" Edan asked.

"The stones are set upright, but well into the ground. The earth around the keystone must be dug out, and the stone toppled. If not the keystone, then at least three must be toppled so."

"But, that leaves the stones to be reset, does it not? Is there no more permanent dismantling?" Rory asked.

"Fire can reduce the stones to pebbles, if it burns long and hot enough." The mayor patiently instructed the squire.

"What do you suggest for our pursuit of the beast?" Rory asked.

"Ferry past Adtur and Shuna to Kilmalieu. That allows you to track the beast well and push across the loch when you need to." Magnus replied. "I insist you allow me to commission the ship."

"Kind Mayor, we will pay you for the ship. And for tonight's feast!" Padraig declared. While the townspeople cheered, Edan wondered if the three pints of mead had contributed to the knight's generosity.

# The Muireall

A cool morning mist hung as a veil over the Sound of Kerrera. Somewhere off in the distance, a seabird squawked in protest of an unseen indignity. The waters were still, barely a gentle lapping at the wharf. Fergus Leoideach looked over his crew as they loaded supplies into his small knarr. This commission for the transport of Sir Padraig and his companions was a bounty, paying him more than he would likely make in the entire season. Besides, mayor Dubhglas himself had asked him to fill the commission. That alone would boost his business, and safe passage of the three would no doubt add further to his reputation. Fergus frequently boasted of the speed of the Muireall, now he would have a chance to prove it, by outrunning a dragoness on the fly!

Ah, the dragoness! The thought both excited and terrified Fergus. Ferrying dragon hunters in his knarr! The Muireall had missed ferrying the Good King on his quest, having been carrying fishing nets to Torlundy at that time. He thought of his young son, barely six years old now. He thought of his crew; redheaded Fionnghal Matasan, half his own age; bald Osgar Sailcirc, a decade older than he, and young Brianan Lios, just a dozen years on God's good Earth. The first two men had children of their own, Fionnghal's son born this past winter. Brianan was the son of Fergus' neighbor. The man left in his knarr on a cargo commission to Ballintoy and never returned. Fergus gave the lad half of his own share on each trip, until Osgar and Fionnghal found out. The two insisted Brianan have a full share. Fergus planned to split the extra income from this commission equally with them, for they were a good crew, deserving of the bonus. But mostly he thought of their children, and how a world without the fear of dragons would be a better place for them to live in.

Fergus saw to the even distribution of the supplies, carefully balancing the load while leaving room for the three horses. Fergus Leoideach may have been young for a captain, but he had learned his craft well from the years he spent on the sea at his father's side.

"We are ready, Captain! The last of the supplies is loaded." Fionnghal shouted.

"And just in time, our fare arrives now!" Brianan's high-pitched voice rang out.

"Hælan, Sir Knight! Welcome aboard the Muireall!" Fergus shouted with great fanfare.

"Hælan, good Captain! Is the wind favorable today?" Padraig called in reply.

"The wind is just right for chasing dragons, Sir Padraig! Your mounts may go 'ere." Fergus pointed to the three spots prepared for the horses, placing Greg in front of the mast, with Gilda and Cailean abreast it. Around them trotted Luag, his tail betraying his excitement.

"We are ready then! Excellent, gentlemen! Brianan, to the lines! Osgar! Fionnghal! Ya know what to do! Look lively, lads, for our guests!"

"Aye, Captain!" Brianan squeaked out.

"Aye-aye, Cap'in!" Fionnghal and Osgar echoed in unison as they readied the sails and oars.

"Away all lines!" Fergus cried.

"Lines away, Cap'in!" Brianan shouted as he leapt from the wharf onto the knarr.

Osgar and Fionnghal pulled at the oars as Fergus hauled the lanyard to keep the sail tight to the faint breeze. They all moved about their tasks with gleeful expressions. To be sailing again! These men all loved being at sea.

The craft sat low in the water under the weight of the supplies and horses, yet moved out from shore with an easy grace.

As the Keep of Oban faded into the morning's mists behind them, Padraig moved up next to Rory.

"Good hunter, the mayor seemed quite happy to fill this ship with provisions for our journey. Be you a friend of his?" Padraig asked with a tilted head.

"We have met before, Good Knight. He is a kind man, a gracious host, and no friend of dragons!" The hunter declared as he stared into the lifting mists.

"Listen!" Fergus admonished.

"I don't hear anything!" Edan complained.

"That is just it. The sea birds, all a chatter, now silent." Osgar whispered.

A bit of a breeze caught hold of the sail, filling it with the ocean's salty scent as it drove the ship forward. Osgar and Fionnghal shipped their oars and took their places at the sail as Fergus moved aft to take the tiller from Brianan.

Luag let out three sharp barks as a warning, then pinned his ears back as he pointed a deep growl at the sky above.

Gilda gave a snort and Greg a stomp, Cailean made a noise none had ever heard from a horse, a low growl as from a bear defending her cubs. Padraig looked up, Excalibur in his hand and the Azure Shield upon his arm, as the dragon dropped from the mists and ripped the sail with her talons, holding Gwenellen as her shield. Padraig was close enough to see the ugly black scar on the dragoness' cheek from Sir Aglovale's blade, and a smaller, newer wound on the shoulder of the beast where Edan's blade had struck true.

"Sister!" Edan cried.

The dragoness carried Gwenellen bound in strips of her frock, tied hand and foot. For a brief instant, Rory captured the maiden's eyes, set in a frightened and weary face, and saw the light of Hope's fire shining through them.

"Edana! Sir Page!" Gwenellen cried hopefully, before the beast carried her from sight.

Padraig glanced at his squire, wondering at the name Gwenellen had used. Quickly the danger at hand banished the question.

"She is beautiful! We must save her, Captain!" Brianan exclaimed.

"That's why we're here, laddie." Rory growled, fingers tight on bow and quiver as he watched the dragoness fly into the mists. "I couldna shoot, least I hit the maiden."

Soon the morning fogs had cleared, and gentile hills of the Isle of Lismore shown in the distance. The ship's captain studied the winds and the waves. And looked to the west for a long while.

"We should make Onich, or perhaps Corran before nightfall," Fergus finally assured the travelers. "We should spend a restful eve'n at either."

"Our route is inland, then?" Padraig asked.

"We should pass Corran and Goirtean a' Chladaich, and spend the morrow's eve'n' in Blaich or Drumfern. Then we head north, and if we time the tides right, we can sail right into Glenfinnan. You have a day and a half's march from there to Mallaig, where you'll sure find easy passage to Skye."

"Four days to Skye, and the final battle with that beast." Padraig muttered under his breath.

"Keep your blood cool for that encounter, my friend. Heed your own sage advice!" Rory placed a hand on the shoulder of the knight. Padraig looked up and flashed a smile.

"A true friend reminds one when he's off course, does he not, Captain?" Padraig bellowed.

"Each time we stray, Sir Padraig! Each time we stray!"

Just then the ship gave a vicious roll, nearly casting Edan into the sea and upsetting the horses. Luag began a continuous yapping.

"Hold on! Whales!" Fionnghal cried.

"There!" Brianan pointed off the bow, where a spout of water and steam rose up higher than the Muireall's mast, then disappeared as a huge dark grey tail lifted up and slammed down onto the sea.

"'Ere! Alongside!" Osgar cried.

Padraig, Rory and Edan looked over to the side, where not a yard from the ship swelled out of the sea a great shiny grey head. On top sat the nostril, open now and expelling the creature's foul breath and a great deal of mist that settled upon them. Then settling back, the great being inhaled deeply. Padraig could just make out the huge eye, as big as his fist, staring up at him from just under the sea. He nearly fell over as that eye rose out of the waves and above the side of the ship, all the while staring directly at the him.

"'Old on!" Fergus shouted, "'E'll drop his head and smash the ship, the better to eat us all!"

But Padraig stood straight, staring back at the great whale, seeing now the long, narrow jaw rise up, with its row of huge pointed teeth along each side, each half as tall as Padraig, with the great pink tongue lolling between. "Be still, my friends. He smiles at us!"

"I think 'e smiles at yer mare, Sir Knight!" Osgar's laughing retort banishing the tension of the moment.

The knight turned and looked at Gilda, who stood proudly shaking her head. He stole a glance at Greg and Cailean; both proud stallions seemed a bit put out, eyeing the whale. With suspicion or jealousy, he could not tell. Luag watched, silent now, tail and ears down, between Gilda's forelegs. Padraig let out a laugh that spread to the others when the great whale slid once more beneath the sea.

Eight of the whales the crew counted, now swimming effortlessly alongside the knarr. They now kept a good twenty feet from the ship, as if escorting it.

Fergus walked over to Rory and said quietly, "It would seem ya 'ave more support with ya on yer quest than ya knew, heh, M'Laird?"

Rory looked at the captain and replied, "A man can never have enough friends with him, good captain." The High King of Dal Riata smiled as he turned and walked over to Cailean, tending to his mount's comfort.

"He is a quiet man when it comes to talking about himself." Edan said to Fergus. "Sir Padraig does not know of the hunter's true position. That it remains so is the wish of the king."

"I dunna understand, squire, but my understanding is not a precondition of my compliance to my king's wishes in such matters," and the captain went back to sailing his ship.

As mid-day approached, the captain called to the squire, and bade him to break out the noon meal of smoked lamb, oat ale, and bread.

"Portion this out for each, then carry the rations to yer knight and the hunter. Leave the rest for me." Fergus instructed Edan.

Edan carried the food with some difficulty across the rolling ship's beam, setting the portions for the knight and the hunter, before placing the squire's portion at the ready. Rory had already seen to the horses, the three great animals watching with feedbags on, refraining from quenching their hunger as they watched Sir Padraig.

A was his custom, Fergus carried his crew's portions to them himself, setting his at the ready. A glance at Padraig, as if an unspoken agreement was being fulfilled, signaled the knight to speak.

"Thank you, God, for these bounties of this World that You have seen fit to place before us. Amen!"

"Amen!" chorused about the knarr.

Edan began chewing an ambitious mouthful of bread while gazing upon the whales swimming away from the ship. The ease with which they seemed to glide through the seas was a marvel to Edan, who watched as, now a considerable distance away, they dove as one out of sight. The squire's eyes gazed across the horizon, then upwards...

"DwMknlws!" Edan pointed while fighting to swallow the bread not sprayed across the deck in the excitement. "DRAGONS!" The squire finally managed to yell, even as Luag began his warning barks.

The men all followed Edan's direction and looked up, scanning the heavens for the dragoness.

Instead, their eyes beheld six huge dragons, circling high above the ship. Greg and Gilda stomped in frustration of their confinement; Cailean shook his feedbag off and readied himself as if to leap, eyes upon the beasts above. Luag growled, crouched down next to Rory, ready to leap.

The circling dragons began their descent to attack the small boat, banking over into a graceful dive. They picked up speed as Rory raised his bow and Padraig lifted his shield, set ablaze by the light blue glow of Excalibur unsheathed. Edan had the claymore at the ready, and noted the crew's claidebs were drawn and held, blades eager to strike.

The first beast, easily twice the size of the bull dragon Padraig had slain, was nearly upon them, when the sea beside the knarr burst upward. The seven would be dragon slayers in the ship stared with great wonder through the exploding water as a grey whale flew up out of the sea at an amazing rate, until the wide tail was above the tip of the Muireall's mast!

"GOOD GOD!" Fergus cried at the sight of the huge beast bending around, the long, narrow mouth of the whale snatching the dragon in mid air! Loud cracking sounds echoed off the nearby hills as the powerful jaw crushed the beast as if it were but a heel of crusty bread. As this whale began to fall back to his own domain, a second burst from the waves, tail wider than the Muireall was long, and another huge dragon found it's destiny in the gullet of one of the great guardians of the deep.

Over and over did the whales meet and dispatch the dragons with rapid succession in the skies over the ship. The third dragon tried to burn the warriors from the deep with his fiery breath, but if the whales felt any pain from the dragon's breath, they showed no signs of it. The dragons that followed in their dive tried to avoid the monsters devouring their kin, but such had been their confidence and eagerness for attack that the speed of their dive now precluded any evasion.

In but a few moments the six dragons were no more, and the seven adventurers set about the challenge of bailing out the waters splashed into the knarr by their protectors' activities.

As the crew and passengers were thus engaged, they did not see the largest whale slide silently next to their ship and lift his great head above the waves near the three horses. Except for Brianan, who watched out of the corner of his eye. He alone looked on in awe as the three loyal mounts tilted their heads in a nod of their respect for their marine kin, while Luag wagged his tail. As the great whale vanished silently beneath the waves, Brianan turned his gaze to the obvious leader of the band; he regarded Sir Padraig very differently now.

Fergus set the Muireall into a small cove near a creek for the night, as the time spent bailing the water from the knarr having slowed their progress considerably. As Osgar made fast the vessel, Fergus and Padraig moved inland to set up camp, while Edan led the horses off the ship. Brianan followed Luag and Rory as they headed inland to hunt the evening's meal.

Fergus placed a hand on Padraig's shoulder, and as the knight turned, the good captain knelt before him with bowed head.

"Sir Knight," Fergus raised his head as he began, "I've traveled most of my life on the seas. Dragons before 'ave attacked me. I've been as far as Rome thrice, and I've e'en been to a frozen island in the west where 'Ell's fires spew from the Earth. Yet I've ne'er seen the likes of what we witnessed today. I believe it is due to yer presence, Sir."

Padraig looked at Fergus, and reached down and lifted him to stand.

"Good Captain, I have no reason to doubt your experience, and your exceptional abilities to handle both your ship and your crew are evident. If what you say is true, I have no knowledge of it, nor any influence upon it." Padraig turned and resumed walking along the shore.

Fergus tilted his head to one side, and stood, staring after Padraig. *This trip will pay you much more than you contracted for, Fergus Leoideach,* he thought as he resumed following the knight.

The camp was set up a few dozen yards from the Muireall. The knarr could be easily seen from this site, and the trees formed a canopy that would deter any dragon attacks from above.

Soon Fergus, Padraig and Fionnghal had a lean-to up and a fire burning. Rory, Brianan, and Luag returned with a deer, the hunter taking obvious glee from showing the young Brianan how to dress it for the fire. Fergus and Fionnghal scouted the area around the camp as the venison roasted. Edan and Padraig returned to the ship to retrieve their bedding as Osgar made fast the knarr.

"Sir Padraig, how are you always so sure of everything?" Edan asked.

Padraig stopped and turned to face his squire, "There is more to your question, my little one, than you ask. Since the hunter has joined us, I hav'na given enough time to your training. I regret depriving you of that. Here, sit, and we will begin." Knight and squire sat on the cool beach next to the ship.

"But, we have had my lessons every morning!"

"There is much more for you to learn than simple fighting skills. That you learn those lessons well I have made sure of, since you may need them when we meet the dragoness. I have been neglectful of your other training, and I must expedite that, for you will need it after I am gone."

Edan rose with a start at those words. "What do you mean, 'after you're gone'?" the squire demanded through trembling lips.

Padraig looked straight into his squire's eyes, remembering the strength of the Good King during his own lessons. "It is a likely outcome that I willna survive this encounter with the dragoness. That is why it is important for you and the hunter to take Gwenellen to safety as I fight the beast."

"But, you've killed bigger, stronger dragons than her! Surely, with Excalibur, she is no match..."

"Keep the sword of the Great King to yourself; knowing it is here would make certain people take actions best for all if avoided. As for the dame dragon, Edan, there is a reason she travels to Skye. There will be many others of her kind there, and no great grey whales to help us."

Edan's jaws clenched as the squire asserted, "I won't see you sacrifice yourself!"

"My little one, I dunna plan to sacrifice myself, for I do love life dearly. There are many things I long yet to do." Padraig looked deeply into Edan's eyes as he continued, "One lesson you must learn is to always be honest in dealing with yourself. My expectation is an honest assessment of the situations we face, not a recital of a desired outcome. I plan based upon that assessment, so we may save your sister. I will fight very hard to survive, and I am more likely to do so if I know that you are taking Gwenellen to safety."

"I am not a strong enough fighter to be at your side. I will work harder, you'll see, I'll get better!" Edan pleaded, nearly sobbing at the outcome Padraig foretold.

"Little one, you have all you will ever need for combat. Few men could trouble you in battle. I've trained you to fight dragons, as I was trained. My instructor told me, 'when you can prevail over dragons, fighting men will not trouble you.' That is how I have trained you."

"The Good King trained you!"

"In many things, he did. But for certain kinds of combat, he brought in a curious man to do that. Short and slight he was, with elfin eyes. He spoke with a funny sound to his words, and often said the words out of order. I do not know if this was to make me listen more intently, or if it was a confusion from his native tongue."

"What was this elf's name?" Edan sat down beside Padraig, becoming focused upon the tale he was weaving.

"He was called Zin. And while he was small, he was fast and quick, and much stronger then he looked. And, about combat, he was very wise. He was not an elf, however, but a man from some land far, off to the East." Padraig stood and gathered up his portion of the load. "Now, my Squire, we must return, for my nose tells me Rory's catch is ready to eat."

Neither noticed the glowing orange eyes following them from the darkened forest.

Padraig had said their Grace, and the travelers had eaten. Luag took possession of a tasty bone, contenting himself with gnawing upon it. The horses grazed, each in a different direction, covering every path into the camp.

Padraig took Edan aside and began teaching the squire what he knew about the ways of man and dragon. Rory playfully tugged on Luag's bone. The sailors tended their ship, Osgar and Brianan drawing the duty to sleep aboard the Muireall this night. Captain Fergus and Fionnghal discussed the day's events. Neither had ever heard of whales leaping so high, let alone eating dragons!

"Surely none will believe our telling of this tale!" Fionnghal asserted.

"Ne'er 'ad we a cause to create such a story. Our reputations will..." Fergus snapped his words off as if with an axe. He motioned with his eyes to Fionnghal, who slowly turned, shaking slightly with the expectation of seeing a dragon.

"Eyes. Many eyes, orange in the firelight. Tigers!" Fergus said in an even voice, afraid of exciting what watched them through those eyes.

Padraig noticed the start in the two sailors, as did Rory. Luag let go a low growl, his bone forgotten at his feet. The horses seemed unconcerned; perhaps they were unaware of the company.

Padraig let out a whistle, followed by Rory, then Edan. The three equines walked calmly to the sides of their riders. The orange eyes had vanished.

"Highland tigers, they are. Can be as big as Luag. Or bigger. Mean, vicious cats. The Romans tried keeping some as pets, like they did the Egyptian cats, but they wouldna tame. I've ne'er heard of them showing up in groups, though." Rory offered.

"I'll be with my knarr this eve'n. Two mayna be safe with tigers about." Fergus stated as he gathered his bedding.

"Edan, with the good Captain, please."

"Yes, Sir Padraig."

Rory leaned close to Padraig so the squire would not hear.

"Wouldn't the young one be safer here? Perhaps I should go, Sir Knight?"

"The tigers would most likely attack us here before those on the knarr. And Edan is skilled enough to have a blade stained by dragon's blood. The assignment to protect the ship will build my squire's confidence. The fighting skills required have already been mastered. Edan knows how to use weapons. My squire needs to learn how brains are best used now."

"And much of that is believing yourself able. Again your wisdom humbles me, Good Knight."

"We hav'na freed the maiden Gwenellen yet, hunter. Yours is the second watch, I will wake thee upon midnight. The sailors need their sleep, as they will be the ones working the morrow. Good night, Sire." Padraig sat near the fire with a grin.

Rory just stared at Padraig. Had that title been intended? After a moment, he motioned for Luag, and the faithful hound trotted up to lay by his master's side.

Padraig watched as Rory quickly slipped into his bedding. The knight took a slow look around the sleeping camp as his watch began. The bright moon lit up Gilda as the roan also surveyed the surroundings while Cailean and Greg slept. Luag lay next to Rory, gazing at Padraig with bright brown eyes, tail twitching softly.

Off to his left, Padraig could see the knarr gently rock with the sea. Edan was on watch, head dutifully turning to and fro. The squire in the knarr had only one direction to watch.

The quiet night perked Padraig's interest. A cool spring night near the ocean should have carried the cries of owls, the scurrying of voles, and the chirps of crickets. The absence of these sounds evidenced to him the apprehension that the

82

dragons had spawned upon this land.

Padraig stood and moved silently around the camp. As he came nearest to the moored Muireall, he noted Edan looking at him. He sent his squire a nod, which was returned.

Much later, as Rory waited for the second watch to end, a low rumble came faintly to his ears. Not quite a growl, the sound brought images of wooden sledges dragging over rocks. A quick glance showed the knarr was still fast, and Osgar now alertly on the watch. The rumble seemed to come from every direction at once. As the sun brightened the morning, the rumbling abruptly ceased.

Later that day, the Muireall was at sea making a brisk pace. No whales escorted them now, for the sea was not of sufficient depth here. Past the towns they sailed, favorable winds shortening their journey.

Twice Brianan had spied the dragoness carrying Gwenellen, flying low over the trees to hide her path. They were very close to her now, and the dragoness was careful to hide her camps from the pursuers.

They approached Glenfinnan near the end of the day. The setting sun cast a golden glow on the western walls of the village. Torches placed on the wharf set a flickering glow onto the water as Fergus brought the Muireall into port.

"There's far too few to greet us, Cap'in" Osgar whispered as he jumped onto the wharf with a mooring line. Fergus looked about, noticing a lone old man walking up the wharf.

The captain made his way back to Padraig and Rory, watching the waterfront as it dimmed under the rapidly setting sun. "There are usually a dozen here to make fast the ship and off load the cargo. Now there's just one old man. Something's amiss. Follow my lead, Sirs, and be alert." With that, Fergus jumped onto the planks of the wharf and strode boldly up to the old man.

"'Arbor Master, how is it that the fine lads of this village sleep while you work!" Fergus called out in good humor.

"Hrumpf! Fine lads INDEED!" growled the old man. "Left ta join that bag o' wind Aengus Mac Mor, they did. Fancy themselves as dragonslayers! Hrumpf! Just shirkin' their work, is all they're good fer. Hrumpf!"

Fergus made a motion, and the Muireall's crew and passengers began off loading their cargo.

"Fear not, Alistair, I 'ave an able and willing crew to unload our cargo. We 'av'na goods for your town today, only passengers and their properties."

"The tax I must still collect, Captain Leoideach!"

"Let me, kind sir," Rory said as he stepped forward and placed something shiny in the old man's hand, "This should cover the tax. If it be over, add another pint of ale to your dinner, eh?"

"It takes more than a pint of..." The old man squinted at the coin, and then at the hunter, his eyes widening to cut off his words. "As you command, Sire!" The old man exclaimed as he began lowering his aching bones to kneel.

"Stand, my good man. There's no need of that today." Rory quietly urged.

"As you wish." Alistair looked at the hunter, then at Padraig and Edan. "May I be o' service to ya?"

"Lead us to a good supper and some warm beds, if you would be so kind," Padraig replied.

"Aye, Brigid's Inn ya want. Straight up the street, two crossroads past. Ye canna miss it!" With that, Alistair turned and began his slow walk back to his shack at the end of the wharf.

Padraig turned to find the horses packed, the hunter and the squire mounted, with Luag sitting on his excited tail. Brianan stood by Rory as Fergus spoke with them both. Presently the young boy reached up as if to mount Cailean behind Rory, but then stopped and turned. He walked quickly to Fergus, and then wrapped both arms about the good captain tightly. After a moment, Fergus patted Brianan's shoulder, and the boy released his guardian. Then he did mount Cailean behind Rory.

Fergus walked slowly to Padraig. Wet eyes gazed at the knight as the captain offered his hand.

"God be with ya, my friend."

"And with you. Are you at peace, Good Captain?"

"I am, kind Knight. The 'unter and Brianan 'ave taken to each other. The lad will 'ave a better life on land than I can give 'im at sea. I am depending upon you, Sir Knight, to assure that he lives a long one."

"I will do what I can, my friend. Safe travels!"

"Safe travels, my friend. Ya are less than two days from yer goal. Should the dragoness move towards Portballintrae, make to the port Culnamean, near Rubha an Dùnain. We'll be there in four days."

"You do not need to do this, Fergus Leoideach."

"Aye, that be true, my friend. But my crew would ne'er ship with me again if I dunna." With that, the good captain turned and jumped into his ship. "Osgar, stand on the lines! Fionnghal, make ready the oars. Look sharp, lads, Brianan's become a land lubber!"

The Muireall faded silently away into the night.

# The Quest Turns

The four dragon hunters found boarding for their three horses at the stables behind Brigid's Inn. The hunter insisted on attending to these details, waiting until the others had left for dinner before engaging the stable master.

"This chestnut mare, is she for sale?" Rory inquired about a fine young horse near the entrance.

"She's for sale, Mister. Very reasonable, too I might add."

Rory walked into the mare's stall, feeling her strong flanks and sturdy legs. He patted her nose, and turned again to the stable master.

"What do you consider reasonable, my good man? Include that fine saddle and reins as well in your price." Rory handed a small bag of coins to the stable master, who stood mouth agape at the offer. "Good, done then 'tis! You drive a hard bargain, my friend. We shall take the mare in the morn."

His business in the stable completed, Rory walked the short distance to the inn. A quick glance down the dark streets raised the hairs on his neck; orange eyes, dozens of them scattered about, flittering and disappearing as his gaze fell upon them.

"To what end portends this?" he whispered to himself as he opened the portal and stepped into the Inn.

Sunrise the next morning found Brianan beaming with excitement at the prospect of riding his own horse.

"The young lad is very observant; he will make a good hunter, don't you think?" Rory answered Padraig's questioning smile.

"Watching Edan's lessons have whetted your appetite, have they?"

The two men laughed lightly as the four left rode out of Glenfinnan, followed by a trotting Luag's forever wagging tail.

The road led due West until almost to the open sea, then North to Mallaig where the four would find passage to Skye. Near midday Padraig motioned the hunter to ride along side of him.

"You are no fool, hunter, so I know you have considered what I mention here. The boy is young, and likely ill prepared for battle with dragons. I will not be distracted with his safety. Nor should you be."

"The boy is better schooled than you believe, Good Knight. 'Twas he who felled the last deer we supped upon. One shot, through the trees, at over two hundred paces. I couldna have made that shot twice for five tries. He ne'er doubted it."

Padraig considered this for several minutes as they rode.

"How is the lad with a dirk or a sword?"

"That I do not know, my friend. This eve'n I'll discover the extent of the lad's training."

"Still, is it right to bring him into such danger?"

"He wants to come. He begged. I've told him that our chances of survival are less than sure in the strongest of terms. The lad is verging upon manhood, and wouldna be denied." The hunter looked into Padraig's eyes directly, "Something tells me it should be so."

"So be it then. This eve'n, you train Edan and I'll see to Brianan."

"Sir Knight, the young lad has joined us as *my* page. While I appreciate your considerable skills, I will see to his training."

Padraig looked at Rory as Cailean slowed to come alongside Brianan's mount. The words from the hunter came in the manner of Gingalain to his subjects; there was no question that they would be obeyed. Padraig smiled, ever so faintly, as he nodded his head slightly three times.

Greg pulled up next to Gilda, Luag riding across the horse in front of Edan, tail wagging in the breeze. The squire squinted, looking Padraig in the eyes; "Is all well, my knight?"

"Yes. Why would you ask?" Padraig suspected Edan's concern was from the tone of Rory's remarks.

"There seemed to be added passion in that discussion."

"Was there? And why would that be, my young squire?"

Edan looked down the road ahead. "You do not think the lad should be with us."

"And?"

"And the...hunter disagrees."

"So, what do you think we should do, Edan?" Padraig's serious face struggled to keep his laughter a prisoner as he brought Gilda to a halt.

Edan stopped Greg. The squire turned to face the knight. "He is still with us, so it has been already decided. As if it were... ordained." With that, the squire rode on, leaving Padraig and Gilda standing until Rory and Brianan rode up.

"It would seem that my squire has a lesser need of my lessons with each day." Padraig Ualas said as he brought Gilda up to a trot to regain the van.

Rory's smile kept growing until it burst with his laughter. *If only you knew*, Rory thought.

At twilight, as the four sat down to their eve'n meal, Brianan asked shyly, "If you p-please, Sir Knight, m-may I say The Grace tonight?"

"Are ye of a good and honest heart, Brianan Lios?" Padraig squinted very seriously at the lad, "Do you live your life in service of The Laird?"

"Aye, Good Knight. I do my best at all of that, as much as a poor young sinner can."

"Then you may give The Blessing, Page Brianan." Rory cut in, winking at Padraig's grin.

"Ave Maria, gratia plena,    Maria, gratia plena,    Maria, gratia plena,    Ave, Ave, Dominus,    Dominus tecum.    Benedicta tu in mulieribus, et benedictus,    Et benedictus fructus ventris tui,    Ventris tui, Jesus. Bless this food to our lips and us to Thine service. Amen."

The three stared at the boy for some time.

"What?" Brianan finally said.

"Where did you learn the Roman tongue?"

"My father ferried Colum Cille to Iona many times. The Friar took to teaching me when he could."

"It would seem the Friar's touch is quite abundant among us. This must be a good thing," Rory smiled.

Padraig turned to the hunter and said, "Well then, let's eat!"

The fine supper of Lady Brigid's haggis consumed, Edan stood to collect the dinnerware for washing. "Brianan, you must name that horse, or she will name you!"

"Lara. I'll name her Lara!" The young boy exclaimed.

As if called, the chestnut mare walked up behind Brianan and nudged him with her nose. The lad jumped up with a start, which brought much amusement to his three companions.

His embarrassment so overcame him that young Brianan did not know if he should run away or cry. Then he saw Greg behind Edan, shaking his head, and Gilda, and Cailean as well. Brianan began smiling as the three horses nudged their riders, whose expressions of alarm elicited great deal of laughter from the lad.

"Well, my squire, it would seem our mounts like the lad, won't you say?"

"Aye, Sir Ualas, It would appear so!"

"Aaaaaaaaaaarwk"

A bone-chilling screech pierced the eve'n air. Dragon call!

"Be alert, though that call wasna for us. Your dragoness announces herself, Sir Knight." Rory's voice was stern yet quite.

"Dawn may find us facing a score of the beasts, I fear. The watch tonight will be two together. Edan and I will take first. Aedan and Brianan the next."

The hunter's head snapped around to face Padraig at the mention of that name.

"Sleep well, Sire." Padraig smiled at Aedan Mac Gabrain, The High King of Dal Riata. "Life may be too precarious from here on for secrets."

Aedan glanced at Edan, whose head shook in denial. "Good night, Good Knight," Aedan said quietly as he crawled into his bedding. Brianan already slept.

"My knight, how did you know?" Edan whispered to Padraig.

"The stable master tried to return a gold coin Aedan had given him for Lara's purchase. He had recognized The High King, but couldna place the face until he looked at the coin; it bore Aedan's likeness. I had suspected such for some time. We are blessed when good men are king, as we are surely cursed when evil rules."

"What do we do when evil rules, Padraig?" Edan's voice came softly to the knight's ears.

"We do what we do now, my squire; we protect the innocent, the good, and the righteous as best we can. It is no different. With the tools we are blessed with, we have an obligation to protect, lest we become, through our inaction, an evil to the people ourselves."

Edan thought a moment. "Some times evil doesna look evil. How do we know?"

"That which cloaks itself in the garb of good, yet delivers only suffering, we will surely know as evil."

"What if we canna win? Must we fight anyway, and perish, or shouldna we reform for a later day, when we may prevail?"

"Sometimes, Edan, the fighting is more important than the outcome. Victory can come a long time after the battle is o'er."

"If it is too hard? What if the tasks are too hard?"

"We are ne'er tasked with more than we can bare, for God loves us. Knowing this helps us find that path to victory that runs through e'ery moil. We needna clear that path, nor pave it, but merely find it and follow it."

"Padraig, do you... have you e'er thought about, um..."

"Thought of what, my little one? Ask, you need ne'er fear the asking, nor my answer," Padraig replied softly.

"Have you e'er, um, do you, have you thought about wanting a family? A wife, children. Do you want to have children?"

"Why ask me such a question, Edan?"

"I'm only thinking of my future, Sir Padraig."

"When I have a wife and children, you will no longer be my squire, this I promise." The knight laughed his answer.

"But, do you want children, a family of your own?"

"A wife who loves you, and children to teach, to watch grow; these are God's greatest blessings, my little one."

"Padraig, look..." Edan motioned slowly at the darkening woods about them; pairs of glowing orange eyes reflected their fire. "Tigers..."

"Yes, but I think we needna fear them. They've been following us for three days now."

"What?" Edan exclaimed.

"Quiet, My squire! It is not time to wake the High King yet."

Edan's angry stare burned into Padraig for a moment. "We've been surrounded by tigers for two days, and you've said naught?"

"Yes. If they had meant us harm, they would have attacked us a long time ago."

"How do you *know* this?"

"Shh! Some things one just knows. Now, at my back, and stay alert. Focus above. Dragons seldom attack at night, but seldom is not the same as ne'er."

"I've ne'er, e'er… seen anything like… hmf! tigers…ha!" Edan mumbled softly.

A noise like a knarr being hauled steadily along a dry, rocky streambed sprang up from all around them.

"Sir Padraig, what is that noise?"

"Our friends seem to be contented, squire. Stay alert!"

The two sat on opposing sides of the fire, backs to the warming glow. Around the camp and up into the clear, starry sky they looked. Edan looked up and gave a big sigh.

"Padraig, have you e'er tried to count the stars?" Edan asked softly.

"Why would one do such a thing? Knowing the number wouldna help you. Not at all." Padraig teased.

"Do you e'er wonder what they are?"

"They are exactly what you most want them to be."

"No, they are not." Edan sighed quietly.

"Sir Ualas?"

"Yes?"

"Do you have… is there, um, a, ah, do you have, are you betrothed?"

"Hah-ha, no, my little one. Not yet."

"Is there some one, one who owns your heart?" Edan's quiet voice asked.

"If I am lucky, the one I love will reciprocate. It could be some one I already know, or some one I hav'na encountered yet." Padraig said with a slight smile.

"Some one, like my sister, perhaps?"

"Some one, *like* your sister. Perhaps."

"Is it my sister?"

"Some things are best left alone, my little one, to see how fate directs us."

As the mid night was approaching, Edan rose and began preparing their bedding while Padraig tended to the horses.

"Padraig, should such a young lad as Brianan come with us? Is it the right thing to bring him?"

"Earlier you were content to let others bare that burden. What think you now, my squire?"

"I want him to be safe. Then, I want us *all* to be safe. But, he is so young."

"He is not much younger than you, my squire!"

"I am fully sixte..." Edan's passion began to rise before cooling, "...I am much older than he, my knight."

"I see," Padraig chuckled. "Well, as you have said before, it has been decided. Time to wake these two logs!" Padraig gave the two a shove, "Up, your watch is here!"

"You do many things very well, Sir Ualas, but being a rooster is not your strong suit." Aedan stretched and arose.

"Did you see any dragons?" Brianan asked as he rubbed the sleep from his eyes.

"None more than in your dreams, young page." Padraig crawled under his bedding, "Good night, King and Page!"

"Good night, Brianan and Aedan!" Edan echoed, before rolling over and coming face to face with Padraig. "Oh!" Came the blushing gasp. "Good night, my Good Knight," the squire whispered.

"Good night, my little one." Padraig answered softly.

"Sire, why did they not know ye?" Brianan asked.

"Because I've worn disguises, and hid my title from them."

"Why would you do such a thing?"

"A king needs to know certain things about his kingdom. About his people. This lesson my father has taught me, and I've lived it for three long years now."

"Why do you need to know your people? And, why are you now hunting the dragons? And, what is a High King?"

"A king needs to know what his people's struggles are, what their joys are, what their needs are to rule well. Five years ago I was but an impetuous boy, ne'er much wiser than you. My task was to learn what I needed to know to rule wisely.

"Along the way, I met a maiden. Beautiful, kind, gentile, with a smile that warms as daybreak and a laugh that... I fell in love with her, and she loved me. We were to be married. Then, the dragon came. Now, I follow the one who murdered my love."

Aedan stared blankly into the fire, "If I do not rid my anger upon the beast, I fear a terrible darkness will grow inside and take hold of me.

"The Good Knight and his... squire happened upon my love just as I did. They were hunting the very same dragoness, so I joined their quest. The Good Knight is a terror in battle, and a kind, wise, and moral man otherwise. I pray to the Laird Of All that I may be so myself, one day.

"A High King. Many smaller kingdoms arose after the Great King Artair's death. Sir Padraig is pledged to King Gingalain, my uncle, who is known as the Good King. Another nearby kingdom is ruled by the Laird O' the Isles, Mac Mor, known as the Great Celt. Both of these men have pledged to me, and I to them. I rule the Isles and Kintyre as part of Dal Riata. We all seek a better life for our people, and rule by the Way that Artair taught us. Each of us is stronger together than we all are when apart."

"I'm sorry about your betrothed, my King. I often dream of my father, at sea, with the dragons after him. The whales didna protect him, I think. Perhaps, perhaps he returned home, to Clonfert."

Aedan looked at the boy for a few moments. *Let him remember his father*, he thought. Then he stood and removed two dirks from Cailean's saddle.

"Here, my péitse," Aedan called as he tossed a dirk past the fire to the lad. The thoughtless reflexes of one so young caught the foot-long dagger before he realized what it was. "Your lessons must be thorough, if brief."

"Sire, if I should injure you..."

"HAH!" Aedan retorted as he thrust hard at the center of the lad.

Brianan slipped easily to his right as he held the dirk in his left hand, slapping the flat of the blade down onto the wrist of the startled king. Aedan spun away, watching his page in the flickering light of the fire.

"You have had training?"

"Yes, Sire. Quite a bit, actually." Brianan said, as the horses neighed in agitation.

"Pray that your training included fighting DRAGONS!" Aedan

shouted the last word as he tossed his dirk to Brianan while drawing and swinging his sword upward in a single motion. The king's arm shook at the impact of his blade upon the large bull dragon above him. He quickly brought his other hand to give more power to his blows, and spun to strike at his tormentor's center.

Between dodging the dragon's blows and delivering his own, Aedan caught brief, flickering glimpses just beyond the fire's glow of other dragons, whirls of blurred crimson slashing across his sight. A white flash, Greg, high in a jump. Luag's growls, barks and now yelps. Then another high-pitched growling sound he did not know. A dragon flashed across his eyes, Luag's strong jaws clamped around the beast's throat. Aedan couldn't think of the others now, for this bull dragon was larger than any he had ever heard of. Fully two heads taller than the king, the powerful beast was not very graceful in the air. When grounded though, he moved like a dark red flame, flickering here and there, difficult to catch in the pre-morning darkness.

Aedan swung and swung again, feinting now, then a powerful blow. The dragon slashed with razor sharp talons, barely missing the royal throat before slicing into king's left arm.

"Aaargh!" The pain only served to fan the fires of rage burning in King Aedan's heart, their heat powering his sword; "Take this, for Murron!" he screamed as his mighty thrust sank the sword's point deeply into the neck and shoulder of the beast. Foul smelling black dragon's blood sprayed over Aedan's face as he pulled the blade back to strike again. But before he could begin his mighty blow, the bull dragon grabbed king by the neck and lifted him two feet off of the ground, talons sinking into the flesh at the nape of his neck while pulling Aedan's head towards those horrific teeth.

Aedan could not get enough power to swing the sword with effect while the dragon held him so, but king was possessed of far too much skill, and driven by far too much desire to let his fight end now. He drew his arm back and thrust the blade into center of the beast, adding his left hand's power to the thrust. As the hilt met the dragon's belly, King Aedan levered the blade up, then to his right. Great gushes of dragon's blood cloaked Aedan

94

with the life that poured from the beast.

As the bull dragon fell dead, Aedan tumbled atop the foul smelling corpse. Exhaustion was the king's next foe. He was breathing heavily as his eyes searched the darkness of the pre-dawn camp. Brianan? Edan? Padraig?

Three more dragons flashed about in the flickering light of the campfire, while Aedan saw that two more dragons lay dead, one cut in half, the other shredded, as if by a thousand small blades, its throat ripped out. Aedan noticed the bedding was aflame, painting its smoking glow over everything.

A pale blue flash energized Aedan, as the recognition that Excalibur was being swung to great effect brought new life to his aching limbs. There!

Padraig moved as a blur into a pair of the dragons, Excalibur slicing red flesh with lightning strikes. Dragon screams filled the night air each time that fabled blade struck. These were older dragons, bigger, more experienced, yet still the glowing blade struck and burned through them. Injured and confused, the two beasts could not coordinate their attack on Padraig. Before Aedan could reach him, the two dragons fell to Padraig's sword.

"Edan! Brianan" Aedan's voice boomed across the camp.

"Here!" The squire's reply turned king's eyes unto carnage. The squire knelt on the chest of the last living dragon, Edan's chest heaving as both hands plunged the claymore deep into the beast, as Brianan thrust a dirk into each side of the dragon's neck and began slicing.

"He is dead, Edan, Brianan. This is the last one, Dragonslayers." Aedan pronounced.

"King Aedan, these six who attacked us, they are all large males. This means but one thing."

"Army. A dragon army."

The four rested as well as they could amongst the stench of so much dragon blood. Presently they began cleaning their wounds, then their weapons. Padraig tended the horses, Lara being the worst off. He touched his shield to the wounds, closing them and calming the chestnut mare. Gilda nuzzled the newcomer, while Cailean stood guard over her on the left, Greg on the right.

Edan and Brianan, their wounds surprisingly light, picked up the camp. They salvaged what they could, some food and enough of the bedding. Most was too burned, torn or soaked with dragon blood to be of further use.

"Luag! Here, boy!" Aedan called and whistled, but the hound did not come or call. A good ways past the battlefield the four searched, but no trace of the hound was found.

High King Aedan sat on a large stone, staring at the ground, his muscles aching nearly as much as his heart. "Murron and Luag, both gone," he sighed.

"Do not give in to the vow forming in your heart. It will only cause you to punish yourself" Padraig Ualas sat next to his friend.

Aedan looked up and saw a large gash from Padraig's left ear to his mouth. "Let me tend to this, Good Knight."

"That is Edan's work. Let us tend to that shattered heart you've been hiding."

Aedan looked at his feet, his head hanging low. "Every thing I have ever loved has died these past few days. I feel like I should ne'er…"

"Dunna go there. It won't help you. Life has a way of bringing the spring blooms after the worst of winter's snow. Your flower may bloom for you when and where you least expect it. Luag may yet turn up. He's a clever one." Padraig stood, then paused a moment. He placed his hand upon Aedan's shoulder and said, "A king needs to love his people to serve them well. A wise man once told me, 'Certain acts, by unburdening the loads of others, will in kind serve to unburden *our* loads, while they also strengthen our souls. Remember that which Friar Colum Cille has taught, and search your heart, for therein The Laird God has set the answers ye seek, but hav'na asked.' You would be well served to learn that lesson."

The king looked up into the knight's eyes. "Fortune has brought you to me, so I may know that others are wiser, and more regal, than I shall ever be."

"I doubt that is so, King Aedan. Your heart will lead you well once your experience has tempered it."

"Are you two going to chatter all day as two old women?" Edan's voice broke with the dawn's light. "We have a maiden to

96

rescue, remember?"

# Dragon Storm

Smoke confused the horizon as the four dragonslayers crested the hills by Beoraidbeg. So heavy lay the acrid mist over Mallaig that the harbor could not be seen, and only a few rooftops evidenced the town.

"My hope is that a worthy craft remains for our passage to Skye," Padraig said to no one in particular.

The four spoke no more as they rode into the town, eyes glancing upward every few seconds. Mallaig had no walls, dunn, nor keep; the hills rose up around the town so steeply that walls need not be built, and the one path of access to it was so narrow as to be easily defended.

The path into Mallaig was deserted. Through the streets they rode, wondering where the townsfolk were hiding. Not even a rat appeared on the smoke-covered streets.

"Every third house has been burned." Aedan whispered, for the village had taken the visage of Tartarus.

"We should move to the harbor. Two on each side of the street as we go. That we canna see up, does not mean that they canna see down," Padraig directed. The four horses moved in tandem, Aedan and Padraig each leading their charges, riding close to the buildings on each side of the path.

"There, Sire!" Brianan's urgent whisper and pointing arm led Aedan and Padraig's gaze to the harbor.

Movement! Some one was about. Or, some... *thing*.

Scurrying between a warehouse and the wharf ran two men dressed in Gingalain's plaid. Each wore a sword and glanced upward with every other step, arms full of bundles and packages. Their hurry seemed a combination of fear and urgency.

"Hælan!" Padraig called to the men. They paused, looked at the four riders, and then scanned the sky once more.

"Hurry, and get thee inside! The dragons will surely come!" One yelled back, then resumed loading the ship.

"Come, quickly now!" Padraig commanded as he urged Gilda into a fast trot. In a moment they were upon the wharf.

"May we assist you, men?" Aedan spoke, his voice again carried by that commanding tone. Padraig looked at Aedan, and spied a change; a green and gold sash across his shoulders, the sash of The High King of Dal Riata.

"My Laird! And Sir Page!" one of the men exclaimed. Padraig recognized the man as one of the Good King's Sergeant-at-Arms, Alistair Donnán.

"Quickly then, afore they come back!" The other man urged.

"Aedan, your bow could be helpful now. Your spare lend to your page, as well," Padraig directed. "Edan, tend the horses while I help these soldiers to get the ship loaded."

In a moment the two bowmen stood watch, Edan gathered the horses, and Padraig helped the men load their bundles into the ship.

"Your vessel is a good size larger than you need for this load. Are you bound for Skye, Mister Donnán?"

"Aye, that we are, Sir Page. The Good King is in desperate need of these supplies. And of two able warriors," Alistair nodded at King Aedan as he spoke.

"What is the gist of it, Alistair?"

"We've managed to hold them off, just barely. We started with nearly three thousand men, including Laird Mac Mor's. But the dragons have bled us down to three hundred." Alistair stopped and looked Padraig right in the eye. "They're an army, Master Padraig, eh, excuse me, Sir, Sir Page. An army of dragons like ne'er you've seen! Half again as tall as a man, and led by one I swear to be Lucifer himself. Twenty feet tall he is, and thick as a draught ox. There must have been ten thousand of them waiting for us, all too big ta fly." Alistair stopped his tale to swallow heavily.

"We've killed dozens, hundreds, thousands even. But they just keep coming, more and more each day. We can see the evil red glow of the henges at work in Rubha an Dunáin. They're coming from there, the Good King says. Are you coming with us, Sir Page?

"You have the room, we are coming. And, Alistair, my old friend, call me Sir Padraig."

The seasoned warrior smiled, "He told me you'd want that, Sir

Padraig, when you had become a leader of men."

"When did Gingalain say that?"

"The day of your twelfth birthday, Sir Padraig!" Alistair laughed.

*To see him again...* Padraig thought of his king, his mentor, his teacher, his...father.

The horses and supplies were loaded onto the ship, with Alistair and the other soldier tending to the task of sailing the vessel.

"Soldier, what be your name?" Aedan asked, seeing that the older man knew his way around a ship.

"My name is Branden Lios, Sire."

Aedan snapped his gaze to the man's face; beneath the grimace of determination laid not a small pool of melancholy. Quickly Aedan glanced at Brianan, relaxing to find the lad tending the tiller.

*The two faces are one and the same!* Aedan thought.

"Where hail ye from, Captain Lios?"

"From Clonf..." Branden stopped and stared at the man before him.

"Tell me, very quietly, please, of your last commissioned voyage." The Young King's command, though whispered, carried such presence that it could only be obeyed.

"I left Oban to ferry a man to Skye. Rascur was his name. When we arrived, there were others waiting for us. They overcame me and my crew, and forced us into servitude, me ferrying their supplies here. I know not what happened to my crew. The dragons took them off.

"When the Good King arrived, I was freed, and I gladly joined him. I've seen the dragons close, closer than any else who've lived. The big one, he's smart as a man, not like the others." Branden's voice trailed off as he stared out to sea. "They delight in causing pain, suffering, hunger, famine; any and every discomfort to mankind. I would see the world rid of such things, or die in the quest."

"Your family, captain? What of them?"

"Four long years has it been since I've seen my son. His mother passed when he was young, from the coughing. I...I had asked Fergus to watch him, as I always did when I was away. What has become of him…I, I do not know." Branden swallowed heavily, then dropped his head to stifle a sob.

Aedan stood, and moved to the tiller. A few words with his page, and the young boy moved forward.

"Excuse me, Cap'n, but King Aedan said I should speak to you about my father…"

Branden's head came up, eyes wide. He turned his head to look at the boy, the voice so familiar.

"Father!" Brianan gasped, but a heartbeat passing before he was flying into those long lost outstretched arms.

"Brian! My lad! Oh, how I've longed to see ye!" Their reunion was interrupted as a spray of water washed over them. The captain seemed as if a great burden had been lifted from him, as he loudly exclaimed, "Fear not, good men, for the whales are here! The dragons willna dare come near us 'til we make landfall!"

Aedan and Padraig turned to look at each other.

"How long have the whales protected you, good captain?" Padraig asked.

"About five trips now. They swim about, and should a dragon come too low, the whales fly! They fly up and snatch the beasties out o' the air, and crunch 'em up for a meal. You would not believe it, but I swear…"

"We believe you, Captain Lios. We truly do."

As the ship neared Rubha an Dunáin, they made landfall in a small cove protected by steep cliffs. A small path led up from the sea.

The two soldiers and their four guests unloaded the ship, packing the bundles onto the four horses. The ship being unladen and secured, the six led the horses up the gentle climb of the path.

Aedan's mood had improved considerably since his page had been reunited with his father. Padraig moved up near the High King.

"What will become of the lad now, King Aedan?"

"My heart tells me he will go with his father. That is where he belongs."

"By bringing him to his father, you've grown in stature before his eyes. What if he wants to stay with you?"

"That I canna see, Sir Padraig. Look at the lad; he adores his father. With him is where he should be. I willna undo that."

"To waste the talents he has would be a sin. A true king would find a way for Brianan to become a knight and be with his father..." Padraig increased his pace and moved Gilda and her load past Aedan. The High King stopped, shook his head, smiled and followed.

*Good Laird, give me this Good Knight's wisdom!*

Presently the six came to the crest of the rise, and beheld a great plain before them. Off to their right, nestled against the edge of a cliff, lay the scores of tents and banners. There was the banner of Oban, and there of Riderch and there Fortrenn, and...

"Hælan!" Padraig's voice boomed out across the plain as he broke into a run at the sight before him.

Gingalain's banner!

Breathless into the camp he ran, heart pounding at the exertion and anticipation of seeing his king, his mentor, as much of a father as he had e'er had. Into the large tent he ran, bursting through the opening... and slamming to a stop at the disturbing sight before him.

Page's heart fell at the vision of the bloodied and torn Gingalain, lying upon his bed with the physicians attending the ugly gashes on his forehead and chest.

"Sire!" Page sobbed, and moved gently to his side. Wet eyes looked down upon the Good King. He looked so old.

"My Page! Good! We are saved!" Gingalain's rasping voice drifted up, so faint and frail as Page had ne'er known it. "You gladden my heart as always, m'lad."

Edan came into the tent and stopped, silent at the sight.

"Hu-ah!" A gasp came from behind the squire. Aedan was taken aback at the Good King's state. Quickly he moved to kneel at his bed.

"My Laird, tell me the news." The High King pleaded.

"King Aedan! Oh, now I see. You, and Padraig. And there, Aglovale's youngest! Tell me you all did not come just to tell an old knight a bedtime story!"

"We're following a dragoness, my King." Padraig offered.

"She's taken my sister, Gwenellen. We've come to free her." Edan added.

"Your father, he is with thee?"

"Father was killed by the beast we seek."

"Vale, my friend..."

"Good King, what can we do that may ease your pain?" Aedan asked.

Gingalain sat up on one elbow, "Don't sound my death knell yet, Young King! Old, tired, and bloodied may I be, but still very much alive, as well!" His voice boomed as Page remembered it, his eyes burned with life.

"HA-ha! The Good King is with us!" Aedan grinned as he exclaimed it.

"Young King Aedan, Sir Padraig, Edana, we are not in a good position here." Edan gave a start at the words, relieved as Gingalain quickly continued. "Thousands there are, more coming every eve'n. All are bigger than any dragon I've seen before, but flightless; their wings get smaller as they grow, it would seem. Their leader, huge is he! Aengus Mac Mor hacked his way to him, and struck him thrice to no avail. Nearly killed the big man with one blow that dragon did. Mac Mor took a hundred men off to the East, so as to circle in behind the beasts. That was two days ago. I fear the worst. Aedan, we need a plan."

"Sir Padraig has a better head than I in these matters, Uncle. Perhaps with Excalibur, he could..."

"Excalibur!" Gingalain sat up straight and peered with wide eyes at Padraig's scabbard. "Aye, it is!" The awed king moved as if a score of years had been erased from his marker. "This surely changes things! The leader, the dragon king must you fight, Sir Padraig Ualas. And we must clear a path for you to meet him!"

"Sire, the maiden Gwenellen, we have to rescue her!" Page pleaded.

"A clever knight would find a way to do both, Sir Padraig!" Aedan smiled at the chance of turning the tables on his friend.

"S-sire?" A timid voice from the tent flap pleaded.

Aedan turned, "Brianan! Come in boy, and Branden as well." The two moved shyly into the Royal tent, heads bowed.

"What troubles you, my page?" Aedan asked, instantly regretting the word.

"My father has told me of the situation. Well, Sires, I ask that you consider something."

"Speak, lad!" Gingalain commanded.

"Sire, we need archers."

"Aedan, who is this boy who can see the answers that we miss? Did you call him your page?"

"Aye, Uncle. This be Brianan Lios, my page, and his father, Branden Lios, your soldier."

"The sea captain has a son. Lad, I see that you are right! But, where do we get archers? We have want of many."

"How many men have ye at arms, Good King?"

"Two hundred forty, lad."

"Give me a hundred eighty, Sire. There are ash trees and deer for sinew to make as many bows. Arrows we need; your sixty men should begin making them now. Puffins for the feathers, flint for the tips."

"Sire, if I may, the armory at Dornie Keep has more than we need, bows and arrows, enough for thousands of archers. I could sail and be back by the morrow." Branden offered.

"So be it! And the sixty, gather all the shields ye can, Branden, and good mail, too; so they may plow the Dragons aside for Padraig!"

"But, Sire, Gwenell..."

"Sire! A dragoness! With a maiden!" Alistair burst into the tent, "She's alighted within the camp!"

Padraig flew out of the tent, a few strides placing him a scant score yards from the dragoness. The evil thing held the bound Gwenellen, talons at her throat, taunting Padraig.

"Let her go, dragon!" Padraig's voice rumbled deeply, portending power as distant thunder before the storm.

"SSSSssss-NO-ssssss" hissed the reply to his ears, "Sssss-she DIES! Ssss-slowly-sssssss-NOW!"

The dragoness pressed her sharp talon into Gwenellen's neck, drawing the maiden's blood. Padraig began to move as he spied the trickle of blood. An angry buzz hit his left ear, and another instantly hit his right. An arrow appeared in the dragoness' right eye, followed in a heartbeat by another in the beast's left. The bound maiden was dropped the as the dragoness fell lifeless. Edan raced in. One slash of the squire's claymore ended any doubt that the beast was finished.

Padraig turned, looking to thank Aedan or Brianan. Instead he gasped at the sight of a bloody King Gingalain, calmly handing the bow and quiver to Aedan.

"I dunna like it when they talk," The Good King said. "I dunna like it at all."

"DRAGONS!" The sentry's cry rang in their ears.

Out of the North they came, six thousand roiling as a crimson sea towards the encampment. Padraig found his shield and sword at the ready, Gilda nudging him to mount. Once up, he looked over the plain ahead. Lit by the orange glow of the late evening sun, tide upon tide of the huge beasts surged relentlessly forward. In their midst strode a giant dragon, at least twenty feet tall.

"Form on Sir Padraig!" Gingalain's powerful voice echoed across the camp.

His heart quickening, Padraig looked to his left: Aedan, mounted on Cailean, Brianan atop Lara, and Alistair on a fine looking grey stallion. On his right, Edan sat atop Greg, the powerful white stallion's head two hands proud of the others. Gingalain rode a brown and white mare, his long time mount having fallen the day before. Around them formed the line of foot soldiers, pikes and axes at the ready.

"Phaaa-laaanx!" King Gingalain bellowed over the din of the onrushing dragon army.

The foot soldiers moved quickly into formation; three rows of twenty men, spears to the outside, shields at the ready, along each side of a square, with the mounted men in the center. Those in the second tier used their shields to cover the heads of the first row as those in the third row covered the second.

The twenty dozen stood as a rock, awaiting the crash of the first wave of the oncoming tide of dragons.

"Padraig, raise up your sword," Gingalain commanded.

Padraig raised Excalibur high, the blue glow brighter than ever. Gingalain's sword was soon raised along side of it, and then it touched the fabled blade; now The Good King's sword glowed with the pale blue light as well. Aedan's bow next caught the blue fire with a touch of Excalibur. The two kings passed the fire of Excalibur along the phalanx; the pale blue glow spreading outward from the center as a great shout of excitement arose from the men.

"Brianan, the big one!" Aedan called as he began sending arrows aloft. His page soon followed his lead.

"We must get to the dragon king. If he be killed, the others will flee. It is our only hope," Gingalain shouted over the din of the onrushing horde.

"Branden, take Gwenellen to your ship. Quickly!" Aedan called out.

"Edana!" Gwenellen cried as the captain Lios carried her away.

Then the dragons were upon them.

# The Battle

Twenty arrows streaked as pale blue fire above the Isle of Skye's battlefield. From Aedan's and Brianan's bows, up and over they arched, unaffected by the deadly clash of talon and steal below. Down they flew, darts to their target, past the screams of dying men and beasts.

Twenty arrows, glowing with a pale blue fire, found the crimson flesh of the giant dragon king. They burned deeply into his arms and chest.

"ssARRAGOOOSHss!" his great cry of pain echoed over the battle, causing many a dragon to turn, to look at their king. Those within range of an axe, sword, or pike perished as they did so.

Anger supplanted pain as the huge monster ripped the offending quills from his body, ripping out chunks of burning flesh with each arrow. Rising in rage, the beast spread his vestigial wings and opened his mouth wide as he took in a great breath.

A torrent of orange fire spewed from the gigantic beast, flames pouring over the heads of hundreds of dragons to batter the shields of the phalanx. The screams of men rose as the flesh of their arms blistered and burned under the blast. Yet no shield waivered or fell.

The phalanx began moving towards the dragon king.

Hundreds of dragons lay dead, impaled upon the spears and pikes, cut by the axes, pounded by the maces, and sliced by the swords of Gingalain's soldiers. The men marched over the foul smelling bodies as the horde of monsters swirled around them.

The flightless dragon soldiers struck with talon and tooth at the phalanx, taking a toll on the men there. Seven and eight foot tall dragons threw themselves at the shields, crashing into the men and opening gaps in the shields. Most of these gaps closed before any men could be killed.

Most of them.

Dragons crashed into the phalanx and others right behind them slithered into the opening, slashing with black, razor sharp talons and tearing into flesh with yellow, needle-like teeth. A score on the outside lines died. As they fell, those in the second line raised up to replace them.

"To the dragon's king!" Gingalain commanded. The phalanx shrunk around them as soldiers died, but closer they moved to their goal.

"There are too many! We'll not make it to their king!" Edan cried over the din of the battle as the squire's blade slashed a dragon's arm clean off.

Relentless was the push of the dragon army, wave after wave pounding the men as they fought within the midst of the horde. The charged weapons of man struck with deadly force, their pale blue glow slicing past dragon scales with good effect. But the numbers seemed bent on fulfilling Edan's prophetic lament. Though over a thousand dragons had been struck down, the men would not reach the dragon king before being overwhelmed.

The foul stench of dragon blood and burned flesh choked the battlefield as the phalanx was reduced to two lines of men, a dozen on each side. Still the dragons came, leaping over the first line to land amid the formation. Gingalain struck down two with one mighty blow, to his left, Padraig another, and Aedan yet another. More and more dragons penetrated the phalanx, the weight of the abominations sending men crashing to the ground.

Now the formation was but a single line around the mounted warriors, and a thousand dragons still lay between them and the dragon king. The shrill screams of the red beasts and the death cries of the men mingled with the thuds of steal striking scale, and of talon striking maille.

Suddenly they were alone. Padraig, Aedan, Gingalain, Edan, Alistair, and Brianan fought desperately from the backs of their mounts. Gilda struck out with her hind legs, her vicious kick sending two dragons flying above the throng.

"Protect Sir Padraig at all costs!" Aedan commanded, using that voice which men must obey, "Only Excalibur will kill their king!"

A large dragon's talons slashed at Gingalain's horse, the mare's head nearly severed. The Good King leapt from his mount before being pinned under her, only to land atop another dragon. Thrust down, withdraw, then slash down, spin, thrust! The king's old muscles rejoiced in the familiar dance of battle. Two more down! Duck, slash, spin. A searing pain ran across his back as talons sliced deeply through his chainmail. Again, on his thigh! Another, at his ribs, and then the taste of his own blood as darkness covered the old knight's pain.

Edan saw Gingalain fall. The Good King was too far away to help! The squire slashed desperately on one side, then the other as Greg plowed powerfully through the dragons, sharp hooves taking as much of a toll on them as his master's claymore. The two worked as one, Greg rising and kicking in time to Edan's slashing blade. The squire was torn for a moment: to aid Gingalain, or to help Padraig try to reach the dragon king? Edan fought the dilemma as much as the dragons, but that battle was much shorter. The squire could not leave the flank of Padraig, slashing at the dragons to the left and right.

Brianan swung his sword to good effect. The lad's blade was covered in dark, foul smelling dragon's blood. But his young arms grew weary, muscles burning in protest at each new arc of his sword. Lara pressed close near Cailean, kicking and snapping with her teeth at the monsters surrounding them. Each dragon that came close felt the sting of Brianan's sword; those too slow also felt the impact of Lara's hooves.

Aedan moved along side Padraig, staying slightly behind the knight, on the opposite side from Edan. The High King wielded his sword as a reaper's scythe at the harvest. Aedan's sword sliced deadly arcs through the air, cutting deeply into the crimson monsters with each stroke. Dragon after dragon fell, Cailean accounting for many. The High King was cloaked in the dark stench of dragon blood as one after another of the monsters fell to his blows.

Yet still the dragons surrounded them as far as their eyes could see.

Padraig moved as a blur, Excalibur felling dragons at an astounding rate, mowing a swath towards the dragon king. Still hundreds of dragons remained between him and his goal. A seed of doubt began to grow in the mind of Gingalain's knight.

"Arrgh!" Screamed Brianan. Aedan no longer felt the lad's presence by his side; his heart broke as he turned and found no sign of the lad.

"AHH!" Edan's voice screamed now, and Padraig's squire was no longer to be seen.

Aedan and Padraig fought side by side, the two alone now amidst a sea of dragons. They swung their swords as fast as they could, a dark gloom fueling their fight. The dragon hordes closed in. There was no where to go, no way forward or back, left or right, too many dragons, too many...

"ARoooooooo!" A long, loud cry as from a wolf echoed across the battlefield.

"By God!" Aedan exclaimed as a dragon's blow spun Cailean around. He could not believe what sight met him there!

"Padraig! Behind us!" he called as he swung his sword.

"Arf! Arf! Arf!" came Luag's cry, the big hound leaping onto the back of a dragon near the warriors. And right on the faithful hound's tail galloped hundreds of highland tigers! Two, three and more of the grey striped cats leapt upon a dragon, scratching and clawing until a dragon's throat presented itself to a cat's sharp fangs. The dragons did not die quickly under the cat's attacks, screaming in agony until the cats would rip out the dragon's throat, and then leap away to attack another.

Aedan ducked as a seventy-pound tiger flew in front of him, front claws holding as teeth sank into an abomination's throat, while powerful hind legs slashed and slashed the chest of the beast. The powerful cat pulled his head back, ripping the throat out of the beast, then leapt onto another. These are what had shredded that dragon at their campground!

As dragon after dragon fell to the cats, Padraig and Aedan found a new energy in their fight. Hundreds of the cats fell upon the dragons, their cries and Luag's barks causing a panic among the beasts. The dragons in front of them had turned, and now the two dragonslayers pursued the dragon army.

Still, as Excalibur sliced the horde before him, Padraig saw hundreds between him and the dragon king. Should they all turn around...

# The Great Celt

Padraig saw it first. Beyond the giant dragon king, a great cloud of dust. It was Aedan who heard the cry.

"TO THE END!" The battle cry thundered out of the cloud of dust rising from under the familiar banner.

"The Laird O' The Isles, Aengus Mac Mor!"

A great din arose as a thousand warriors crashed into the rear of the dragon army. War cries of both Celts and Norse could be heard among the death knells of the dragons. Padraig caught the glint of the setting sun upon a throng of horned helmets. Laird Mac Mor had brought the Northern Raiders!

The Great Celt could be seen even through the battle's confusion, swinging his battle-axe left and right through the panicked beasts. The dragon ranks broke!

Confused and unnerved, the dragon army was now in a state of complete chaos. Between Mac Mor's men and the highland tigers, the crimson beasts ran in all directions. In the center, dragons fell in huge numbers as Aedan and Padraig fought with renewed vigor. Despite the bellows from the huge dragon king, panic had taken the fire from the dragon army. The rout was on.

Only a few more dragons, and the dragon king would be before him, Padraig thought! His hair raised in excitement, as he could taste his goal now. A flash to his left...

"Aedan!" the Good Knight yelled, but no reply came. Gilda gave a startled snort, and then fell beneath him, his shield flying off into the fray as he fell. Rage boiled in Padraig's veins as he fought to his feet and swung Excalibur up, down to the left, up, down to the right, forward, forward, dragons falling about him, sliced in two by his blows. Talons ripped into his back, but still he moved forward. Slash, chop, cut, thrust...

Suddenly Padraig stood alone. He looked up and before him stood the giant dragon. A score of wounds dripped with his foul, black blood, gifts from the bows of Brianan and Aedan. Towering over Sir Ualas, the huge beast spread his tiny wings and took in a deep breath...

Padraig moved as if his Azure Shield was again on his arm,

and indeed it was! Quickly he crouched behind it as the giant dragon let another torrent of fire pour from his evil mouth. The hair on Padraig's arm singed, his flesh screamed at the heat, the shield glowing brighter and brighter as a pale blue glow surrounded him.

And then the fire ceased. Padraig looked over the shield in time to see the great hand of the monstrous beast crash into him, sending him dazed a dozen yards in the air, Excalibur flying off into the battle. A few great strides brought the monster over Padraig as he shakily regained his feet. Then another blow, and Padraig again flew far through the air, crashing to earth upon his shield with a great impact. Stunned, Padraig was but to his knees when the huge beast stood again over him, drawing his hand back to strike, this time with talons open...

Time slowed for Padraig now. He could see past the dragon king, where the Norse and Celts behind Mac Mor closed in. Off to the south, the cats were shredding the remaining dragons there. A strange taste of copper filled Padraig's mouth, and a warm wetness ran down his back. The Azure Shield felt heavy as Padraig tried to raise it one more time. He looked up again at the monster before him, the blurred battlefield too slowly clearing as something red seeped into his vision. He saw the beast's arm was poised to strike him again, then two blue streaks! And two more!

"Rise, Good Knight! Now's not a good time to be napping!" Aedan's voice commanded.

"Kill the damned thing!" Brianan echoed as he notched another arrow onto his bow.

Padraig struck as Zin had trained him, sending the Azure Shield at the monster with all his might. The glowing silver disk flew spinning up into the twilight at an unreal speed, a pale blue blur, faster than lightning against the darkening sky. Up into the giant dragon king, where the neck met the shoulder, neatly burning completely through.

The dragon king stood for a moment, legs wobbling as his severed head fell from his shoulders.

The dragon king was dead.

Padraig collapsed in exhaustion. A bloody hand reached out

and pulled the hair from his eyes. The battered knight smiled up at his friend.

"He lives!" Aedan exclaimed.

"Let's get him to my tent," Gingalain's voice boomed. "Here, men, Sir Ualas!"

Padraig tried to speak, but only pieces of his broken teeth came out of his mouth. He felt Luag lick his face as the darkness embraced him.

# Maiden Strike

"Let me GO!" Gwenellen demanded, her shouts drowning out the din of battle that rapidly fell behind them.

The girl's fists pounded his back as Branden Lios carried her to his ship. *A fine, strong young woman, she was seemingly little the worse for her ordeals in the captivity of the dragoness,* Branden thought.

"Two kings and a knight bade me to take you to safety. I'll take their direction o'er yours, M'Lady," Branden replied. "Just a bit more to the ship now."

The maiden had been nothing but a protesting bundle of fists and feet on this trip. Branden considered that he'd be less in danger fighting the dragons than watching over this one. But his main concern was his son. After four years, to see him so grown, the chosen page of the High King! He was so very proud of the lad, but he had seen him only for so short a time.

"Let me GO!" Gwenellen's fists again beat Branden's shoulders as he carried her to the boat.

"A week under the dragon's wing should see you a touch more grateful to be safe, M'Lady!" He scolded.

"My sister! She's back there! I cannot leave my sister!" Gwenellen screamed.

Branden set her down, keeping a solid hold of her arm. "What sister? You be the only woman that was in the camp," he challenged her through squinting eyes.

"Edana, my sister! She was with Sir Page!"

"Edan? The knight's squire?" Branden stared at the girl.

"Edana. My father called her Edan and dressed her as a boy to hide her from Rascur, that lecherous sheriff. She's my sister, a full two years my younger. Now, let me GO!"

Branden thought a moment. "You'll do as I say, and follow my directions?"

Gwenellen took two deep breaths, tightening her mouth.

"If you'll take me to my sister, I will." Gwenellen frowned her reply.

"Come then, M'Lady, we..."

The dragon dug his talons into Branden's shoulders as the beast's long neck bent forward, the dragon's teeth closing around the captain's throat and tearing it out mid-word. The beast dropped the man's body and grabbed for the shocked girl.

Gwenellen nearly fainted at the spray of blood from the captain's throat, but she still managed to grab the captain's dirk as the dragon snatched her and took off, following the setting sun to the West, flying high out over the sea.

"I've had all I will take of this!" Gwenellen screamed as she plunged the dirk's fourteen-inch length into the breast of the crimson beast, twisting and pulling it up and to the right. A torrent of dark, foul smelling dragon's blood poured over her as she continued to cut through the dragon's chest.

Brianan rode over the crest just as the dragon took off with Gwenellen. He glanced down the hill towards the ship, seeing the body lying there. He turned and watched the dragon carry the girl out to sea. Too far for an arrow! Then he saw the dragon fall, releasing the maiden.

He kicked Lara into a full gallop towards the falling maiden. He cast a glance at his father's body as the tears ran down his face.

# The Pyres

"Good Knight, how do you feel?" The familiar, expected voice enlightened Padraig's muddlement.

"I feel as if a huge dragon has been pounding me all day. Tell me, Edan, what happened?"

"Good Knight, I am Gwenellen." The maiden took a deep breath before continuing, "Your squire... has not been found."

"My little one is..." Padraig fought to keep the bile down, swallowing hard and breathing deeply. "My squire is not dead," the words fell as gravel from Padraig's lips. Padraig took a few deep breaths before opening his eyes.

"I am glad you are alive, Gwenellen. What of Brianan? Gingalain? Aedan?"

"All alive, though the Good King has many wounds, and needs to rest for some time." The maiden looked into Padraig's eyes while holding his hand tightly.

"You have some deep wounds as well, Sir Knight. Rest, and get well."

Padraig looked back at Gwenellen, and then closed his eyes to keep them from weeping. "I now have time to count the stars, it would seem."

"My Page, how be you?" Gingalain's voice boomed in the tent. "Three thousand dragons did we kill, with the cats. Aengus Mac Mor and the Norse another two thousand and a half. You slew their king."

"The henge?"

"Aengus and the Norse have toppled the stones, trapping the dragons. The younger ones could fly off, but not the army. That is why they attacked so late in the day. The Norse brought in masons behind the warriors to break the keystones. These henges will ne'er bring the dragons again."

"Sire, you should be resting!" Padraig cried, half in concern, half in glee for seeing him.

"A –GAWF! A leader must attend to his men before himself. Hadn't I taught you that?" Gingalain turned, and spit the coughed up blood outside the tent flap.

"Sire, if you could stop this tent from spinning long enough, perchance I could remember a few of your teachings!"

"Gwenellen, stay with him. Send word if needed." Gingalain's powerful voice carried these words on a blanket of tenderness.

"Aye, my king." The maiden spoke her confirmation as the Good King left the tent to tend to his own injuries.

"Sir Ualas, there is something I..."

"Shh, not now," Padraig whispered through closed eyes, "Now is not the time. Later will I hear of such things," Padraig said quietly, giving Gwenellen's hand a squeeze as he drifted off to sleep.

The tent's flap flew open as Aedan peered in. The Young King stopped upon seeing his friend was asleep. His gaze turned to Gwenellen.

"He is asleep? Out of peril?"

"Yes, Sire." Aedan's shoulders relaxed at the maiden's whispered answer. Gwenellen looked up at Aedan with pleading eyes.

"Edana? Has she been found?"

"Come, then. Now." Aedan laid Excalibur and the Azure Shield down next to Padraig, in awe at the pale blue glow that covered his friend the instant he released them. He then held out his hand to Gwenellen, nodding towards the tent flap. She rose, took Aedan's hand, and followed him out of the tent.

"King Aedan, what troubles you? The look on your face, it frightens me."

"Gwenellen, your sister, Edana, has been carried off by dragons."

"Wha, what? She, she was on the battlefield, she, she... "

Aedan caught her as she fell. He marveled at the feelings her touch awakened in him as he held her. He looked at her pretty face for a moment before he carried her into the tent with Padraig, laying her down next to the Good Knight. He sat down next to the maiden and his friend, watching over them both.

He was still sitting that way when Brianan came into the tent. The lad sat down next to Aedan. The Young King was still watching the sleeping knight.

"We have but a day, my page. Then we must set sail."

"Where is it going, Sire?" Brianan asked quietly.

"Portballintrae, no doubt. 'Tis the only way home for the beasts." Aedan stood and looked seriously at Brianan. "Are you ready?"

The lad looked down for an instant, then rose, "Aye, my King."

Brianan rose, Aedan placing his hand on his Page's shoulder. The two left the tent and made their way to the funeral pyre. Gingalain limped over to Aedan and Brianan, placing an arm over the young lad.

"Too many brave men died here, King Aedan. I did what I could, but too many still died."

"King Gingalain, Artair himself could not..."

"Don't!" The Good King snapped as he grabbed Aedan's collar, "Dunna speak of the Great King and me like that. I'm not long for this earth, I will not stand such undeserved comparisons just to sooth my own feelings." He released Aedan's collar and walked a few steps away, where he coughed and stumbled a bit. Brianan ran up to support him as Aedan walked to stand in front of the Good King.

Aedan looked Gingalain in the eye, High King to King, and said, "You feel the loss of each man is a personal responsibility. Such is the reason you are rightly known as the Good King. If God is willing, I pray that some day I will be half the King you are today!"

Aedan turned and faced the pyres. Brianan was praying in the Roman tongue as the pyres were lit.

Aedan watched the flames rise, knowing Brianan's father was there. He looked at the lad, steadfast in his resolve to be all grown up and stoic.

"My page, be prepared, for good and strong men cry at such times." Aedan's voice cracked as he said this. His own tears ran down when he felt a powerful old hand squeeze his shoulder.

"And, it is right that they do." The deep voice of Gingalain added, more powerful in these quiet tones.

"We have more work to do, King Gingalain. Be you with me?"

"King Gingalain is not, Aedan. Sir Gingalain pledges to thee my life and my lands."

"Accepted, my friend, should Sir Ualas pledge the same. I

dunna believe we could prevail without him."

The three watched the fires burn. Brianan tried to make sense of what these two great men had said and how they had acted. They expected him to cry, he was certain, but no tears came. He watched the two closely. He so wanted to be what these men expected him to be. *Someday, perhaps, I will understand.*

The Young King of Dal Riata and the Old Knight of Artair's Table looked into the flames. Each life carried aloft by the flames these felt as a blow to their very core. Such was the character of their souls.

# The Pursuit

Padraig reached up and stroked the big stallion's face. A large brown eye looked back at him.

"We'll find your master, Greg. I promise."

The big horse nodded once, then raised his head and neighed at an earthshaking volume. Padraig waited for the cry to end, then walked back to Gilda and mounted his roan mare. Behind him, Sir Gingalain mounted Greg, giving Gwenellen a hand up. In a moment she was holding tightly to him.

"Away, then!" King Aedan called, as he kicked Cailean into a fast trot towards the road to Culnamean. Gilda, Greg, and Lara followed, baring Padraig, Gingalain and Gwenellen, and Brianan. Behind them, those men pledged to Laird Aengus Mac Mor, both Celt and Norse had begun moving Northeast towards Portree on the far side of the Isle of Skye, where the Norse ships waited.

"Captain Leoideach awaits us at Culnamean. His ship will be faster than the Norse boats, as Mac Mor's men'll weigh them down. We'll be at sea for a full day afore they will reach their ships, and then they'll have to sail around the island. We'll be at Portballintrae five days or more afore 'em." Padraig called to Gingalain. "Did Aedan tell you of the whales?"

"Aye, Page. Between the whales and the highland tigers, you've recruited all of Creation, I believe!"

Gwenellen glanced at the Good Knight, smiling politely. Then her face turned up to Aedan, and Padraig saw her cheeks blush.

"Hah-ha! All is as it should be, Sire!" Padraig called as he pushed Gilda even with Cailean. "Sire, it would seem you've trapped a maiden's heart, eh?" Padraig smiled his whisper to Aedan.

The King's eyes opened wide, and he glanced back quickly. Nervously, he looked at Padraig; "What do I do now?"

"Relax and be yourself, Aedan. That should suffice!"

"Are you..." Aedan fired a serious look at Padraig, "Are you still my friend?"

"There, ahead, the Muireall!" Padraig called loudly, trotting ahead of the others, and then letting Gilda gallop the last league.

Aedan's face grew worried. The maid was pretty, and his few moments with her entrancing. But Padraig's friendship... he prayed he would not have to choose.

"Hǽlan!" Captain Fergus Leoideach called.

"Hǽlan!" Aedan replied. The group dismounted and led the horses onto the Muireall. Aedan moved so he was next to Padraig as they helped Gingalain climb aboard. When the Good King was secured aboard the ship, Aedan placed a hand on Padraig's arm.

"You are my friend, Sir Ualas. Tell me that I am yours as well." He spoke straight into the Good Knight's eyes.

"You canna be my friend, Aedan Mac Gabrain." Padraig's voice carried a seriousness Aedan had not heard before. The knight moved the cloth with Gingalain's seal from the hilt of Excalibur, and withdrew the mighty weapon.

All stared in silence at the two men on the shore.

"I had told Rory, the hunter some days ago that there would come a time when I would pledge to him. Now..." Padraig withdrew the great sword, and presented Excalibur, hilt first, to Aedan as he knelt before him. Looking up at the High King of Dal Riata, he continued, "...is that time. To you, King Aedan Mac Gabrain, I pledge my life and my lands, for as long as you require them."

Aedan's eyes widened as he reached out and lifted Excalibur. The fabled blade did not glow, but neither did it burn his hand. He touched the sword to each of Padraig's shoulders, and said in a quivering voice, "Rise, Good Knight, Sir Padraig Ualas of Kintyre. I have great need of you now. Both as a knight, and as a friend." King Aedan rested the blade of Excalibur upon his forearm, hilt offered to Padraig.

The Good Knight stood and accepted the sword from Aedan, carefully sheathed the mystical weapon, and then turned to face Aedan.

"You have me as both, Sire. As long as you have the need." The two men then grasped each other's shoulders and smiled.

"Are you two done playing yet?" Gwenellen called out, "We still have a rescue to effect!"

The two men jumped aboard, and the Muireall set out to sea.

"Where to, Good Knight?" Captain Fergus called.

"Portballintrae!"

# The Irish Sea

"How can the dragons fly so far out to sea?" Brianan asked his twentieth question of the hour.

"If there be two or more, one will be carrying Edan. The others will fish or 'unt sea birds and share their catch," Fionnghal explained.

"Or they may 'ave just brought a sheep." Osgar added.

"The wind is good to us. We should be at sea only two days, I'd say." Captain Fergus looked up as he spoke, and then he scanned the waves around them. His crew was convinced that the whales would protect them now as before, but he had seen no whalesign. He was worried that the protection they offered had ended.

"Brianan, tell me your tale of these past few days," Fergus wanted to give the men a break from the boy; they loved him as their own little brother, but their work was hard, and dangerous for those distracted from it.

"Cap'in, I found father!" the lad began. "He'd been captured by the men who called the dragons, and forced to serve them. King Gingalain freed him and father pledged into his service. While we fought the dragon army, he brought the maiden Gwenellen to his ship. A dragon killed him, but Gwenellen took his dirk and gutted the beast as he flew off with her!"

Fergus stared at the lad, not knowing what to say. His heart ached for the boy, and for his friend; oh, how he wished he could have spent but an eve'n with his friend Branden again!

"He told me to thank you for taking care of me."

Fergus closed his eyes at the lad's words, seeing his old friend saying that himself in his mind's eye. A deep breath almost stifled his sob.

"Your father was a good man, Brianan. You should be very proud of him." The good captain swallowed a large lump, and said, "But what of the battle, boy? Tell us!"

"You should have seen it! King Gingalain had the men around us in a big square, a "fall-shanks", and..."

"Phalanx, lad. Phalanx." Gingalain gently corrected the boy.

"...Fa-lanx. Right! And, the dragons couldn't get through it! King Aedan and I let loose some arrows at the dragon king, and every one hit home! That just seemed to anger him, though, even with the fire from Excalibur. The dragons were huge, even too big to fly! The dragon king was twice as big, twenty feet tall! And when they came close, our spears and axes killed them! But most of our men died, because there were thousands of dragons crashing into them."

The excited lad paused hardly enough to breath; "Then, we were alone, just Padraig, eh, sorry, Sir Padraig, King Gingalain, King Aedan, me, and..." Brianan now paused long enough to swallow and look from Gwenellen to Padraig before continuing, "and Edan. We hacked and hacked at them. Sir Padraig was a blue blur, chopping dragons down by the score!

"Then a bunch of them crashed into Lara, and knocked us down. All I could see were these huge dragons, so I just kept swingin' my sword. Finally, my arms could not hold it up anymore, I thought they'd eat me for sure, when Luag jumped in with a whole million highland tigers! They went from one dragon to another, ripping the throats of 'em clean out!

"All of a sudden, I saw Sir Padraig fling his shield, and it cut the head of the dragon king right off! The rest of the dragons tried to flee, but Laird Mac Mor was there with thousands of Norsemen, and they finished the stragglers off."

Brianan sat down, apparently as exhausted by the telling of it as he was by living the battle.

"The squire was taken by a dragon that flew from the dragon king's back. I saw six of them fly to the Southwest. The only standing dragon henge is in Portballintrae. That's why we're headed there," Gingalain added.

"I hear they make a descent whisky there, but not quite up to highland standards." Osgar added, hoping to break the mood.

"Brianan, how many? How many of the beasts did ye slay?" Fionnghal asked.

"I couldna count, and I dunna want to exaggerate, but I think about seventy-five or eighty," he replied with great consideration before continuing, "I went looking for my father, and saw the dragon take off with Maiden Gwenellen. I could not have shot an arrow that far, so I started to follow when she killed the thing. How she fell so far and lived I could not say!"

"Brianan's father was a very brave man. He fought the dragon well, but he had given me his dirk, so he had only his hands to gouge at the beast." Gwenellen said with head lowered.

Aedan leaned in and whispered, "Thank you, fine maiden, for that gift to the lad." His lips barely touched her ear as he spoke.

"I owe your father my life, Brianan Lios." Gwenellen blushed as a tear ran down her cheek.

"Sire, we will have need of a good watch tonight. Fionnghal, Osgar, and myself will take one each, but a second set of eyes wouldna hurt." Captain Fergus said to Aedan.

"Good thinking, Captain. I'll take first with you, then Gingalain, then Padraig," Aedan replied.

"Sire, please let me take the Good King's watch, for he sleeps already!" Brianan pleaded. "Not fully healed yet, is he."

"My page misses nothing, as usual. All right, you've earned you place, Brianan. Second watch!" Aedan turned to Gwenellen, "You'd best find a place near the Good King, M'Lady, lest ye be disturbed at each change of watch."

"Yes, My Laird," her blushing reply smiled at the Aedan.

"Good night, my King," Padraig offered Aedan. "Good night, M'Lady, good night, Brianan." Padraig pulled his bedding about him and rolled over.

"My King, what of these dragons at Portballintrae? What of our trip there?" Fergus quietly asked.

"Good Captain, I know only that the henges at Portballintrae were destroyed by my father, only to be restored by that bastard Madadh," Aedan spat the name into the sea.

"I dunna know that name, Madadh." Fergus noted at Aedan's discomfort too late to refrain his words and change the topic.

"My half brother. His Pict mother disguised herself as my mother, and bewitched my father into siring the cur. All that he touches comes only to suffering, sorrow, and death. Part of the reason my father sent me to Kintyre was so he could deal with that scum while keeping my hands clean of it."

"You canna gut a fish an' keep ya hands clean, M'Laird." The good captain gave Aedan a sympathetic look before gazing up at the clear, starlit night. "God has provided us with spectacular things to enjoy," now he glanced at Gwenellen, covered in her bedding next to Gingalain. "Some times, he asks us to defend these things, to protect 'em." Fergus looked back at Aedan Mac Gabrain. "He ne'er places such special things before us to be defiled and discarded."

Aedan gave a start at Fergus' words. Who was this man to speak to him so? A deep breath brought his father's teachings back; it was to meet and know men such as this, the reason for his trip to Kintyre in disguise.

"Good Captain, I thank The Laird above that men such as yourself live within Dal Riata," Aedan leaned in closer to Fergus, whispering, "I intend to make her my Queen, should she consent to it, and Padraig bless it. But this is not to e'er pass from your lips, my friend."

The captain smiled at king Mac Gabrain, "As you wish, Sire." The Captain looked at the stars again, brighter as the fully set sun had darkened the night. "It makes a man feel, well, small, does it not."

"Oh, my friend, it can make a man feel very big at times, as well. What are your plans, after we have finished this affair, good Captain?"

"I'll return to my wife, an' my wee one. Stay home, for a time. Then I'll be out sailin' again, Sire. No doubt."

"You've done a fine job with Brianan. You've taught him well, prepared him for life as a good father should."

"I canna take credit there. Branden ferried the Monks across this sea, an' brought the boy with him. When he had other commissions, he left the boy with the friars. They've taught the lad what he knows, not me, Sire."

"You're a smart and able man, Fergus Leoideach. But you're wrong on this account. For sure the boy learned the Roman tongue from the monks, and learned to shoot a bow and wield a sword from the friars. But his important lessons came from you as well as his father.

"He's learned to put others before himself. And he's learned to fulfill his duties and obligations, no matter the pain he's in. He did not learn that from the friars and monks. He learned it from the men who loved him enough to teach him the morals of a good and honorable life, by word and by deed. Who loved him enough not to let him stray from those morals. He learned that from the man who loved him enough to treat a boy as his own, because it was the right thing to do.

"He's pledged to me as my page, but he'll always be your shipmate, Captain. A grateful King sits humbled beside you."

Fergus kicked at the wooden planks of the knarr's hull, uncomfortable under the burden of praise just laid on his shoulders by the High King.

"M'Laird, I've only just done what seemed ta me ta be the right thing. Nothin' more, nothin' less," came his quiet reply.

"How many scant meals do you eat, so your wife, growing with child, and the lad, growing to manhood, could have full bellies? And your crew, taking the lad in as one of their own, as a brother, demanding you pay him a full share, even though it cut into theirs?"

"I canna take credit for their..."

"A crew follows the path chosen by their Captain, Fergus Leoideach. They do as you've taught them it is right to do. I didna mean to weigh you down with praise, Captain. But I do thank ye for being a right, fine, and honorable man. There's no sin in being that. I am glad to know ye." Aedan sat back and stared at the stars.

"Sire!" Fergus whispered. Aedan looked at the Captain, who pointed near Gingalain.

"Well, I'll be!" Aedan whispered his exclamation.

"He-he-he!" The quiet giggle came from the side of the knarr, where Gwenellen leaned over, reaching out to run her hand softly along the glistening grey skin of the whale's head. After petting the giant a moment, she pulled her hand back, and the whale slid silently back into the depths.

"You two were much too loud, and not very good look-outs at all!" The fair maiden exclaimed. "You did not even see the whales!"

Fergus and Aedan looked at each other for a moment, then back at Gwenellen.

"If you two will be quiet, I will try to get some sleep!

Thankfully, you did not awaken my Godfather Gingalain. Now, good night." With that she crawled back into her bedding.

"How much do you think she heard?" a wide-eyed Aedan whispered to Fergus.

"Oh, I heard enough!" Gwenellen replied, keeping her grin hidden from the two men.

Aedan closed his eyes. He didn't know whether he should be happy or terrified. He decided to let his sleep decide the issue, but first he must awaken Brianan.

Fergus woke Osgar as Aedan woke his page. The old salt and the young lad took their place at the tiller as the king and the captain climbed into their bedding.

"What was it like, wee 'un, hacking inta those beasts?" Osgar's otherwise rough manner was always softened for the lad.

"I was afraid, but too busy to know it, I guess. It feels funny to hit something alive with a sword. It's not like hitting stuffed sheepskin at all. The dragons smell bad, but they smell worse when they bleed. Have you ever been in a battle, Osgar?" Brianan rubbed his left shoulder, where a dragon's talons had dug deeply.

"Aye, lad. One or two. Ne'er ag'in dragons, though. Jus' men. Norse men, wild as an angry sea. Big they are, as a rule, and tough, like Fionny. Aye, it does feel different to drive yer blade into living flesh. What's it like, being a page? Does he treat ya right an' proper?" Osgar kept an eye on the stars as he adjusted the tiller.

"Sort of like being on the Muireall. I get to run and fetch this and that. King Aedan also teaches me things."

"Such as what, lad?"

"Things about leading men, helping those in need, doing things the right way, stuff like that. Like what the Cap'in taught me, only more...involved. He says I already know how to use a bow and a sword well enough."

"That ya do, Brianan. Fionnghal taught you well. Does the king treat ya well?"

"Oh, yes. He's really very nice. And he ne'er lets me slack in my lessons."

"He does seem the right sort. Brianan, I'm sorry about yer

father. I mean, I'm happy ya got see him ag'in, but I'm sorry he was killed."

The boy stared at his knees in silence for some time. Finally he leaned into Osgar's chest, wrapped his arms around the big man, and began to cry.

Gwenellen began to sit up at the sounds of Brianan's sobs, but a strong hand held her fast.

"This is between the boy and his friends now, Gwenny. You'll have your own to comfort in time." Gingalain's whispered voice calmed her a bit, and she snuggled closer to him.

"I still can't bare to see one so young hurt so! Makes me think of Edana..."

"Shh. None of that, now," Gingalain's arm wrapped her in it's protection.

Luag rose from his master's side and came to Brianan with ears down and eyes saddened. The big hound laid his chin upon Brianan's lap, and quietly waited for the lad to feel better.

Lara turned towards her rider. Unable to move closer, her big brown eyes kept watch from near the mast.

"I've known yer father since many years before ya were born, Brianan. A fine an' 'onorable man, he was, an' a good an' loyal friend. I will miss him." Osgar sheltered the sobbing lad in his big arms.

"Osgar," the lad sniffled, "when this quest is over, and I go with king Aedan, I will miss you, and Fionnghal, and the Captain. I wish, I wish you could all come with me."

"Are ya sayin' ya wish to stay part of the Muireall's crew?"

"Part of me does, but I know I should go. I should be with king Aedan. It is where I belong. But that won't stop me wishing for my friends to be near."

"We will always be with ya, lad. An' ya with us. Now, 'tis time to wake the lazy Fionnghal an' the Good Knight!"

"Fionny's not lazy!" Brianan laughed, wiping the tears from his face.

"Ha-ha. No, he's not, or we wouldna have him on the Muireall now, would we? Hey, sleepyhead! Time for work!" Osgar tapped his foot into Fionnghal's back a few times for punctuation.

"Sir Padraig, time to wake up, Sir!" Brianan shook Padraig's shoulder lightly.

"Yes, well then Brian, get some sleep, lad."

"Sir Padraig?" Brianan's face betrayed his dilemma; should he correct The Good Knight?

"Brian. You're grown enough for a man's name now. I'm sure the dragons would agree, had ye left any alive!" Padraig's face was as even as the calm sea as he spoke to the lad.

"Thank you, Sir Padraig."

"Yes, Brian it is. Thank you Sir Padraig. Now can we please go back to sleep?" Aedan growled.

Padraig and Fionnghal took their position in silence, Fionnghal at the tiller and Padraig nearby. Neither man spoke for some time.

"You're worryin', Good Knight." Fionnghal said simply.

Padraig turned to look at the fair-haired sailor, but Fionnghal was studying the stars with a frown.

"About yer squire."

"Yes. I, well…"

"Quiet, Sir Padraig, please." Fionnghal suddenly whispered. He swung the tiller in great arcs back and forth, then fastened it and moved closer to the side of the knarr. He peered into the darkness for a few moments, rubbed his hair, and then returned to his place by the tiller. But, he did not take hold of it. He let out a big sigh as he sat down.

"What troubles you, Fionnghal?" Padraig asked.

"Sir Padraig, we look ta be movin' at a brisk pace, dunna we?"

"Aye."

"Look at the sail."

Padraig glanced at the large, flaccid cloth, a pale yellow with a red highland tiger, faded from years in the sun…

"The sail hangs limp! Yet we move. Fionnghal, how is this so?"

"Good Knight, 'twould seem ar friends from Loch Linnhe be with us again. Look o'er the side."

Padraig peered over the side of the knarr, staring into the darkness below. After a moment, he sat back, eyes wide, a slight smile upon his face.

"Whales! Carrying us, they are!"

"Good Knight, ask yerself this; if the Good Laird sent these beasts ta protect us, would He let any 'arm come to yer squire?"

"The Good Laird's plans are not for us to unravel, my friend; too many have died, and many more will yet. The Good King still bleeds inside from his wounds. Even Artair's shield does not heal him. But your words do comfort me some. Tell me, Fionnghal, how you came to be here; Oban is not your home. You're a Norseman, are you not?"

"Aye, I was born some ways East, around all the Na h-Eilean Siar an' well past Orcas. I was born in a village called Skarbovik. I was but of Brian's age when I came with my father on a raid to Stornoway. It was to be me first battle. A great storm pushed us off course, an' stranded us on a strange shore. It was the isle ya know as Scalpay. Only me father an' me self survived the wreck.

"After a few weeks, me father went inland ta scout. When he dinna return at the appointed time, I disobeyed 'im, an' I went inland, seeking 'im. I came across 'is body a day into me quest. 'E 'ad fallen, perhaps o'er a tree root, an' stumbled into a ravine, smashing 'is 'ead. I buried 'im, an' then sat down ta think.

"I decided to walk as far as I could along the shore of the island. Soon, I found a village. A ship had just tied up to the wharf, an' was loading cargo. I crept in an' 'id among the goods. The captain knew I was there, yet 'e pretended to 'discover' me only when we were far out ta sea. The captain of that ship was Fergus Leoideach. 'E took me in as if I was 'is younger brother. I've been with the man e'er since. I've married 'is sister. Where 'e goes, I will e'er follow.

"What of ya, Good Knight? 'Ow 'ave ya come to be 'ere this morn?"

"Norse raiders attacked our village when I was but two winters old. They attacked our house, where my father killed several, and drove them off. A large one came, and killed my father. He went after my mother next. I took a knife and I stopped him, but I was too late. My mother had been killed in her struggles with the man.

"Gingalain came just as I finished the task. He took me in and raised me as his son in manner, but not in title. The Good King always hoped for a son of his own.

"Some months ago, he left. He told me not of his mission. After a time, I followed. I came upon the village of the maiden Gwenellen. The dragons attacked; two I killed, but the third one carried her off. I followed the dragon to Skye to free the maiden.

"The rest you know."

The sunrise seemed to signal the end of Padraig's story. The two peered over the side of the knarr, and saw that the ship was carried upon the backs of two great whales. Fionnghal threw the knotted rope over the side ahead of the ship, and counted as it moved past and he pulled it in.

"Twenty knots! The Muireall's a fine ship, but she's ne'er sailed s' fast!"

"We've only half a load, Fionnghal. Remember that!" Fergus yawned as he rose. The captain moved back to the tiller and unlocked it as he carefully found the Morning Star to guide his hand. When he pushed the tiller to correct their course, he nearly fell over from the absence of any resistance.

"We're not *in* th' sea, Cap'in," Fionnghal explained, "look." He pointed down over the side.

Fergus looked over the side of the knarr, but instead of the expected spray and foam thrown up by the ship's passage, his eyes found two huge dark grey backs baring the ship a few feet over the waves.

The good captain looked first at Fionnghal, then at Padraig.

"Well, then, with what shall we break our fast this fine morning?"

Fionnghal sliced the smoked haggis, and Osgar poured the whisky and the water rations. Gwenellen was quick to the task at hand, as were Aedan and the sailors. Padraig watched Gingalain down the whisky on a mighty gulp, then turn back into his bedding.

Aedan moved over and sat beside the brooding knight.

"Noon will see him with a better appetite."

"I canna stand to see him this way. He's always been so strong of limb and soul."

"Mistake not the strength of the Good King's body with that of his soul, my friend. The whales below couldna break that. The whisky will help him. I'll fetch him more, mixed properly with the water, presently.

"I sense another issue pulling at you, Padraig. Your squire."

"I should have kept my squire closer to me in the battle."

"In that mêlée? How would you have done that, now? Do not trouble your soul with things beyond your control, my friend. Your squire was in possession of both dirk and sgian dubh when carried away. You yourself know how fast that young one is with both. You've taught your squire well, and I'll wager that dragon will find a bit of personal Hell near landfall."

Padraig looked at Aedan, a flicker of hope growing in his eyes.

"You know, of course. You've known for some time."

"Aye, I've known. When did you see it?"

"I knew it the eve'n when we met you. The scolding of you as you mounted Greg, the panic over the bathing, the midnight bath. The ruse was so dear to her mettle I couldna take it from her. Later, as I grew to know her, I became, well…"

"And she for you, my friend." Aedan stood to go tend Gingalain, but stopped and turned to Padraig; "If she finds out I told you *that*, I'll ne'er survive it. Oh, Gwenellen tells me her right name is Edana. "

"You will always be safe where I am concerned, Aedan." Padraig smiled at his friend. "Thank you."

"I have dire need of you, Sir Padraig. The pledge I gave to you still stands, and always will."

"And my pledge to you will always stand as well, my King."

# Scourged

Edana looked about as much as she could without moving. She had awoken about an hour ago, nearly screaming at the pain in her head as well as at the sight of the sea so far below. The cold wind, the dark talons, foul smell, and crimson scales told her what she needed to know.

A dragon carried her.

She could see enough to know there were at least four others flying with them, most likely five or eight more, since they always grouped into threes. Twice now she had seen one dragon dive into the sea, and then burst out with a good size fish. One of these was passed to the dragon carrying her.

*Well, at least that means I'm not just food for a long trip*, Edana thought. *They haven't bound me, so they must have left in a hurry.* She moved her hand down by her belt...*Yes! It's there! Now, if I can swing my arm down to my calf...yes!* Edana smiled to herself, *it's good to have sharp things when dealing with dragons!*

Trying to keep her movements as subtle as possible, Edana managed to look in the direction they were flying. Through the morning mist she could see the rocky peaks of high hills in the distance. *Too far to swim from here, too rocky to fall into the sea close by. Besides, dragons can swim!*

"Sssssso, you awakesssssssssss"

Edana's head snapped around at the sound in her left ear. A dragon's face was but an arm's length away from her own! The dragon seemed to sniff her, and then hissed, "Ssssssssmellss of bloodsssssssss!"

Edana's eyes widened. She shivered with the thought of these beasts discovering her secret. Then she realized the battle had left her with several wounds. She narrowed her eyes and moved her head a little closer to the beast's face.

"HAAAH!" Edana blew a hard breath into the dragon's face. The beast dove away, screeching his displeasure. "It would seem that we smell as bad to dragons as they do to us!"

Her head throbbed as Edana skillfully moved her dirk from its sheath and, keeping the hilt in her hand, hid the blade up her sleeve. She repeated the motion with her other hand for her sgian dubh.

*I think I can kill the one carrying me, but what of the others?* Her thoughts were interrupted by the eight dragons escorting her captor, who were all flying within her sight now. They stared at her, but from two full yards distance.

Edana crossed her arms and glared back through narrowed eyes.

"Come a little closer, so I may introduce you to death, as I have for so many dragons before you," she challenged.

The five dragons moved further away from her. A quick glance brought both comfort and fear; her blades cast a pale blue glow to her arms that the dragons must have seen, but that glow told her that the power of Excalibur lived in her blades.

*If only I could get this one down on land!*

Edana looked ahead again. There, just behind the parting mist, shining sand and green trees rising up from the sea.

Land!

The nine dragons flew over the land as the sun rose behind them, casting long shadows from the high cliffs and rocks. A short distance from the shore, Edana noticed more water. This was an island!

As the sun burned the mist from the land, a long, rocky island shaped as a wolf's leg. High cliffs arose to the right. To the left, where the land sat closer to the sea, a grassy plain hosted grazing sheep.

The dragon carrying her began descending, sparking Edana's heart to race. If the dragons were looking to the sheep for a meal, then they would land amid the trees for cover.

She would soon have her chance!

Branches lashed at her as her captor dropped closer to the ground. This one was not experienced with bringing captives to earth. As the forest floor rose up, Edana struck upward with both hands, scissoring her two blades in the dragon's belly. The beast screamed in pain as its dark, foul smelling blood poured down over Edana.

The dragon released her as it died.

A large branch knocked the wind from her as she fell, then she hit the ground. The pain in her head screamed anew at her, her eyes blurred as the forest spun about her. Everything began to dim into darkness. Eight crimson beasts screamed at Edana as they swarmed through branches and around the trees, their din keeping her from slipping into a peaceful nescience. She fought to her feet and staggered to a close copse of buckthorn.

Edana took several deep breaths to speed her head's clearing. As she had lost her dirk in her fall, she was armed only with her half-foot long sgian dubh. The dagger's blade no longer glowed, but the dragons would still find her soon. The buckthorns would not protect her from their fire.

*Dear Laird, please help your humble servant.*

One of the bulls landed in front of her. Silently, she stood as the dragon turned his back to her. Her attentiveness to the lessons with Padraig served her well. She reached out quickly and silently sliced the beast's throat. Only the gurgling of dragon's blood filling a severed windpipe, followed quickly by the thump of the dragon hitting the ground could be heard.

Edana moved through the buckthorn to a position well hidden near the fallen dragon. Her patience was soon rewarded as two dame dragons found the body of their mate. As one fussed about the fallen bull, Edana leapt from the thorns and struck quickly, grabbing the nearest by the chin and slicing her throat before her companion could react. As the second dragoness turned to see her sister fall, Edana was behind her, again slicing through the crimson scales.

Three dead, five alive.

Edana quickly moved to another bushy buckthorn, searching for the other five dragons. Her head throbbed, and something warm ran from a burning on her hip down the back of her left leg. Her heart was racing, and her lungs ached for deeper breaths as she struggled to remain as silent as possible.

Another dragon moved near, searching for her. The foul stench of dragon blood filled Edana's nostrils; she was covered with it. Was the smell as strong to dragons, would it help them find her?

The monster in front of her stopped too far for her to strike safely. Edana sat back, waiting, praying; *Please come a little closer...closer...*

A roar from her left, and a searing pain along her back sent her out of the suddenly burning buckthorn. She had no choice as her pain threw her into the beast before her, slashing at it as she could. Her blows were true, and the fourth dragon fell to her blade. As the beast hit the ground, Edana turned, as she'd been trained, ready to strike at anything behind her.

The dragon struck her first.

Black talons ripped through the blistered, burned flesh on her back. Edana screamed as her eyes focused on the dragon in front of her. Recovering quickly, she brought her arm up to strike...

Again, talons ripped into her back, as a second dragon struck her, the blow knocking her backwards into a third attacker, the pain too sudden and terrible to allow Edana's scream to escape. Now the third abomination slashed her, the blow pounding the breath from her. She staggered under the blow, gasping for air even as she tried to scream. Then she stood before the fourth crimson terror.

Another staggering blow sent the pain screeching throughout her being as the black talons ripped into her skin yet once more. Still again Edana reeled under the dragons' claws. And again. And again. On and on, a never ending vacillation of pain and horror, from one blood-red beast's ebony talons to the next...

She could not scream, she could only feel the strange sensation of the talons shredding her flesh.

Yet another powerful blow spun Edana around once more, eyes closed now in silent prayer; *Please take me, now, Laird. Let my relief be quick.* She lifted her chin as she waited for the final blow. Her battered mind brought forth visions of Rory's betrothed, the beautiful girl's neck and belly slashed open, her liver eaten. Another moment and it would come, the end to this.

"I'm so sorry I never told you, my Padraig!" she cried into the forest.

Edana took a deep breath. And another.

*What are you waiting for?*

Another deep, precious breath. Sobs tore from her throat. Agonizing pain poured through her veins, she could bear it no more!

"KILL ME!"

Edana's scream opened her eyes.

She struggled to stand, quivering as the pain flooded down her bloodied back, spinning her head around. The trees started moving up, over her, the sky falling before her face…

"Shh. Easy, my little one," the strong voice wobbling as it comforted her, "You're safe now. I have you."

Edana's bloody face looked up towards that voice as powerful arms lifted her to safety.

"Padraig!" she gasped before the darkness engulfed her.

# The Galloglaigh

Padraig Ualas paced anxiously before the fire, the flickering light doing little to conceal his nervous shivering.

"We needna rush in, now that she's safe. We all have our wounds to heal," the old knight advised his two companions. "Artair's Azure Shield no longer speeds the mending of our flesh, and the glow from Excalibur is no more. We must rest, to gather our strength."

"Padraig, Gingalain speaks wisely. There is enough game here to feed us while we mend. We canna meet the dragons as we are now and win." Aedan's words were more of a plea than a decree. Both he and Gingalain knew from the past hour's congress that Padraig was close to rushing off alone.

"My King, every day we delay means more of them will come. If we can destroy the henge, then we can retire and refresh our forces.

"I am not saying we should fight them as we did on Skye. Nay, we should fight as Odysseus did at Troy. With our heads." Padraig tapped his finger to the side of his head as he implored his friends.

Aedan and Gingalain studied Padraig for a moment before Aedan's sigh broke the silence.

"What have you in mind? I've nay agreed with your position, but I will taste the meat of it."

"I believe I can get to the henges and destroy them with fire. I'll lay wood around the bases and paint it with pitch. It should burn good and hot, enough to weaken the stone. They should be easy to break and topple then."

"Page, where would you get the wood? The pitch? Think it through, Page!" Gingalain's deep voice quieted some as he continued, "How would you carry it unseen to the henge? How would you carry enough fuel for your plan to work?" Visions of the young Page trudging bundles of firewood through the Feast of Stephen's snow flashed through the old knight's mind. "Most likely the henges will be well guarded."

"I'll find what I need there... some where..." Padraig pounded his fist into his thigh.

"My friend, your blood is too hot right now, its fire veils your reason." Aedan moved to Padraig's side. "She *will* heal. It will take *time*."

"I..."

"You know he is right, my Page. When we are stronger, and Mac Mor's forces have joined ours, something like your plan may work. It does give us a good foundation to build upon." Gingalain placed his big hand on Padraig's shoulder and said, "Padraig, my son, she needs you to be with her now."

Page looked up at Gingalain.

"Son. You called me... You ne'er...you called me your son."

"Aye, and a finer one no man has e'er had'" the two men's eyes welled up, before Gingalain's words took on a fatherly tone again; "But it's time for you to stop mullin' about and go see her. She'll heal all the faster for it. Merlin's magic or no."

Padraig nodded, and the three men moved out of the tent. Gingalain walked slowly, limping to his tent, while Aedan strode briskly, nearly dragging Padraig by his arm to the tent of the Aglovale sisters.

The knight's heart was wrenched by the thought of Edana's suffering.

"I should not have brought her along. I knew she was a girl, I should not..." Padraig mumbled as they walked.

Aedan stopped and spun to face Padraig. "You blame yourself? All that was about blaming yourself for Edana's plight? Your plan was ne'er about burning the henge stones, but it is about punishing yourself for her wounds!"

Aedan softened his tone just a bit as he beseeched Padraig; "You've known her as I have these days past. You could ne'er stop her from any of it, anymore than I could have stopped you. Edana knew what she was doing. She was helping the strongest warrior she knew to save her sister, to end the dragon's scourge. Her motives were noble, and for that she deserves our allegiance and our kindness. But you, if you're to live the life I know you are destined to, you must stop being so damn selfish and begin thinking of *her*!" With that, Aedan turned and lifted the flap to Gwenellen and Edana's tent.

Padraig took a deep breath. *He is right. I've been trying to punish myself. Oh Laird, I canna bear to see her suffer! Please help her!* He finished his prayer and followed Aedan into the tent.

Edana lay on her right side, wrapped in a cloth from her shoulders to her knees. Her left arm was also wrapped, but her right was free. The cloth was soaked with blood and seepage from her wounds, the nidorous smell assaulting Padraig's nose. A large swollen bruise colored her left cheek to above her eye.

"I'll return in the morn to change 'er bindings. I've made a poultice of birch pitch, herbs, an' 'oney that should keep 'er fever down." Fionnghal stood to leave, adding in serious tones, "keep 'er warm, an' make sure she drinks an' eats well."

Padraig's eyes went about the tent, avoiding the scene that so grieved his soul. Gwenellen sat by Edana's legs, holding her sister's hand as Aedan's arm around her shoulders comforted her. Luag sat by them, gazing at Edana, his eyes pleading for her to get well.

Padraig knelt by her head, and reached out with quivering hand to brush the hair from her eyes.

"My little one. Can I do something for you?" Padraig whispered.

Edana's eyes opened, shining with a life that surprised Padraig.

"My Knight!" she beamed, "I knew you would save me!"

The warmth in Edana's eyes brightened Padraig's soul. He sat, smiling at her, stroking her cheek.

Morning found the dragonslayers asleep in their positions, having passed the night where they passed the evening.

Edana was the first to waken, and she spent the first hour of the day gazing at Padraig's sleeping face.

*How I've dreamt of awakening thus,* she smiled to herself.

"Padraig. Padraig." She whispered. Again, louder, "Padraig!"

"Hrumbl. Huff! Umm...What? Where? Edana! Are you all right?"

"Yes, Padraig. Would you please bring me some water?"

"Of course, of course," Padraig rose, noticing the others still slept. "Have you taken your swim yet?"

"PADRAIG!" Edana shouted her whisper at him, her pale face

now blushing brightly.

He grinned as he pushed through the tent flap, walking out into the camp. The water was just a short distance ahead.

"WOOF!"

Luag's call froze Padraig in place, causing the arrow to pass inches in front of his face.

The knight turned to face the direction from whence the dart came. He saw them as they ran down the small rise behind the Aglovale sister's tent, a motley score of raggedly dressed men, screaming as they came. Their manner gave Padraig no cause for alarm, but he knew that their blades would still kill.

"ALARM!" Padraig's powerful voice thundered throughout the camp as he ran for Gilda. In a moment he was astride the roan, shield on arm and sword in hand. Aedan and Brian soon rode up abreast of him, Brian with drawn bow taking aim...

The arrow sped straight and true into the center of the attackers. A tall soldier, slightly ahead of the others, fell as the arrow smashed into his thigh.

The three mounted warriors let out great yells, and urged their mounts to full gallop. Cailean, Gilda, and Lara sped their riders at the invaders, Luag barking a great chorus at their rear.

While the score of foot soldiers greatly outnumbered the three mounted warriors, the horses gave an advantage. They could strike with such speed from above, that the ground soldiers had little chance of defense or attack. The truth of this suddenly hit the men rushing down the hill, bringing their fear close to ruling their actions.

The appearance of Fergus, Fionnghal, and Osgar running at them from the other direction, brandishing swords and screaming loud war cries convinced them of their folly.

They turned and ran away.

Aedan kept Cailean at a gallop, even after Brian and Padraig slowed. He rode up behind the man limping from Brian's arrow, and pounded the man's head with the hilt of his sword, collapsing him into a heap. A few more yards forward to be sure the rest still retreated...

Padraig rode up and dismounted. He picked up the benumbed man and tossed him over Gilda's back.

"We'll put him in my tent. Gingalain can move in with me," Aedan directed.

The trip back into camp was short. Gingalain, not yet ready for full combat, had moved to defend the sister's tent. He now followed Padraig, Fergus soon joining him. Fionnghal and Osgar took sentry positions outside the tents.

Padraig carried the man into the tent, laying him down on his back. Aedan knelt with his sgian dubh at the ready, and carefully cut out Brian's arrow. "Now we should awaken him."

The man was tall, but not stocky. His face was grimy and unshaven, his dark beard and hair were uncut and tangled. He wore a simple heavy cloth skirt, fastened with a flaxen rope, which also held a leather scabbard for his Roman short sword.

Gwenellen opened the tent flap, tossed the water onto the man's head, and left the tent.

"Oh, me 'ead. Damn" the captive complained as he sat up. "Ow!" He reached down to rub his thigh as his pain reminded him of the wound there.

"Who e'er took the arrow oat, I thank ya." He said as he looked around the tent. His eyes hit on Fergus, Padraig, and Gingalain before settling upon Aedan.

"I knows ya, Aedan Mac Gabrain. These others, I dunna know. 'Ad I knowed it was ya 'ere, we wouldna attacked this way." He rubbed the large lump that Aedan's sword had placed upon his head.

"What is your name?" Aedan asked.

"Brude Mac Maelchon, ya can call me."

"How do you know me? I dunna know you."

"I fought with yer father. An' I fought ag'in yer grandfather." Brude said as he leaned back against the bedding.

"How come you fought for and against the same clan?" Gingalain asked.

"Heh! The price was right! Me men fight fer 'ire. Life is much simpler that way. We get ta choose the battles we fight"

"Why did you attack me? Did some one pay you?" Padraig's words did little to conceal his contempt.

"No, we 'aven' been paid to attack ya 'ere. You be on me land. The Island of Rathlin be mine. The sheep ya hunt an' eat be mine.

We were just protectin' what be ars."

"How do we know this is true?" Fergus challenged. "I've been here before. I dunna remember you."

Brude narrowed his eyes as he looked at the captain. "Nor 'ave I seen ya. But if yers be a trading ship, ya will know Endaé, the 'arbormaster."

"Aye, I know 'im well, an' 'is wife, Macha."

Brude relaxed at Fergus' words, "Then ye be traders? Ye seem well armed for such."

"We are hunting dragons." Gingalain explained. The captive's eyes grew wide, and his shoulders retreated at the word.

"Dragons! Why are ye 'ere, then?"

"We are the vanguard of a force which defeated a dragon army on the Isle of Skye. We are pursuing the survivors. We mean to destroy the henges they use to come here."

"I dunna know of such things." Brude's eyes landed upon the hilt of Excalibur and widened just a bit. "I be a simple man who tends 'is sheep an' leads 'is galloglaigh when the price is right. Dragons are beyond me. Unless, unless ye be willin' to 'ire me band?"

"Those twenty men who ran at the charge of three horsemen? What will they do ag'in dragons?" Brian chided. Aedan passed his page a discouraging look.

"Hmpf! Ye faced me shepherds, not my galloglaigh. The shepherds run now t' get 'em. They should be 'ere by mornin's first light."

"Really? I do hope they enjoy Norse company. Mac Mor should have them here by then." Gingalain countered.

"Well played." Brude's eyes narrowed. "So, whaddya intend t' do with me?"

"I intend to pay you for your sheep, and for the use of your land." Aedan offered a small bag of coins to Brude.

The mercenary's eyes lit briefly. He accepted the bag, judging its weight without looking inside.

"Stay as long as ya like, but less than a moon. I'll 'ave some sheep penned 'ere for you. Now, if one of ya will 'elp me up, I would take kindly t' a ride back t' me 'ome. My galloglaigh dunna like the Norse. 'Twould be a loss fer us both if they were t' meet;

144

there wouldna be a profit int."

Aedan helped Brude to his feet, allowing the man to lean on his shoulder. They walked out to the horses, Aedan mounting Cailean as Padraig steadied Brude, and then helped him onto Cailean's back. Brian had already mounted Lara, and Padraig was quick to mount Gilda.

"Which way, Brude?" Aedan asked.

Brude pointed, and the three rode off at a brisk trot.

"Luag, stay. Guard them." Aedan sent the big hound back to the camp.

As they rode over the small hill, Gwenellen returned to Edana's side, and Fergus to Gingalain's. Osgar turned to Fionnghal and slowly shook his head.

"I fear nothin' good will come o' this."

"Then what would ya 'ave us do?"

Osgar looked to the direction of the riders.

"We should know that, me friend, when the time comes."

"Agreed. Now, 'elp me gather some more bark an' 'erbs. The ill ones need us," Fionnghal said, heading into the woods.

# The Mending

Inside the Aglovale tent, Gwenellen removed the last of the bandages from Edana. She tried not to gag at the smell, wondering if her sister could smell it as well. She would bundle the bandages for washing. There was a stream nearby that would do nicely, and the ship's pot would serve to boil the sickness out.

Gwenellen's eyes fell upon her sister's wounds. She couldn't stifle her gasp.

"Does it, do I look, is it that bad, Gwenny?" Edana sobbed out the question, as much from her fear of the answer as from her pain.

"Eddy, it looks... better. It will take some time. Does it hurt much?"

"Yes. But, sometimes the pain fades. A fresh poultice, or when you, or Padraig...Gwenny?"

"Yes?" Gwenellen wiped a tear from her cheek as she gathered up the bandages.

"Do, do you, your one... is it Padraig?"

"No, Eddy. Not Padraig. He wouldna have me anyway."

"He's be a fool not to, you're so pretty."

"I've seen the way he looks at you, Eddy. 'Tis not me his heart beats for."

"You're just saying that because I'm dying." Edana burst into sobbing, the tears released from all the times she'd held them back; her father's death, Gwenellen's capture, Aedan's dead fiancé, the dead soldiers around her on Skye, the times she was sure Padraig would never love her...

Gwenellen's heart broke. She wanted nothing more than to comfort her little sister, to hold her and make the world leave her be, but her wounds forbade it. Her own tears began falling, for their father, the dragoness binding her and carrying her off, for the abominations she witnessed that evil beast commit, for Brian's father, and for her sister's wounds.

Fionnghal opened the tent and found the women crying before him.

146

"Are ya two all right?" He knew not what he could do to help them.

"Y-yes, I'm better now." Gwenellen took a deep breath, and another.

"Fionnghal, am I dying?" Edana's voice creaked the words out.

Fionnghal laid his bundles down and began applying his poultices to Edana's wounds.

"Now, fair lass, would Fionnghal The Lazy be goin' ta all this effort if ya were dying? Ya'll be fine. It'll take some time, but ya're 'ealing fine."

"I'll be ugly. So scarred and ugly no man would want me," she pouted. "OW!" Fionnghal couldn't help slapping the poultice on a bit hard at hearing those words.

"I'll 'ave no talk o' that. Yer back will have scars, I wouldna lie to ya. But, any man who fixes on that dunna deserve the rest of ya, lass. Besides, the one ya're concerned about has just a bit more character in 'im than that."

"Does everyone in Creation know my heart's secrets!"

"Lassie, I've seen ya enough, an' I've 'eard yer calls in yer sleep. Mostly it's his eyes, the way he looks at ya. An', there's not a one of us 'ere who's not your friend."

"Edana, it's not me he protects by sleeping outside the tent. It's not me he wept over as he carried you here, ne'er letting another touch you until Fionnghal was ready to dress your wounds. Edana, it is you that he loves. And, if you love him, you'll get better to spare him the anguish he feels at your pain."

"You've always made me feel better, Gwenny. When father made me live as a boy, you'd sneak me to your room and dress me in your finest gowns. Thank you."

"Well, you fought dragons for me! I think we're all even now!"

"There, all dressed. Miss Gwenellen, be sure those bandages boil till half the water's gone. Now, if there's n'more I can do fer ya, I'll tend to Sir Gingalain."

Gwenellen leaned in and gently kissed Fionnghal's cheek. "Thank you."

"Thank you, Fionnghal." Edana added.

The blushing sailor nodded once and left the tent. Osgar met him with the bundles for Sir Gingalain.

"I've boiled the bark as ya've said, an' added in the moss an' flowers. It should be cool enough for 'im t' drink now. 'Ow is the wee lass?"

"She is a tough one. She'll be fine. Let's tend t' the Good King."

The two men entered the tent where Luag lay next to Gingalain. The Knight coughed as they neared, wiping the blood on his sleeve. From the look of it, he'd been coughing a lot.

"Good King, I've something to ease yer cough." Fionnghal said quietly.

"Stop tip-toeing around. I willna die today."

Gingalain sat up and took a long drink of the brew.

"Sire, let me look at yer leg." Fionnghal moved to Gingalain's left leg, pulling back the wool of his léine to expose the large man's thigh. He carefully bent the knee, lifting the thigh up, and began unwrapping the bandage.

"Sir Gingalain, ye must stay still as much as possible. Every step re-opens this wound. It'll ne'er 'eal like this."

"I'll not live to see it healed, good man. The fevered poison grows in me, and the broken ribs keep cutting me lungs. Should I stay here, or go on, I'll last a week, no more."

Osgar stared at the Knight, then glanced at Fionnghal in time to see his affirming nod.

"Sire, can we do anathin' to 'elp?" he asked.

"Aye, what you're doin' helps a great deal. Fionnghal's brew dulls the pain and stops the cough. I'd have more of it, and stronger, if that can be."

"I'll bring ya more, but too much an' ye'll sleep the week away." Fionnghal looked into the old man's eyes, awaiting the answer.

"I'll die awake. And with a dragon's throat in me hands, God willing!"

Osgar and Fionnghal both let out a deep breath. The dressings having been changed, they left Gingalain to rest.

"They'll not like tha' news, my friend. Bloody 'ell, I dunna like it." Osgar watched the ground as he walked.

"Nor do I. We'd best keep it to arselves. They all 'ave 'nough ta bear. We should care fer ourselves now. The whisky waits at the Muireall."

# The Agreement

"Hǽlan! Oscail! It be Brude!" Brude called as they neared the collection of houses.

A score of armed men trotted out into the open at the call.

"Brude, be ya all right?" one shouted.

"Relax, these men 'ave paid their rent fer the land, fer the wounds to myself, an' then some. Sionn, have Finnean bring some mead, an' 'ave Rós an' Sileas prepare some food. Our guests would contract us!"

A cheer went up from the men, and then each moved quickly to their well-rehearsed duties.

"You may set yer 'orses there," Brude pointed to a three sided pen, "An' follow me. My 'ouse is thisun, but we'll be in the common 'all tonight. If one of you would be kind 'nough t' 'elp me down?"

Brian took the horses as Padraig and Aedan helped Brude into the common hall. No sooner had Brude taken his chair at the head of the table did Finnean arrive with a half barrel of mead. Well-practiced hands had the cask tapped and the mead flowing presently.

Aedan began.

"Brude, I was always told Rathlin Island was unsettled. How is it you and your folk are here? Surely there is easier land to live from?"

"When ye 'ire yer men an' their blades t' fight fer the 'ighest bid, ya dunna want those ya fought ag'in t' 'ave easy access t' ya. The gifts of the land 'ere be sparse, but it be 'nough."

"What is your price for your galloglaigh to fight the dragons?" Padraig wielded the question as a hammer.

"Well, that's the gist of it, now, init? Will ye 'ave need of all me men?"

"That we will." Aedan responded, passing a blank look to Padraig. Brian watched, nervous energy twitching his hands.

"Well, then our price is twice what ye gave me so far."

Padraig started at the cost, but Aedan spoke to stifle him.

"Agreed. A quarter now, the rest after."

"Agreed then. Ah, 'ere is the supper! More mead!"

A great cheer rang up in the hall as the haggis was passed around.

"Tell me, Sir Padraig, how ye came ta be chasin' dragons?" Sionn asked between bites.

"A dragoness carried off a maiden from the village I was defending. I set out to free the lass. Now we are here. There's not much more to it than that."

"With dragons involved, there's always more ta it. But, yer business is jus' that, yers. Will ye be stayin' the night then?" Brude asked, downing a large gulp of mead.

"We must return, to prepare for the others arrival!" Brian said quickly.

Aedan and Padraig locked eyes for a moment, and went to Brain briefly before Aedan spoke.

"The lad is correct. Your hospitality is welcome. We must leave now, however." Aedan placed a bag of coins on the table as he stood, Padraig and Brian standing with him. "Your payment, Brude."

"Aye, an' I thank ye, Aedan Mac Gabrain. D'ye know yer way back?"

"I'll find where I need to be, Brude. Good eve'n."

"Good eve'n." Brude nodded, but did not stand.

The three dragonslayers were soon mounted and headed back to their camp. As they crested a small hill, Aedan spoke up loudly.

"A good trot will exercise our mounts, don't you think, Good Knight?" The Young King pushed Cailean into a fast trot, Gilda and Lara keeping pace. After a good time, Aedan spoke again, more quietly.

"Brian, what did you see?"

"As I was tending the horses, one of the men ran off, down to the sea. I took my time with the mounts, and soon I saw a small boat leaving."

"It seems your page still has good eyes to go with his keen mind, my King. What do you expect?"

"The man is going to tell Madadh I am here. He will try to bargain a better price from him than we have offered. We have two days, at most before they come."

"Edana can not be moved. We hav'na the blades to defend here. There must be another answer." Padraig thought out loud.

"Why dunna we make them think we've left?" Brian asked. "They dunna know Edana is with us, they've ne'er seen her. There is a small copse by our camp. Edana could hide there. We could make it look like we've left, leaving our tents there, putting the horses on the knarr, and then have Cap'in Fergus sail the Muireall past their port where they're sure to see it."

Padraig and Aedan stopped their horses and stared at Brian for some time. Finally Aedan spoke.

"All right then."

"All right then." Padraig echoed.

The three rode at a gallop back to camp.

# Betrayed

"Easy, Padraig. Be gentle!" Gwenellen begged.

"I can feel no pain when I'm in his arms, sister!" Edana's grimaces betrayed her lie.

"Quiet, both of you. They could be rather near, you know." Padraig whispered as he carried Edana deep into the woods, to a place protected by rock outcrops on three sides. A shallow cave, dark but dry, was nestled into one outcropping. He laid Edana upon a bed of pine needles and soft mosses there.

"Gwenellen, it's time for you to go. You must be seen on the Muireall."

"Yes, Sir Ualas. Be careful, and take care of her."

"I will. Now, go."

Gwenellen ran off to the Muireall, and was soon aboard with the others. Gingalain sat conspicuously, with Brian, Aedan, Gwenellen and the crew flitting about the horses. A sack, stuffed with straw, sat on one side of the knarr, dressed in Gingalain's garb, as the old knight wore Padraig's shield and attire. To any looking from shore, it would seem that the entire party was aboard the Muireall.

The knight and his squire sat alone in the cave as the sun rose.

"Padraig, may I ask you something?"

"Of course, my little one."

"Do you, will, oh, damn!" Edana took a deep breath before continuing, "Do you think I'm pretty?"

"I dunna think you are pretty. I know it as fact that you are."

"Will my scars bother you?"

Padraig turned from the cave mouth and moved back to Edana's side. He looked down at her face, and stared into her eyes for a long time.

"I would not live a life that didna include you. That is all I will say now, lest I become too distracted to protect what I must."

Padraig went back to his vigil at the cave's mouth. Edana's heart raced. Oh, how she wanted to jump up and throw her arms around his neck and lose herself in those powerful arms! She began to move, and the pain hit her hard.

"Ow!" She gasped.

Padraig was next to her in a flash, his hand holding her head, lips lightly brushing her forehead…

"Padraig!" She gasped.

"Edana, my love!"

"PADRAIG!" Edana slammed her fist into his shoulder. "Look!"

His eyes opened and went down to her face. The pale blue glow covered her. *The pale blue glow covered her!* He looked further, to where Excalibur lay across her leg. The blade glowed again!

He sat back, pulling his lips from her face and his hand from her head, and the glow faded away.

"What, where…" Padraig stumbled for words. *She was to be healed, and now it's stopped. WHY?*

"It helped, Padraig. I feel stronger." Edana reached up to touch him, her hand falling upon his wrist.

"The glow! It's back! Edana, we must be touching for it to work! Stay still, let it heal you! Oh, My Laird, thank you!"

They sat for most of the day. Once, some one walked near enough to be heard, but Padraig could not see them. He snuck a glance out of the cave towards the campsite; everything was gone, even the tents. As he sat back down, Edana spoke;

"Padraig, it's getting dark. Won't they see the glow? We should move apart now. I feel much better. We can begin again in the morning…"

"Shh." Padraig broke from Edana, the cave becoming very dark now that it was absent the sword's glow.

A crouching figure limped through the woods, followed by a taller figure with a fine maille shirt and a helmet that glinted in the twilight. While the crouched man made no noise, the taller one's sword clanged as he walked.

"Right, they arna here then. You be sure it was Aedan?" The taller man cried.

"Quiet; they could still be 'ere!" Padraig recognized the whispering voice of Brude.

"And, why exactly, my mercenary friend, would they be hiding here? My brother gains nothing from that. In the end, it willna matter. I have new friends now, and their army will crush all before us. Here is the rest of your payment, Brude. Greedy thing, having me pay you half in front of your men so you could keep the rest for yourself! Here."

Padraig could hear the coins in the bag jingle as the money was given to Brude.

"Now, turn ye back, I've a secret spot near here..." The coins clanged again as Padraig watched the bag fly past him to land on Edana's bandaged leg! She bit her lip hard to keep silent, her fists clenched and her eyes squeezed tightly shut against the pain.

"What do ya need now, Madadh?" Brude asked.

"Bring your galloglaigh, follow me to Portballintrae. Camp in the woods to the South of..."

The two figures moved out of hearing as Madadh spoke. Padraig could not hear the end of the instructions, but he knew he had heard enough.

Brian's plan was for Fergus to sail around the island and land nearby, rejoining them tomorrow. They hoped that Edana would be well enough to sail a few days after that.

"Are you all right, my little one?"

"That sgúm will be back, Padraig. We canna stay here through the night."

Padraig thought a moment. He looked into the back of the cave; it was not big enough to hide in. Edana was right. He began packing everything into his pockets.

"This may hurt. I'm sorry..." He bent down and picked her up, walking hunched over until they were out of the cave. They both glowed with a pale blue aura.

Edana reached up and clasped her arms about Padraig's neck, and then nestled her head into the nook between his powerful chest and neck.

"Ah, hmmmm." She sighed.

Padraig froze in mid stride;

"Are you all right? Did I hurt you?" he whispered in a panic.

"I couldna be better." She punctuated her words with a kiss to his neck.

"Edana, can you walk?"

"I dunna *want* to..."

"That is not what I asked..."

"Yes. I'm fine. Mostly."

Padraig looked down, finding her sky blue eyes smiling up at him. He smiled, and gently set her down.

"Easy, now. Take some time to get your feet under you."

"I'm fine, really...oh, wooah!"

Padraig caught her as she teetered.

"OK, I'm fine now, really. Just let me hold your arm."

The two moved on into the woods.

# The Sea Chase

Luag lay on the floor of the rocking knarr, ears flat and tail still. The faithful hound was not enjoying the rough seas one bit.

"Watch the lines, Osgar! Fionnghal, look sharp on the sail! Brian, keep the 'orses still!" Fergus directed his crew as he turned the Muireall to port. "We'll be passing their 'arbor soon. Everyone ready!"

"Will they try to intercept us, Fergus?" Aedan looked out towards the small harbor coming into view.

"We're still light, and making good speed. This sea's choppy enough that they'd need a big, fast ship, like a galley or a Norse raider to catch... Damn!" Fergus cut his words short at the sight of a sleek Norse ship leaving the harbor and turning in their direction. "They be 'alf way 'ere already! Fionnghal, tighten the sail!"

"That's the Drakos, Madadh's ship." Aedan moved to the stores, retrieving his bow and quiver. "Four left!" he sighed as he counted his arrows.

"To the left, Sire, under my bedding!" Brian called.

Aedan looked where his page directed, and pulled out two score of fine arrows.

"I did a little trading in the village." Brian announced.

"Well done, lad! Well done, indeed!" Gingalain called. "King Aedan, a bow, if you please."

Aedan tossed Brian's bow to the old Knight, and took a position in the bow of the Muireall.

"Madadh will be the tall one with the polished helmet." Aedan called to Gingalain.

"Can we turn to a wind more favorable for shooting, Captain?" Gingalain asked.

"M'Lady, gentlemen, they'll be upon us soon. That ship carries thirty men, an' is faster than we are. Even more so, in this sea. 'Tis no matter which wind we choose, as they'll 'ave it too. Miss Gwenellen, ya should stay low behind the horses."

The big Norse ship moved steadily closer.

"Wait till they're an actus from us, then we'll fire!" Aedan called.

"Aye, Sire." Gingalain replied.

At two hundred yards a score of arrows flew from The Drakos towards the Muireall. All landed well short.

"Steady...NOW!" Aedan called as he let go his arrow, loaded, and fired again. Gingalain fired as well, the two men's arms a blur as they loaded, aimed, and fired.

A second round of arrows from The Drakos flew through the air, hitting the sea around the Muireall. One shaft hit Cailean, the big horse screaming his protest but standing fast.

The arrows from Aedan and Gingalain hit the Drakos. Three men fell there, and Madadh slumped as an arrow lodged in his shoulder. He stood and screamed orders as the Drakos gained speed.

"They'll be upon us soon!" Aedan cried, making the rounds of his charges; Fergus, Brian, Gingalain, Osgar all held their swords at the ready, and Fionnghal pulled up a particularly nasty looking battleaxe. Gwenellen stood defiant, staring at Aedan.

"And now, what do I do, show them m' leg, so you can run them through as they swoon?"

Aedan, dumbfounded, stared at the lovely girl. Fionnghal bent into the hold of the knarr, and arose with a fine Gladuis.

"'Ere, M'Lady!" He tossed the blade to her as he called.

"Thank you, good sailor!" Gwenellen deftly caught the short Roman sword by the hilt, and then bent to pick up Padraig's shield. She moved up to a place near the Muireall's bow, raised her sword and shield while letting loose a blood-curdling war cry!

Aedan was shocked to see pale blue light flash around the shield, and several men on the Drakos shrank back from the gunnels in fright!

The Drakos still bore down upon the Muireall, however. Madadh shook his sword as he cried to Aedan.

"I'll have your head, brother!"

"Come and try! You and I, alone, coward!" Aedan's response thundered across the waves.

"Oh, Laird, be with us in our hour of need!" Brian calmly prayed.

The Drakos was but a stone's throw from the Muireall, her men now at the gunnels, ready to leap upon the smaller ship's crew in another heartbeat...

"Sire!" Fergus exclaimed.

The bow of the Drakos suddenly rose up out of the sea, carried high on a glistening grey head. Men fell into the sea as the Drakos' keel broke, planks shedding from her hull. The screams of Madadh's men were soon silenced as great whales surged from the sea, now falling back down upon the Drakos and her men. Once, twice, three times did the great leviathans rise over and fall upon Madadh's vessel, smashing it into kindling.

The crew on the Muireall watched in awed silence.

The whales then vanished beneath the waves, leaving more than two score of men floundering in the rough seas.

"Shall we save them, Sire?" Fergus asked softly. "We can drop them off on that beach yonder."

"They are my citizens, traitorous as they may be. How many can we take on, Good Captain?"

"A dozen or so; no more than 'alf."

"Any injured men, we will take you to shore!" Aedan cried as Fergus turned the Muireall. "Brian, keep your eyes open for any treachery. I'll be looking for Madadh."

"Keep alert. They may be less than grateful for their bath." Gingalain warned.

"There, Sire!" Brian called, "Near the sail!"

Aedan turned his eyes to where Brian pointed. Near where the battered sail floated, a group of six men swam urgently towards the shore. One of them sported the broken shaft of an arrow on a near useless arm; Madadh!

"If you go after him, these men will drown." Gwenellen was at Aedan's side, her hand on his shoulder providing a decidedly comfortable feeling.

"Aye, M'love. I canna do that."

Gwenellen slid her arm about his, and rested her head upon his shoulder.

"A hand here, you two!" Gingalain's deep voice boomed.

Aedan moved to the gunnels of the Muireall, and looking down at the men struggling in the sea, called to them.

"Do ye pledge your lives to me, for now and evermore?"

"Aye!" The men chorused in reply. Aedan reached down and grasped the arm of the nearest man, hauling him up into the knarr.

"Help my men out of this sea!" The Young King commanded.

The crew worked quickly pulling the men into the Muireall. Four refused to pledge, and swam off towards the harbor, clinging to bits of flotsam. In the end, eighteen men were saved. They sat shivering in the breeze.

"Sire, the men want to thank you for saving us," a stocky grey haired man stood and spoke.

"What is your name, good man?"

"Fiachnae Mac Demmáin, Sire."

Aedan looked at the man for a time, and tilted his head slightly.

"I know you."

"Aye, Sire. I would call on your father every year, bearing the tithes of my father, Demmáin Mac Cairell. I was at your christening, Sire. As I left, Meirleachas attacked my procession, captured me and sold me into slavery. I have been bound to the oars of the Drakos these past nine years."

"This explains the attacks by your Uncle Báetáin Mac Cairell. No doubt he sees your loss as a treachery on my father's part. You must stay with us, and make your way to Duiblinn. When we land, take my stead. Cailean is a fine ride."

"Sire, I have pledged my life to you."

"And I have given you direction for that life. No more will be said of it. Will these men follow you?" Aedan swept his hand across the beam of the Muireall, indicating the men saved from the sea.

"Aye. Many are my men, captured over the years. Each of them had pledged to me before they pledged to you."

"I release these men to your service. Fiachnae, you must get to your uncle and tell him what you have told me, before war drains the blood from both of our houses."

"Aedan, you have your father's character. I will do as you bid." The two men clasped each other, hands on arms.

"Sire, the arrow in Cailean, it is deep." Brian called.

Aedan's eyes got wide as he moved quickly to the horse's side. Gwenellen was there, as was Fionnghal. Fiachnae followed.

"The dart is deep, it could bleed him dead if we remove it." Aedan's dejected voice cracked as he spoke.

"Let me see, before ye kill the poor animal," a powerful voice parted the onlookers. Gingalain limped up to Cailean, running a powerful hand soothingly over the black steed's flank. The big horse quieted, standing very still.

"Gwenny. Come here, girl, and bring the Azure Shield."

Gwenellen picked up the shield, marveling at the sliver and blue designs. She held the armor out for Gingalain.

"Here, Sir Gingalain."

"Hold it up to the horse, Gwenny. Careful not to cut him now…"

A pale blue glow spread out as the maiden held the flat of the shield against Cailean's side, just below the protruding arrow. Gingalain reached up, wrapping his powerful fingers around the shaft. With a blindingly swift move, he pulled the arrow straight out of the horse's flank. The shield's blue glow faded, and Gwenellen brought the silver and blue disk down to the deck.

Cailean took one step sideways, coughed once, and was again still. Aedan reached up to the spot where the arrow had been, running his hand over the horse.

"There isna wound!" Aedan gasped.

Gingalain held up the arrow, it's head and shaft covered with Cailean's blood.

"What be this?" Fiachnae asked, and then squinted his eyes at Gingalain. "You! You're of Artair's Table!" he gasped. "Does the Great King live?" he looked up, eyes pleading with Gingalain as much as his tongue.

"Naye, Artair, lives n' more. This be his shield. Why Merlin's magic works for her, I canna say." The old knight turned and limped back to his place to rest. Gwenellen followed him, bringing the shield.

"Aedan, you've fallen in with some interesting people, I would say." Fiachnae commented.

"Sire, we're at the spot." Fergus called.

Aedan looked up at the beach, scanning the trees and shrubs.

"He's not here."

"We must give 'im some time. I'll beach the Muireall, an' we can look. But, Brude will begin searching soon, so we must be quick." Fergus offered.

"Brian and I will mount Cailean and Lara to search. If we dunna return within two…"

"Hælan!"

"Padraig! Edana!" Gwenellen called as she jumped into the surf and ran ashore.

"Woof! Woof!!" Luag barked from the knarr's gunnels, tail wagging frantically.

"Gwenny!" Edana cried, running down the beach.

Padraig trotted right behind her.

Within moments, all were onboard the Muireall as she sailed towards the beach East of Dunseverick.

# Éireann

"Sire, to the West, look!" Brian called.

"Where, my Page?" Aedan followed Brian's pointing finger, but could find nothing of interest.

"Above the hill, circling... dragons!" Aedan climbed up the rise to stand beside the young lad. Behind him Fiachnae and his men helped unload the Muireall and guide the horses onto the beach. Edana followed Padraig, still performing the duties of a squire. Gingalain limped along the sand, finally sitting to rest on a small rock.

"Aye, Brian, your eyes are good. I see them." A group of dark shapes circled above the far off hill. "They're a ways off yet. Keep watch, lad." Aedan turned and trotted down to Padraig.

"Aedan, may I have your ear?" Fiachnae called. Aedan stopped near the stocky warrior.

"I leave now for Duiblinn. One of my men has purchased two good horses from that nearby farm. I'll take one to Duiblinn, and Niall has departed, riding the other to Ballynahatty, to try to contact your father. The rest of my men will stay and fight with you. Maon is a capable leader, they will follow him, and he will follow you. This was not my order, 'tis their desire.

"Aedan, I've been close to these beasts, and I've heard Madadh speak with them. He thinks he controls them, but they use him as a striapach. We must prevail, or all will come under the dragons' claws."

"Fiachnae, take Cailean and Lara and two more men. You must get through!"

"You'll need the horses, and I will be faster alone. And harder to find." Fiachnae placed his hand on Aedan's shoulder, "Good hunting, King Aedan."

"Godspeed you, King Fiachnae."

"Aedan!" Padraig's voice hit the King's ears. "Here!" Aedan took one step, then turned back to find Fiachnae riding off to the South, over a hill. He turned back and walked to Padraig.

"What is it, Good Knight?" Aedan caught the look of fear and panic in Padraig's eyes

"Gingalain, Sire." The two men ran to where the Old Knight lay on the beach.

"Edana! Fionnghal!" Padraig cried.

"Gwenellen!" Aedan called.

Padraig placed Excalibur across Gingalain's chest as Edana arrived.

"Take my hand," Padraig instructed without lifting his eyes from his mentor's pale face. Edana grasped his hand, squeezing tightly at the sight of the Good King.

"Gwenellen, take Padraig's shield. Hold it against Gingalain's leg."

She slipped the Azure Shield off of the Good Knight's back and moved to place it as Aedan had directed.

There was no glow.

"KROUGHF! You all can relax. I be not dead yet." Gingalain's low voice came full of dust and gravel, not the powerful resonance they had known. "Soon, but not yet. Now, will you let an old man rest!"

The crew from the Muireall and the soldiers had gathered at the commotion. Fionnghal pushed through the crowd, and placed a flask at Gingalain's lips. After two swallows, he withdrew the flask and handed it to Edana.

"Good strong whisky. N'more than two drams, lest 'e sleep 'is life away," he looked at Padraig; "Ye'd give him too much, Sir Ualas." The he stood and backed away.

"Thank you, Fionnghal," Gingalain said, his voice appreciably stronger.

"Excuse me, Sir, am I to understand that the old knight has broken ribs?" A thin red haired man asked.

"Aye. Can ya help him?" Gwenellen answered.

"I'd been a healer before I was a soldier. My name is Sólas. We need to make a binding for him, so that moving doesn't re-open his wounds inside." He stood up, and motioned to two men, "Maon, Laise, listen: Maon, gather me some strong wood, about as thick as yer wrist, and as long as yer arm. Laise, I need some rope or vines…"

"I've plenty of rope on the Muireall." Fergus eagerly offered.

"Good, I was hopeful you'd offer." Sólas turned to Gingalain and continued; "Now, Sire, sit yourself up here. Lean forward a bit. There, that's it."

The men came with the wood and rope, and Sólas soon had a splint for Gingalain's side secured and in place. As Sólas stood, Gingalain's voice boomed again;

"Sólas, thank ye. Now, will you all leave me be!"

Satisfied that no more could be done for the man who taught him life itself, Padraig returned to packing Gilda with provisions. His return to the task at hand prompted the others to return to their toils.

The next evening, after all was prepared, Aedan and Gwenellen, Brian, Padraig and Edana, Fergus, Gingalain, and Maon sat together.

"We are but two hours walk from the henges at Portballintrae," Padraig began outlining his plan. "We could send the men South, then West, where they would attack the Southern lines of the Dragons. We then ride into the henges, and set them aflame."

"I've no better thoughts on it. Sir Gingalain, your thoughts?" Aedan turned to the old knight.

"I would do as Padraig says, but add to it thusly; Maon, how many bowmen do you have with you?"

"Fully a third of us have our bows and quivers, Sir Knight. But many a quiver is but half full."

"Aye, you won't need too many arrows, just enough to grieve 'em some."

"We've been anxious for that, Sir Knight."

"Fergus, you take the bowmen on the Muireall, and sail close to the henges. When the guards come out, the bowmen strike."

"Aye, an' after that, I'll put the Muireall up at the dock. When ya 'ave finished, come there if too many be upon ya."

"Sire, let me send four bowmen with the others to the South. 'Twill look more like a proper attack that way."

"Good thinking, Maon. Any other ideas?" Aedan asked.

"What of Gwenellen?" Edana blurted out.

"Edana, Gwenellen, Brian, and Gingalain will be with the Muireall."

"WHAT?" The two women chorused.

"You are all skilled with a sword; Brian and Gingalain also with a bow. The Muireall will have a dozen strong arms to defend her. Maon and Laise, to lend credence to their attack from the south, will ride Greg and Lara while leading that group. There will be no further discussion on this matter." Aedan stood tall, his voice leaving no room for argument.

"When?" Padraig asked.

"Maon's men should move a full day's travel South, to get into place without discovery. The sun sets soon. If we time the attacks correctly, we can all attack before sunrise while the beasts still sleep two days after the morrow. Maon, you should begin your attack just before sunrise, on the third day from now. You leave in an hour, so your men will have a little time to rest before their attack. In three days, the Muireall sails. An hour later, Padraig and I ride.

"Now, is there anything to eat?"

# Dragon's Gate

"Perhaps we should have done a reconnaissance?" Padraig whispered as he sank back down behind the low stonewall.

"Sure, *now* you mention it!" Aedan shivered as the cold stones on his back seemed to suck all the warmth from his bones.

"Well, you did say there wasna more discussion on the matter..."

"Oh, be quiet. I saw your relief when I assigned your squire to the ship. Do you think mine was any less?" Aedan looked behind them, seeing Gilda and Cailean standing quietly behind a small copse of trees.

"They willna stay, you know. As soon as they get to the dock, they'll be after us." Padraig peeked over the stones once more.

"What else could I do?"

"Send them with Fiachnae?"

"Yea, they surely wouldna done that. Can you see anything?"

"Hold on... nothing. We should have brought Brian. His eyes are like..."

"There are two guards atop the rise just outside the nearest henge."

"BRIAN!" The two men chorused their whispers into the darkness.

"The furthest henge has a wall around it. I think they've fortified it."

"Why be you here?" Aedan's whispered scream demanded.

"Gingalain said you could use an archer. I can hit the guards from here, while you be riding fast into the henge."

"That sounds good."

"Then what does he do, Padraig? We'll be up there, and he'll be alone, back here."

"Shooting arrows. He will be hard to spot." Padraig turned to Brian, "Just remember to stay under something, and to look up afore you come out to shoot!"

"Yes, Sir Knight."

"Good thinking Padraig. Are you ready?" Aedan asked as he looked over the cold, damp stones again.

"That I am, Sire."

"Brian, time your arrows well." Aedan asked as he moved past the lad.

"I will, My King!" The eager Page replied.

"Remember, look up!" Padraig patted the young man's head as he slipped past him into the darkness. Brian's whispered Roman prayers faded with the distance behind them. Padraig road Gilda, and looked over at Aedan atop Cailean.

"I'm almost glad your sword and shield aren't aglow, my friend. Almost. It would betray us here, but it was a comfort in battle..."

"We should go, Sire."

"Away then!"

The two rode at a gallop to the henge, Gilda carrying skins of pitch and Cailean bundles of firewood. Up the slight rise they rode, fast as a gale's winds. As they came to the top of the mound surrounding the henge, they looked for the guards.

They found them near, to their left, an arrow providing permanence to the slumber of each.

"There! That one's the keystone!" Padraig called, riding to his right.

"Here then!" Aedan pulled up at the massive stone's base. As wide as Padraig was tall, the stone towered over the two noblemen. Intricate carvings covered the surface, with writing of a form that Aedan didn't recognize. At even intervals gold and silver rods protruded from the sides of the stone, from the level of Aedan's head to the top of the thirty foot high menhir.

Aedan laid the firewood around while Padraig readied the pitch. As Padraig spread the pitch over the wood, Aedan took the lines Fergus had given them and climbed up the stone, using the rods as a ladder.

"Ready!" Padraig called up.

"Ready!" Aedan called, "Look out," as he jumped to the ground, landing hard.

The morning twilight began to spread its subtle glow across the henge as Padraig struck the flint over the pitch. Again and again he tried, with no success. The sky was becoming brighter as Aedan tried the flint, also failing to produce a spark.

"Perhaps we can topple it with the horses alone." Aedan's

statement was as much a wish as a question.

"Even if we did, they'd have it raised again too soon. We need the fire."

Padraig pulled Excalibur out of his sheath. That familiar glow greeted him, and guided his hand as he struck the flint with the fabled blade.

Two strikes and a gentile breeze had a strong, spreading flame licking at the base of the stone.

"Now!" Aedan called from Cailean's back.

Gilda and Cailean began pulling the stone, the strong, trusted ropes singing under the strain of the two powerful horses. The sun's rays broke ground, and struck the stone as the flames rose up around it.

Off to the South, a great commotion demanded their attention as Maon's men attacked. Padraig looked from atop Gilda, scanning the grounds around the henge.

"My Laird!" His gasp caught Aedan's attention. The king looked about, and was taken aback by the sight lit by the flames and the rising sun.

A score of Madadh's soldiers lay dead around them, many but a few yards away. From each neck, a single arrow's shaft betrayed the protector of the two dragon hunters.

"Brian's work".

Aedan began searching for his page, looking along the low stonewall where they had planned his role. The wall seemed to glow red in the morning sun, but the lad was not to be seen.

"Aedan!" Padraig's urgent call brought Aedan's mind to tasks more close at hand. "Look!"

The stone they sought to topple was aglow with a crimson brightness far above the level given by the fire and the sun.

"Look around the henge, Aedan. All the stones are glowing. Dragons are coming!"

The red glow from the stones spread inward, to the center of the henge. A large glowing orb formed in the middle of the henge, and in that orb's center, a great emptiness began to grow. Larger and larger, until the dark nothing at the center was sufficient to hold half a score of men.

Then the first dragon came through.

The ten foot tall crimson beast stepped onto the grass of the henge and looked around, his attention resting upon Aedan and Padraig. As the beast's mouth opened to roar a warning, an arrow flew in and pinned the beast's tongue. Even before the dragon could reach up to remove the dart, another hit his shoulder. A third centered in the Dragon's chest, and a fourth pierced the left eye of the beast.

The dragon crashed to the ground, dead.

"I'm out of arrows!" Brian called from behind the nearest stone to the right of the two dragonslayers, "I'll protect the fires about your stone!" The lad ran quickly to a spot behind the fire, which now roared about the base of the huge stone pillar. From his position, the dragons would have a hard time seeing him through the fire's glare.

"We're not going to topple this now. We've got to give the fire time to weaken the stone." Padraig had to shout over the fire's roar.

"Aye, follow me!" Aedan dropped the rope, and spun Cailean around towards the henge. The big black stallion came in just behind Gilda on the roan mare's right as the two galloped into the circle of stone pillars.

Padraig's hand held Excalibur, his arm the Azure Shield.

"It would seem you are given comfort in battle, my King!" Padraig cried. Aedan glanced at the Good Knight, aflame with a bright pale blue glow brighter than Aedan had ever seen.

A great commotion arose from the East, and Padraig's heart fell as he glanced to see the harbor over flown by a score of dragons. Smoke billowed up from near the sea, but he could not see the fires, nor could he see the docks.

"Keep your mind here, Padraig! Take comfort in your training of Edana!"

Padraig Ualas brought his head around as the two riders found the center of the henge populated with two huge, flightless dame dragons, enraged by the slaughter of their bull. As Gilda sped faster than Padraig had ever ridden her, Excalibur rose and fell faster than the eye could see.

One dragoness fell, cleanly halved from shoulder to hip.

Aedan's war cry echoed through the henge as Cailean spun at

full gallop to deliver a stunning kick from both hind legs to a dragoness' chest. Back the beast staggered, roaring in rage and pain. The flanks of the black stallion glistened in the sun as he spun yet again, bringing Aedan's sword into range. Up, over his head, and down in a powerful arc the king brought his blade to meet the dragoness' shoulder, cutting deeply into the foul flesh there. Down the red terror went, onto one knee, odorous black blood gushing from the wound. A second powerful blow from the High King of Dal Riata cut deeply into the beast's neck, ending its pain forever.

Three larger dragons roared out of the emptiness in the center of the henge. Padraig was upon them even as Aedan first saw their presence. Never had the Young King seen or heard of the likes of this; horse and rider but a bright blue blur in and around the twelve foot tall abominations, sword slashing and cutting crimson flesh too fast for the eyes to follow. Before Aedan could return to the center of the henges, all three dragons were dead.

Yet now, there were six big beasts, newly emerged from the emptiness of the henge. Aedan urged Cailean to Padraig's side to support the knight even as he glanced back at the keystone.

"Good Knight, the fire sears that stone well. We need but a short time hence."

"They will keep coming through. We need another plan!" Padraig shouted in response, "Attack!"

The two men flew into the maelstrom of crimson scales, coal black talons, and yellow fangs.

Aedan used Cailean's spins and kicks to add force to the blows of his own sword. Timing his swings to good effect he had soon slain two more crimson beasts while his powerful steed had crushed another.

He looked for Padraig, but instead found a dozen more dragons emerging from the emptiness at the core of the henge. A glance towards the harbor made his heart drop, as scores of dragons were coming his way. A look to the South found a hundred of Madadh's men and a large group of dragons running into the walled henge. Aedan looked back to the battle at hand.

Padraig and Gilda were nowhere in sight.

"So be it, then!" Aedan's anger growled through clenched teeth. He raised his face to the Heavens and let out a thunderous battle cry. A kick to Cailean sent him into the crimson horde, tears streaming as his sword slashed head and arm of the beasts.

Aedan thought of Brian, surely slain by now. Rage at that thought fueled the powerful strokes of his weightless sword as dragon after dragon fell around him. He thought of Padraig, and his sword slashed out again with even greater violence, cutting a swath through the red beasts. The Young King thought of Gingalain, of Edana, of his lost Murron, of the lovely Gwenellen. His anger-driven blade felled dragon after dragon.

But Aedan knew his anger and rage would expire long before the last dragon did. Still, on he fought, his sword becoming as heavy as his heart with each swing now. Talons caught Cailean's flank, and then Aedan's back. Still they fought, sharp hooves and sharp steel meeting crimson scales and black talons.

Another blow hit Aedan's arm, and he nearly dropped his sword. A copper flash emerged from out of the emptiness at the henge's center, and sped past his eyes as he spun Cailean into his attacker.

Gilda!

Cailean snorted and roared, as he had seen the riderless roan too. Aedan's blows hit home, his spent muscles refreshed by a slim hope. His sword hacked and slashed, Cailean kicked and bit, horse and rider bloodied but still fighting with terrible effect. Beast after beast fell under the pair's blows.

But more dragons surrounded that empty portal at the center of the henge. Aedan's hope faded with his strength, even as Cailean's kicks and dodges slowed. Another talon blow staggered the great steed, and another nearly toppled Aedan from his mount. A large dragon roared in front of Aedan before he could regain his balance, the great arm drawing back those black talons to deliver the deathblow.

As Aedan watched, a steel blade emerged from the beast's chest, quickly withdrawing as foul dark blood spewed from the dying dragon. As it fell it revealed Gilda and her rider.

Brian swung his sword again from Gilda's back, striking the head of a nearby dragon. Aedan, still stunned, searched around.

The roars of angry and dying dragons, loud as thunder to his ears, parted under a fierce war cry. Aedan's first thought brought his eyes to Brian, but his page was busy attacking dragons with youthful enthusiasm. Another cry sounded, Aedan's mind now clear enough to recognize the sound.

Mac Mor!

Aedan sat higher, swatting a dragon's arm with his sword, and looked towards the harbor. The two score of dragons rushing to the henge from there had arrived, but they rushed to escape, not to attack. Behind them came hundreds of screaming Norsemen, wielding maces, axes, hammers, and swords to deadly effect. At their head rode Aengus Mac Mor, seemingly larger than life. The Great Celt chased the dragons, swinging his fearsome battleaxe to gruesome effect.

As the dragons surrounding them panicked, Aedan rode towards Brian.

"Brian! The Keystone! With me!" Aedan shouted. He galloped to the ropes, giving thanks that they had somehow not burned.

He and Brian dismounted and took the stout lines, fastening them to Gilda and Cailean. The two horses began pulling, but the stone would not move.

"Would ya like some help, King Aedan?" Maon's cry rang out.

Aedan turned to find Maon and Laise, bloodied but grinning, sitting astride Greg and Lara. Soon the four horses strained the ropes again. Greg pulled out ahead, the rope taught as steel under the pressure of the huge white stallion. Standing two hands prouder than the other horses, Greg lowered his head, the ropes quivering under the strain.

"It's not moving!" Brian cried.

"Keep pulling!" Aedan commanded.

A loud CRACK thundered across the henge as the keystone crumbled at it's base and toppled over. Quickly the men released the ropes and mounted their horses, heading back into the henge.

The red glow from the henge stones had vanished. Aedan saw the great portal of emptiness at the center of the henge was rapidly shrinking. He looked at Gilda.

"Padraig!" He screamed, galloping to the collapsing portal, but the great emptiness was gone before he could reach it.

"Oh, Laird, what have I done! PADRAIG!"

# The Emptiness

Scores of Dragons surrounded Aedan and Padraig. Padraig could see that the number of dragons coming through the portal was turning the battle from them. The fighting had moved them closer to the portal when a familiar voice sang in Padraig's mind. *Close the portal from the other side!*

"They will keep coming through. We need another plan!" Padraig shouted to Aedan, "Attack!"

The knight fought atop Gilda until the two were next to the portal. "Now, girl! Through!" Gilda leapt into the emptiness.

Suddenly Padraig was surrounded by a black nothingness. There was naught to orient to, no up, no down, no ground or sky, no sounds, no smells, no light. There was only a pale blue glow from Excalibur and The Azure Shield that reached but a few feet into…

Dragons!

The only thing Padraig could see was an endless mass of dragons moving to the portal, their red scales shining black in the pale blue light. They swarmed the knight and Gilda as they relentlessly streamed to the portal.

Padraig wielded Excalibur with vigor, Gilda kicking into the crimson throng. Again and again he swung Excalibur and The Azure Shield, killing every Dragon within reach.

At least they were no longer moving through the portal!

"There, girl! That way!" Padraig kneed Gilda to move towards a bright blue light in the distance, but the faithful mare refused to move away from the portal.

"Go, girl!" *I don't know why, but I've got to reach that light!*" Still Gilda refused to move.

"Home, then. Go back!" he shouted as he jumped from her back.

Gilda vanished into the picture of the henge that was the portal as dragons surrounded the lone knight.

# Respite

"We canna find a living one, Sire." Maon reported to Aedan. "I think we've killed 'em all."

"Only the ones not inside the walled henge." Aedan's weary voice replied. The king flinched as Sólas stitched his wounds. "We will have to breach those walls and destroy that henge." The words were more of a sigh than a call to arms.

"You'll not be fighting for two days, Sire. These wounds are too deep." Sólas reminded Aedan.

"The dragons will not wait, good doctor. Maon, ask Mac Mor to come see me please. I wish to thank that man properly this time. OW!"

"Pardon, Sire." Sólas apologized.

"Yes, Sire" Maon left the tent as Gwenellen held the door flap open.

"What is this talk of more battles? I will not have you dead before..."

Aedan looked at the beautiful woman peering from the tent flap, the relief, rage, and fear streaming down her cheeks. He did not know he was smiling, nor did he see her battle torn, blood stained garments. He saw only those eyes...

"What are you grinning at, Aedan Mac Gabrain?" Gwenellen chastised as she burst into the tent, grabbed his head, and kissed him hard.

"Maiden, I, I, I..." Aedan fumbled for words, his tired and battered body screaming with a sudden, new ache. The tent flap opened again, and Edana stepped in.

"Oh, I'm sorry." She blushed, and turned to leave before spying Sólas and turning back.

"Aedan," Edana sobbed, "I canna find him."

Aedan's heart sank at the thought of telling her. He decided that not to would be an unforgivable cruelty.

"Come in and sit, Edana." Aedan ordered as he took a deep breath. "Edana, we won't find him. The henges are some kind of portal into the dragon's world. This one had opened even as we set to destroy it. The dragons came to our world through it.

Padraig went into their world."

Edana sat down hard, staring at Aedan.

"You saw him go in?"

"I saw Gilda return without him. She would ne'er have been in there without him. And she would not have left him there if he lived."

Edana sat, silent and unmoving, staring blankly at the tent wall. Tears ran down her cheeks. Gwenellen held her younger sister for a moment and then pulled her to her feet.

"Come, Eddy," she said quietly as she led her out of the tent.

Aedan swallowed hard and closed his eyes.

"Laird, these trials you've set for me are hard. Yet there must be a way. How do I comfort them?"

"You will find a way to, Sire." Sólas quietly replied. "Your heart will lead you to it. Now, try not to move your arm too quickly, and keep these bandages on 'til the morrow."

"Thank you, Sólas." Aedan sat alone as the healer left the tent.

His mind shivered as he thought of what had happened since he first met Padraig. He was, now that he contemplated it, a selfish man before. Not that he was without charity, but every goal he had set had been for his own betterment. Even those goals of helping others had been for the satisfaction it would bring to his own pride. He thought of his lessons from Padraig, and of the Pyres, the lesson from Gingalain that night.

He thought he understood.

Aedan rose, willing the pain and stiffness away. He walked to Gingalain's tent and quietly entered.

"Good King, forgive my intrusion," Aedan began. The tired eyes of the old knight looked at him, and a smile twitched briefly across the old scarred face.

"Your loyal subject awaits in your service, Sire."

"Stop the pomp, Gingalain, for it doesna suit you. You are and always will be the Good King to me, pledged or not. I am in need of your counsel. We must destroy the walled henge."

"Yes, we must. Your wounds willna bear another battle for some time, I can see. You lose confidence in light of Padraig's absence. And your heart aches for those your commands sent into the arms of death. You now know the reasons I would shed the crown if I could. My advice? You have everything you need, Aedan. That is my advice."

Aedan sat, disappointed, thinking.

"Gingalain..."

"You willna see it. I must slap your face with it. So be it.

"Aedan, you feel the burdens a good man feels as King. The pains of compassion torture your soul. Yet, what do you seek from me? What is it you want me to tell you?"

"How do I comfort them? How do I remove Edana's pain, and the pain of scores of others like her? I hav'na the means to make it better for them, so, how may I comfort them?"

"Aedan, you are a true High King. You dunna ask how to lessen your own burden; you seek to lessen the burdens of those you rule. That is what you need. It is all that you need. Just go among them and be yourself. That will comfort them more than you would believe."

"Sire..."

"When you have done so, you will be tired. Rest then. When you are refreshed, come to me. We have a siege to plan."

Aedan rose and limped out of the tent. Sólas the healer had told him to avoid too much movement, lest his wounds re-open. He wasn't sure he could move that far, so ached his weary flesh.

He walked about without conscious direction until a loud and boisterous voice called out to him.

"My King!"

"Aengus Mac Mor! My friend, you've saved us yet ag'in!" Aedan placed a stiff arm upon the Great Celt's shoulder. "Come to sup with us tonight." The words were spoken and heard as a command.

"Aye, that will be me 'onor!"

"Your men, did you lose many? Tell me of the battle." Aedan didn't notice the gathering of soldiers behind him.

"We came upon the Muireall as she was heading into the 'arbor. We pulled our boats well behind her, an' landed quickly as they engaged the 'arbormaster. The dragons attacked 'em, but their arrows sent the beasts back afore we 'ad beached our boats.

"Then the soldiers came. I thought they'd be after the dragons, but they fought alongside the beasts! We lost some good men to me error, but we killed e'ery one of those brathadóirs, an' a good number o' the dragons.

"We took off after the dragons as they fled. We came upon the 'enge, an' all the dragons there..." Aengus continued in hushed tones, "King Aedan, there were two 'undred of the beasts, 'acked ta death in that circle of stones when we arrived. I dunno how ya did it..."

"Padraig did most of it, and Brian some. I... was just there."

"Aye, ye did a bit more than take up space in that 'enge, I suspect. Brian tells me when the knight's horse took 'im to ye, there was but four dragons standing." Aengus looked at king for a moment, judging the man's aversion to accepting the praise. "What 'appened to the South? Fergus told me o' the plan. 'Ow did it go there?"

"Maon and Laise attacked the South of Madadh's camp; there was a weak defense at that place. They killed many of Madadh's men, and several flying dragons, forcing them to break and run into the walled henge."

The group of soldiers behind Aedan began to disperse, eager to pass on what they had heard.

"Another gateway they 'ave, behind the wall? That'll be a tall task indeed!"

"Laird O' The Isles, will you sit on Gingalain's right tonight?"

"Twould be an 'onor to."

"I will see you then." Aedan walked further into the camp then, feeling a little less stiff now. He stopped among groups of men, Norse and Celt alike, listening to the stories of their battles, deflecting their questions of his battle. He thanked them, and he thanked the tears they shed for the fallen.

After a considerable time Aedan came upon the pen holding the horses. He gave a start as Cailean snorted his greeting; the wounds on the big black steed were deeper and more numerous than he had known. As he reached up to run his hand over the horse's cheek, he realized that the wounds had been treated.

"Hold still, girl. That's it."

"Sólas!" Aedan walked around Cailean to Gilda. She had taken much worse than Cailean, Aedan cringing at the thought of where she had been. The healer worked along her flank, rubbing a salve into her wounds.

"Sire. Be careful, and move slowly please. Both for your wounds and theirs," he motioned to the horses.

"Sólas, how many have you treated this day?"

"All who required treatment Sire. There are many wounded. I am nearly finished with the horses that need me, and then I can tend to the less severely wounded."

"Those can wait for Fionnghal. You will rest when you are done here." Aedan used that voice which mere men must obey.

"There will be rest enough when all are tended to, Sire." Sólas said simply, without looking up.

Aedan took a step back. Shock painted his face, that he would be disobeyed in such a manner.

Then the king's mouth turned up at the corner slightly.

"Sólas, you will sit with me as we sup tonight." Aedan turned and quickly walked away, trying to leave before the healer could refuse.

"Aye, Sire. As you command!"

"Ha-hah!" Aedan chuckled a little at the small victory. He walked up to another tent, stopping before it. Dread shivered his soul as he stared at the tent flap. Aedan took a deep breath to gather his courage.

He opened the flap and stepped in.

Gwenellen sat before him, rocking gently as her arms sheltered Edana. The younger girl's sobs flowed out in a torrent, matched by the pain in Gwenellen's eyes.

"Edana." Aedan spoke softly as he sat and touched her cheek.

Red eyes peered through the sobs at The Young King.

"I loved him, Aedan!"

"I know. And he loved you, Edana. He told me so." Aedan sat softly next to her.

"Why? Why did he go in there? Why did he?" The sobs controlled her once more.

"He saved us, Edana. What ever happened in the Hell he went into, he saved us all. No dragons came out after Gilda returned."

"He could still be alive, Edana." A small voice called from the tent flap.

Edana's eyes looked up at Brian. The lad looked every bit the battle worn soldier. "Gilda thinks he is. She keeps looking to the walled henge."

"Brian, my page, would you see to the supper tonight? Find us some fat deer, and ask Fergus and Osgar to cook them, please." Aedan commanded.

"Aye, Sire." Brian nodded and left the tent flap.

"I've not been handed a false hope, Aedan. The lad's trying to comfort me, leave him be." Edana managed through her tears. "For I know, even if Padraig lives, you must destroy the last henge, his only means of return."

Aedan's eyes met Edana's. The decision was his alone, and it sat so heavily upon him that his gaze dropped to the ground. He breathed deeply once, twice, and again.

"I must think of all, Edana. As much as I love Padraig," he lifted his heavy eyes to meet those of the grieving girl, "I must close that portal."

Aedan stood and walked out of the tent, pausing without turning at the flap.

"How I wish it werna so," His broken voice said before he left the tent.

As he entered his own tent, Aedan fell in exhaustion onto his bedding. His aches of body and soul followed him into a fitful slumber, broken when Brian awakened him for the meal.

"The venison is ready, my King." Fergus whispered to Aedan. The Young King sat in the center of the table, Gingalain on his right with Mac Mor; Brian, Gwenellen and Edana sat to his left. Sólas, Maon, Laise, Fergus and his crew filled out the table. The entire troop was gathered, Norse and Celt, but for those few with sentry duties.

Aedan stood, and the hum of a thousand conversations was abruptly ceased.

"Good men, a moment, please," Aedan called out, his words echoing over the camp above the smell of well-roasted venison.

"We are here on the eve of yet another battle. Ne'er before has an army of such brave and good men been assembled. Our enemy is powerful, yet twice have you vanquished the demons and held the field!"

Cheers erupted such as Aedan had never heard. His neck bristled as he waited for din to settle before continuing.

"Sir Padraig once told me, 'Think only of the urgency, of the importance, and the nobility of your task, and you shall gather an ample strength to accomplish it!'"

Cheers again rose up, and again Aedan paused for them to quiet.

"Twice has your steel cut into the dragon's resolve, and sent them fleeing in fear! Yet, once more must we cast our flesh into the battle's tumult. Padraig told me, 'Think not of your body's hardships, focus instead upon thy soul's purpose. Remember, each of us is placed where we need to be, so we may help those we know can lest help themselves. It is our duty, assigned from above! Take heart, and know *this* is your reason for being born so smart, so brave, and so strong!'"

Again the cheers rose. Again Aedan waited.

"But your victories have come at a great cost. We shall ne'er forget those we have lost," Aedan swallowed hard, and took a deep breath, "Those who have given life itself for our cause, a world where our children can play, can grow, and live free from fear of the dragon's breath! Remember those now, who have died so our children may live in freedom!

"Yet, there are heroes still among us. Here be one; Aengus Mac Mor, rise."

The Great Celt stood and Aedan moved towards him.

Aedan drew his sword, and nodded to Mac Mor, who protested greatly until a great chant arose among the men.

"Aengus! Aengus!"

The Great Celt knelt before Aedan Mac Gabrain, shaking with the moment.

"Aengus Mac Mor, Laird O' The Isles, do ye pledge yourself and your land to the service of thy people?"

"Aye, I do, My King!"

"I pronounce thee Sir Mor." Aedan touched his sword to Mor's left, then right shoulder.

"Arise, Sir Mor!"

A cheer went up from the men, and Mor moved back to his place next to Gingalain. The men were seen to exchange some words; the content of their conversation remained unheard.

"There is another among us who has worked tirelessly to ease our pain. He has tended our wounded, even our animals, before attending to his own needs. Sólas Mac Ailein, arise and come forth."

The men cheered again, each recognizing the one who had eased their own pain.

Sólas stood uneasily, looking from the crowd to the king. After a moment's hesitation, he moved to stand before Aedan, whispering, "Sire, please. I am but a simple man..."

"Sólas Mac Ailein, kneel before your King!" The healer complied to that compelling voice as Aedan raised his sword.

"Do you pledge yourself to serve those pledged to me, in the art and practice of Healing?"

"I do, my King"

Aedan's sword touched Sólas' left and right shoulders.

"Arise, Sir Sólas!"

The cheers rose again, and Aedan motioned for his page.

"Brian, would you please." Aedan's strong voice quieted so only his page could hear as he continued, "Nice and loud, now, lad."

Brian stood, and, stepping forward, he began the prayer in a surprisingly strong and loud voice;

"And He took the bread, gave thanks, and brake it, and gave unto them, saying, 'This is my body which is given for you: this do in remembrance of me'. Like wise also the cup after supper, saying, 'This cup is the new testament in my blood, which is shed for you.'"

"You men, in the rear, come forward!" Aedan commanded, "Yours is the second choice. Gingalain, Brian, Mac Mor, Maon, Laise and myself; we will take the first choice, so we may serve those on sentry duty. The rest of you men, EAT!"

Cheers again erupted as the six men carried the best meat from a dozen deer to those standing watch. Upon the completion of this task, they returned to their seats and, at Aedan's direction, sat patiently as their men ate.

The soldiers could not believe this; common soldiers eating before their captains, the captains before the generals, all before the king and the nobles ate.

A rumble began, slowly spreading through the men. The lines stopped, and a mixed group of Norsemen and Celts moved forward towards the king's table.

"King Aedan, the men, they, well..." as the well-scarred Norseman fumbled for words, a gristled old Celt standing beside him spoke up.

"The men, Sire. They willna eat 'til ye does, M' King. They say it would 'onor 'em t' eat with ya. They say, I say, well, we'll all go with ye into the fires of 'ell 'ere, Sire!"

Gingalain gave a nod to the trembling Aedan, the corners of his mouth twitching upwards ever so slightly.

# The Dragon's Keep

Gingalain looked around the group, gauging the faces of Aedan, Maon, and Mac Mor. The council had yet to agree upon a plan to attack the walled henge.

"Gentlemen, we have been fortunate that the dragons hav'na flown out to attack us thus far. They willna wait much longer. We have healed enough to attack, we need but a reasonable method."

"Gingalain is right. We must 'ave a plan!" Mac Mor blustered.

"A poor plan is worse than no plan. We need to be wise as to our means of attack." Aedan cautioned.

"I propose we build a siege engine to batter the walls, then we storm the henge."

"Four brave men, all afraid to attack!"

All eyes turned to see Edana standing hands on hips at the tent flap.

"You canna decide how to breach a six foot wall? Each of you has more sense than that. Instead, you all stall, hoping Padraig will appear to save your bloody arses.

"Well, I have news for you all; Sir Padraig isna here. We need to proceed accordingly. Stage a strong, but false attack on the door. See how they respond. Be prepared for them to hit back with everything. Draw them out. Then attack in full when they be exposed."

Aedan looked at Gingalain, then at Mac Mor, and Maon.

"Agreed then. Tomorrow at dawn, we attack the door. Mac Mor and the Norse will storm the door, which looks to be of heavy wood. If there be no resistance, we'll light a fire at the base and burn the door down.

"Maon will keep the rest of the men in reserve. Gingalain and I will be mounted, moving in and about to better assess the battle."

"Aye, a good plan, Aedan!" Mac Mor's embarrassed voice rumbled.

"A good plan, Edana! The head of an Aglovale and the heart of Gingalain will aid our victory!" Aedan added.

184

"Aye!"

"Aye!"

"Very well. See you at dawn!"

The group split up, each leader going to their men to explain the plan. Aedan moved to Edana and touched her arm.

"Edana. Thank you."

She lowered her head, not turning to look at Aedan for an uncomfortable moment. She turned her head up, a tear running down her cheek;

"Promise me you'll come back. For Gwenellen. Please!"

"I..." Aedan swallowed. "Edana, I want nothing more than to spend eternity in Gwenellen's arms. Nothing but a world free from dragons."

Edana reached up and grabbed Aedan's arm tightly;

"Then tell her that. Now. While you have the breath and the chance!" She released him and ran away into the night.

"Woof!" Luag added his opinion, and then trotted off behind Edana.

Aedan walked through the camp until he found himself before Gwenellen's tent. As he reached for the flap it opened before him. Gingalain walked out of the tent.

"Good. You need each other now." The old knight said as he held the flap open. As Aedan walked into the tent, Gingalain sat beside the tent flap. After a few moments, Luag trotted up, tail wagging. He lay down, head resting upon Gingalain's lap. The two spent the night that way.

# Attack!

Just before dawn, the Norse troops were ready. Aedan rode Cailean along the front lines, silently inspecting their resolve. Aedan gave a nod to Mac Mor, who motioned with his hand, sending the Norse off at a brisk run to attack the door.

A tenth of a mile lay between the Norse and the door. The men made short work of half that distance before the arrows rained down upon them.

Half of the Norse fell in the rain of darts. The others did not hesitate, but increased their pace to the door. Each carried a bundle of wood and pitch. A few more paces, and they would be at the door.

The sun broke over the sea behind the walled henge, covering the sky with an orange glow before lighting the land. The Norse seemed like streaking shadows against that orange glow at first. Until the fire came.

"DRAGONS!" Aengus Mac Mor's voice roared over fields and walls.

Aedan called to the men in reserve, "Bowmen!"

The Celtic arrows flew through the morning sky. A few found dragons, but only proved a nuisance. Again the beasts dove, the growing morning light shimmering off their crimson scales. Aedan had seen that glow before, from much closer.

"Gingalain! The henge is open!"

A mere score of the Norsemen had managed to reach the door. They set their fuel at the door's base as a screaming soldier ran among them, his cloak aflame. The dying man threw himself upon the wood and pitch. The fuel ignited, and soon flames crackled and licked at the entrance to the henge. The remaining Norse pushed their backs against the wall on each side of the door, trying to gain some protection from the dragon's attacks. Madadh's men inside the wall poured hot oil over them, the fires at the door spreading to Mac Mor's brave warriors.

Mac Mor rode along the wall, trying to protect his soldiers from the flaming arrows raining down upon them.

"NO!" The cry escaped Edana's lips as she watched Mac Mor

and the Norse warriors vanish in a wall of flame.

Just then the morning sun shone on Maon's men, and Madadh's archers took advantage of it. Darts rained down upon the men, and another score fell before they could move.

"This way, men!" Maon shouted, moving South to avoid the arrows.

"The door's aflame!" Brian called "It's down!"

"Attack!" Aedan called, as he and Brian rode at a gallop into the breach. Close behind came Gingalain riding Gilda, followed closely by Edana atop Greg. Seeing the horses galloping to attack rallied the men, who let out a great cry as they rushed the wall.

Aedan's men numbered less than a hundred by the time they cleared the opening in the wall. Again the dragons came from above, slowing their advance.

A great war cry from ahead turned Aedan's ear. He knew that evil tongue, and the polished helmet it wore.

"MADADH!" Aedan screamed as he drove Cailean forward at his half brother. Scores of Madadh's soldiers crashed into Aedan's men as the two leaders closed for combat.

Gingalain swung his sword with a practiced precision, ne'er a movement wasted as Gilda waded through the foe. Edana was equally effective with her claymore, slashing and stabbing on each side with amazing speed. Brian was giving a good accounting with his blade but hung back as Lara had taken a half dozen arrows.

More and more of Madadh's men poured into the fight. Gingalain and Edana were near, Brian behind as Aedan fought his way to his nemesis.

"FORWARD!" A loud battle cry rang over the henge, echoed from the mouths of a thousand mounted warriors speeding up from behind Aedan. Brian spotted them first, and called out.

"The banners are Mac Demmáin and Mac Cairell!"

The arrival of these mounted men sent Madadh's men into a panic just as Aedan had hacked his way to his half brother.

The two men hesitated for just an instant before they began their battle.

Madadh swung his blade with a fresh arm, but still suffered from Brian's arrow he had taken at sea. Aedan 's wounds had still ached that morning, despite the ministrations of Sólas and the rejuvenating touch of Gwenellen. Yet, though his arms carried the weight of a long desperate battle, having his foe at hand amply renewed his vigor.

The High King of Dal Riata leapt from Cailean's back.

Aedan swung up and to the right, blocking Madadh's clumsy blow. He spun under the blow, bringing his sword in a full circle to strike Madadh's legs.

Madadh jumped up to avoid the blow, but Aedan anticipated this. His blade rose to follow the movement, slicing deeply into Madadh's thigh. Madadh's sword came down at the same time, biting into Aedan's side, glancing off of his ribs.

Madadh fell heavily, Aedan bent over, gasping. Most of his old wounds had reopened, but he knew Madadh was badly hurt. He moved in to finish his work.

A crimson flash appeared before him, and Aedan found a ten foot tall dragon between himself and Madadh.

"I've no time for you!" Aedan called as he thrust his sword into the beast's chest, pulling the blade down and to his right. Surprise shown in the dragon's eyes as the life drained from them.

Madadh was trying to crawl away, but making poor progress with one leg and one arm. He was bleeding profusely from his leg, the blood leaving a wide trail along the turf of the henge. He gave a look at Aedan, smiled, and threw his sgian dubh at him. The blade hit Aedan's shoulder, slicing into his flesh deeply before falling to the ground.

"AAAArgh!" Aedan called as he rushed forward and ended Madadh's quest for Aedan's throne with a powerful thrust of his sword.

A quick movement then caught Aedan's attention. A glance to the henge showed that glowing red light, with the endless emptiness at the center. Dragons were coming through by the score!

Fiachnae's horsemen sliced through Madadh's men and soon surrounded the henge, but the dragons now outnumbered them. The High King whistled for Cailean, the horse neighing to Aedan as he ran up to him. The view from Cailean's back made Aedan gasp; bodies lay everywhere, most of men, but many a dragon as well. Brian ran up, blood dripping from a gash on his shoulder, Luag at his side;

"The Good King! Come quickly!"

Aedan rode the few yards to where Gingalain lay, near where Gilda had fallen from the spear lodged in her too still chest. Gingalain was on his side, Edana cradling his head as she wept.

Aedan knelt next to Gingalain, hearing the gurgles of his breathing. Four arrows stuck out from his chest, bloody bubbles moving around them with each breath.

"My King!" Aedan whispered. He looked deeply into the old man's eyes. Gingalain nodded once, and Aedan turned to the battle. Dragons and horsemen fought and died amidst the red glow, even as more dragons sprang through the portal each minute. He glanced back at Edana.

"The end of this is now."

He mounted Cailean and forged right into the fray.

Edana was torn between Gingalain and joining the fight with Aedan. The red glow was becoming brighter. She turned to Brian;

"Stay with him." She stood and called loudly, "Greg!"

She repeated her call when the huge white horse did not come. Desperately she looked around the henge, her eyes falling upon the white stallion's still form to her left.

"Greg!" Edana sobbed as she saw that there was no movement in him.

"Woof!" Luag called to them as he trotted around Brian and Gingalain.

The noise inside the henge was deafening; steel on bone, hoof on scale, and talons on flesh. Cries, screams, and roars filled the ears as acrid odors of burnt flesh and fresh blood gagged the throat. Aedan swung his sword and Fiachnae hacked away with a huge battleaxe. Dragons and men died by the score.

And all the while still more crimson dragons poured through the opening.

Bravely they fought, but the men of Mac Demmáin and Mac Cairell fell, one by one. Back the dragons drove them, back towards the wall's portal.

Aedan looked and found himself next to Brian and Gingalain, with Edana close at hand.

"Edana, go to your sister. NOW!" Aedan commanded.

"I'll not leave this henge, Sire!"

"Edana!" The High King called between slashes of his sword. "Aedan?"

"It's been an honor to fight with you!"

A swipe of a dragon's taloned hand knocked Aedan from atop Cailean, and Edana lost sight of him. She was pulled down as well. A large dragon loomed over her, Luag on it's back, his fangs sunk deeply into the beast's neck. Edana fought to her feet, running her sword into the dragon, only to see another dragon dive towards her. A large broadsword swung over her head and beheaded the beast before it's talons could reach her.

"Stay close, Edana!" Fionnghal roared. Edana took heart as she saw Fergus and Osgar swinging their blades in defense of Gingalain. The Good King coughed, blood dripping from his mouth. *He looks so pale in this blue light,* she thought. Her eyes widened.

*BLUE LIGHT!*

The entire henge shone now with a pale blue glow. Edana found Aedan, near exhaustion amid dead dragons, staring at the center of the henge. Her eyes followed his there, where a brilliant blue light had replaced the dark emptiness in the portal. Out of that light poured an army of armored warriors, each half again as tall as a man and wearing a hooded, light blue and silver cloak. They moved as one, swinging to great effect heavy curved swords. Each of these glowed with that familiar pale blue fire, slicing into the red dragons before them. And at the front of them all strode Padraig Ualas, Azure Shield and Excalibur shining brightly. The Good Knight was a blur as the army following him cut through the panicked crimson dragons, mowing them down quickly as the cloaked warriors fought towards Edana and Aedan.

Edana's heart leapt to her throat as she watched Padraig fight his way to her. *Could it be? Dare I hope?*

Aedan spun around. The cloaked warriors spread out now, pursuing the fleeing red dragons with a relentless ferocity.

Presently, less than a score of the red dragons remained, with nearly a hundred cloaked warriors chasing them down. When a cloaked warrior caught up to a red dragon, the fight was brief. A slash across the red Dragon's chest or to the throat ended it. Where a red dragon did manage to strike a cloaked warrior, the talons slid harmlessly off of the armor beneath the cloak.

In a few moments, it was done. Scores of cloaked warriors marched back into the center of the henge, a score forming a guard there while the rest returned through the bright light. One cloaked warrior slowly walked, head down, towards Gingalain. This cloaked figure was different from the others. His dark blue cloak was covered with golden stars and the same strange writing that was on the henge keystone. Shorter than the others, he also carried a staff in place of the warrior's curved swords.

Nearby, Padraig stood staring at Edana. Now she could see wounds he had suffered, on face, arms, legs, and body. Her eyes came up to his face, to his smile. His smile.

"PADRAIG!"

"Edana!" he held his arms wide as she leapt into them, the two wrapped in each other's embrace. Padraig spun her around and around, praying the moment would never end.

# The Rest

"Tell me. What happened. In... there." Edana's quiet words fell on Padraig's ears as her tears hit his shoulder.

"I heard the widow Gwenever's voice. It told me to go through the portal, to close the portal from the other side. So, I went through it. There was... nothing there.  No ground, no sky, no wind, no light, no sound, no smell. Nothing but dragons. I fought them, it seemed, forever. They just kept coming.

"There was a light, far off. Gwenever called me to it, but Gilda... Gilda would not move away from the portal. I had to send her... back..."

Edana held her love a little tighter, giving him the time he needed.

"What did it look like, from that side? The Portal?"

"I could see the henge, as through a window. The light was... different. I killed dragon after dragon. There seemed to be no end to their numbers. I could only fight in place, but when I glanced again at the light, it seemed much closer.

"I began to tire, and talons made it past my shield. I felt I would die. Excalibur became heavy, harder and harder to swing.

"Then, the dragons fled. The light embraced me, and I could see! I was in a beautiful blue meadow, under a light green sky, surrounded by dead black dragons. Behind me, the henge shown through the portal. In front of me stood a cloaked figure. I could read the writing on his cloak. It said, 'Merlin The Great King of Dracon'.

"He lifted his hood, and I saw his face. A wise, kind, human face. A face covered in small light blue scales.

"Edana, Merlin is a dragon. The warriors he sent with me are dragons. Good dragons. They fight an eternal war against the evil reds.

"But, Merlin was...father told me he was a Wizard. He was magic."

"Yes, he is. He opened the first portal and came here long ago, at a time when the blue dragons had nearly defeated the reds. Merlin thought he could teach us to live good lives, so we could avoid the endless wars his world had endured. But the last few reds managed to steal the portal, and their evil grew. Here, and there."

"Oh, Padraig. Will we ever be rid of the evil ones?"

"This is the last portal. Merlin will destroy it when he leaves. When it is closed, Excalibur and The Azure Shield will be just...steel."

"Padraig! We need you!" Aedan's voice rang out.

The exhausted knight released Edana with a kiss. There was one more task left for them.

It was the most difficult thing they had ever done.

Padraig gazed at Gilda as she lay peacefully upon the pyre, next to Greg. All around, huge pyres had been built for the dead, with the respectful help of the cloaked warriors. Soon enough these fires would be lit.

"We must. Now, Padraig." Edana's tears reminded him.

They joined the others inside the tent.

Another stood alone in reflection nearby.

He waited patiently as they gathered inside the tent, the dark blue cloak accentuating his height. He longed to comfort them for their losses, to teach them how to avoid such bloodshed. He thought of how he had tried helping them once before, how he had almost succeeded before it all fell apart.

Right now, it was not his place to be with the mourners. The old knight, a good man, he had known briefly long ago. But he could not steal these last moments from them. When they were ready, then he would pay his respects, his retribution, and take his leave.

The rules were different here, he now realized. Powerful forces shaped good and evil here, in a way much different from his world. Forces he did not, could not understand. The humans would have to find their own way through those forces. He could not help them on the road they must travel. Perhaps some day...

Inside the tent, they were gathered around the old knight. Sir Sólas had made a potion to compliment Fionnghal's poultices, helping to blunt Gingalain's pain. The old eyes looked from Aedan to Padraig, from Fergus to Osgar to Fionnghal, from Edana to Gwenellen to Brian to Luag, from Maon to Fiachnae. Then they fell to rest upon Padraig again.

Good King Gingalain took a deep breath and smiled as he passed on.

After a moment, Aedan motioned and those gathered quietly left the tent. After Fergus, Osgar, Fionnghal, Maon, and Fiachnae had left, Aedan held his hand out to Gwenellen. Edana's tear filled eyes looked up at the High King, who motioned for her to stay as Aedan and Gwenellen left the tent.

They walked over to where the others had gathered, near the newcomer. Covered in a hooded blue cloak, with the unreadable writing like on the henge stones. The gathering of the survivors was far too small, Aedan thought. Less than a score remained. They all looked up at the face under the newcomer's hood. Bright blue eyes glowed on the face of a wise, kind man. A face covered in small, pale blue scales.

The seven foot tall blue dragon removed his hood and bowed his head in a graceful gesture of respect to Aedan.

"High King Aedan, too many of your people have died at the hands of our evil ones. I am very sorry for your losses."

"Merlin, thank you for your kind words. And thank you for your help here. Please, tell me how was it that you came to be here?"

"The Azure Shield and Excalibur sang to Padraig, and brought him to us. He fought through the hordes of evil ones to reach us. We did not think it possible for a human to do so, but he has... he is a powerful warrior, with powerful tools. Excalibur and The Azure Shield are the only things with such power in both your world and mine. They are forged of the good and faith from both of our worlds." *And they are the greatest magic I have ever created, though I know not how I did it*, he thought "Still, no one has ever used them as well as he.

"He told us of your world's plight. We did not know; I had thought all the portals were closed when I left before. I was lax in my duties, I should have known that the evil ones were here; they had been very quiet recently. We are sorry for your pain. We came to make sure that this could never happen again."

"Will you stay and dine with us, Merlin?"

"I cannot. I have learned after my earlier meddling that it is

194

not wise for me to... linger in your world. There are forces of good and evil here that I do not understand, I cannot use. Once before I tried. I placed the warrior as king, thinking that the chosen of the sword would vanquish evil here. Much suffering resulted. This time, the warrior is greater, but I will not interfere. I will make sure that this portal is forever closed, to protect your world from the evil in ours."

"We are grateful for your help."

Merlin reached under his cloak and removed something, holding his hand out to Gwenellen.

"A token of our sorrow, M'Lady."

The pale blue fingers unfurled from the sleeves of the dark blue cloak, revealing bright silver talons holding a large pale blue gem.

"Oh, Merlin, it's beautiful!"

"Soon after Padraig comes out, I must go." Merlin said.

After a few moments, Padraig and Edana came out of the tent. Padraig walked over to Merlin and clasped his hand.

"Thank you, Merlin. If only I could repay you."

"I thank you, Padraig. My arrogance, my pride allowed the evil ones to come to your world. Your bravery has provided for our healing. Goodbye, Sir Knight."

Merlin shrugged on his cloak and walked through the center of the henge, holding that heavy silver staff in his hand. As the blue dragon king vanished, he tapped the staff on the ground. The henge's keystone flew through the bright blue light even as that light shrunk into nothingness.

Later that evening, as the pyres were lit, Padraig pulled Edana close as they gazed into the flames.

"We have the time now. Will you count stars with me this night, fair maiden?"

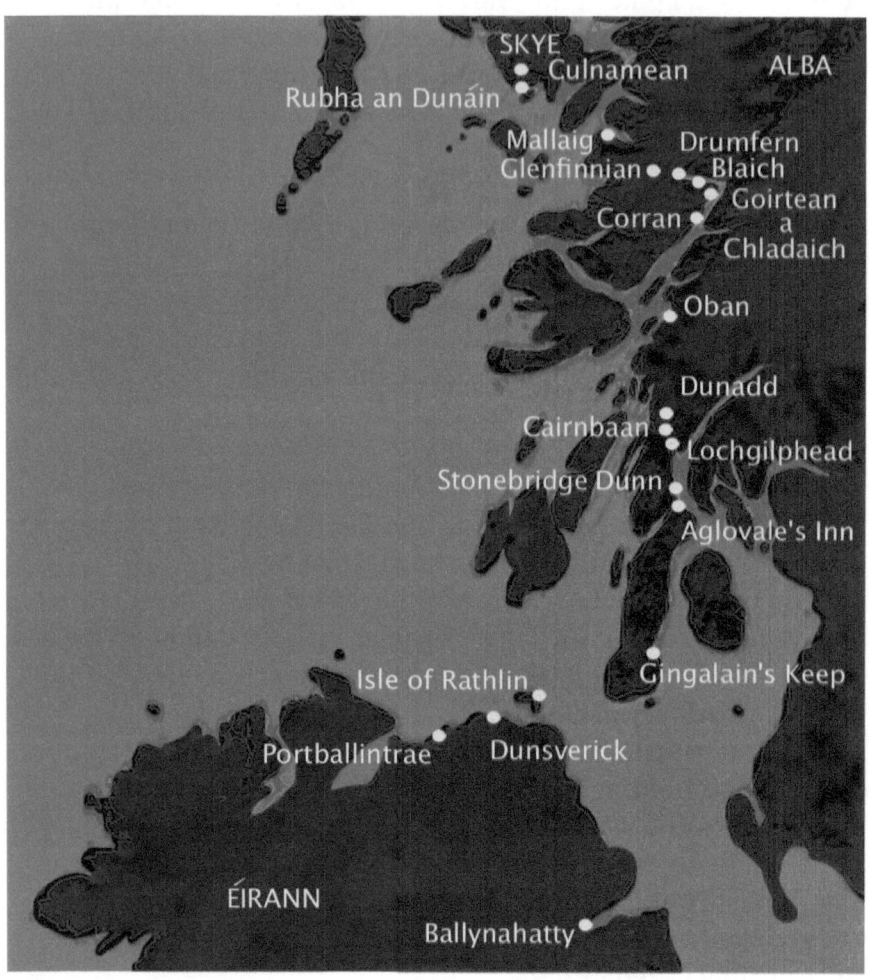

I hope you enjoyed my story. If you did, please leave a review and tell others about it.

# About James W. McAllister

I am a Registered Respiratory Therapist living near Syracuse in Central New York State. Currently I am employed in Healthcare Accreditation. I founded Fortiter Publishing LLC in November 2013 as a vehicle to get all these great Science Fiction and Fantasy stories out of my head.

"FORTITER" is inscribed on the MacAlister Clan Crest. The word means "to go forward, boldly." I am grateful for the Clan Chief's permission to use the Crest and Tartan in my company's logo, and to use "FORTITER" in my company's name.

I have been interested in science fiction since reading the Lensmen Series of books by E. E. "Doc" Smith in Junior High School. TV shows like Star Trek and Battlestar Galactica, and movies such as Robinson Crusoe on Mars and Star Wars further peaked my interest in the genre.

See my Amazon Author's page here:

**http://amazon.com/author/jwmcallister**

**Other books by James W. McAllister**

STARCLAN Book I
THE TURRET
Starclan Foundation

STARCLAN Book II
THE BEST LAID PLANS
Birth of the Starclan

STARCLAN Book III
A MATTER OF HONOR
Starclan Chrysalis 2016

STAGED FRIGHT
A John Martin Adventure

RODS
Another John Martin Adventure

THE UNIVERSE,
While You Wait
28 short stories to read
while you're waiting

www.ingramcontent.com/pod-product-compliance
Lightning Source LLC
Chambersburg PA
CBHW030247130626
46549CB00002B/421